LOTUS BLOSSOM UNFURLING

Also by Toni Morgan

Echoes from a Falling Bridge
Harvest the Wind
Queenie's Place
Two-Hearted Crossing
Patrimony

LOTUS BLOSSOM UNFURLING

Then There was Peace

A Novel By

TONI MORGAN

Adelaide Books

New York / Lisbon

2018

LOTUS BLOSSOM UNFURLING
Then There was Peace
a novel
by Toni Morgan

Copyright © 2018 by Toni Morgan

Cover design © 2018 Adelaide Books

Published by Adelaide Books, New York / Lisbon
adelaidebooks.org

Editor-in-Chief
Stevan V. Nikolic

For any information, please address Adelaide Books
at info@adelaidebooks.org
or write to:
Adelaide Books
244 Fifth Ave. Suite D27
New York, NY, 10001

ISBN13: 978-1-7320742-1-7
ISBN10: 1-7320742-1-6

In loving memory of Scottie and Donald

"Like a raindrop makes its way back to the ocean
that gave it birth, the cycle of life continues."

The lotus blossom unfurls.

A frog leaps…splash!

The morning dawn has broken.

Contents

BOOK ONE
1946-1970
And then there was peace

1

YOKO

Japan

Throughout the fall, the few husbands and fathers who'd survived the war and New Guinea returned to their homes in Nishimi. Tired and defeated, many suffered from the ravages of starvation, malaria and chronic dysentery. A few came home in body only, their minds shattered by what they'd endured. Although Yoko was puzzled when Takeda failed to appear right away, she was not disappointed. Eventually, her husband would show up—likely when she least expected or wanted him.

Old Mori's son, whose hair was now almost as gray as his father's, was among those who stumbled home. He was accompanied by his wife, who'd spent the past several years with her parents in Sakayama. She'd been unable to bear living in Nishimi after the earthquake killed their two children.

Hobbling on crutches, unable to go back to his job with the local forester, young Mori often came to the pottery factory at afternoon tea time. Yoko wondered what the man sought from them. Normalcy, perhaps, though each time he visited, it was the war he spoke of—even though her potters, except for Mori and Ishihara, were women; the young men of Nishimi and the surrounding farms, including Yoko's husband, had either been conscripted or sent to work in industries the government had considered essential to the war effort. Mori and Ishihara, who'd been too old to fight, had been the only men.

One afternoon, as they drank tea and ate bean-paste-filled pastries in the pottery factory's combination office and showroom, young Mori regaled Yoko's workers with the story of a bridge in New Guinea.

"We'd been marching through the mountain jungles for over a month, trying to escape from the Australians. Their weapons were superior to ours and they'd quickly driven us from the city of Finchhaffen and from our positions around a nearby airfield. Up and up we went, starving, our uniforms rotting off our bodies. Bugs and insects drove us mad, as did the birds screeching over our heads. Frogs, no bigger than my thumb, made a booming sound so loud it was like huge beasts lurked behind the trees. Many men dropped out of the line from weariness or disease, while close behind us, the enemy pressed."

Despite her professed lack of caring about what had happened in the war—she'd had too much to worry about just running the pottery factory in her husband's absence— Yoko leaned forward, drawn into the young man's account.

"The rain never stopped, our weapons were rusted and useless. Then, Buddha answered our prayers; we came to a suspension bridge over a deep ravine."

"But why was it an answer to your prayers," one of the potters asked.

"Because, if we crossed it and then destroyed the bridge, the enemy would be cut off, unable to follow"

Yoko nodded then shifted once again in her desk chair, as eager as her workers to hear what happened next.

"Our orders were to wait until everyone crossed the bridge. But someone set the charges off early." As he said this, he eyed Yoko.

Yoko frowned. *What was that about?*

Turning back to the workers clustered around him, young Mori lowered his voice to just above a whisper. "I couldn't believe my eyes. Many men had yet to cross, but others were on the bridge when it fell. Some, thinking to get across in time, ran onto it. At night, I still hear their screams echoing off the walls of the ravine as they spiraled downward through the rain to the rocks and river below."

Shocked gasps came from his listeners.

Young Mori drew a deep breath. "Those who'd fallen to their deaths and those left on the other side were sacrificed."

Asai, seated on the packing platform, looked grim. "Sacrificed. Yes. They gave everything for the Emperor and for Japan."

As did we all, Yoko thought, remembering the many years of near starvation. Before the war, the surrounding mountains and valleys had been dotted by farms growing rice and millet. But most of those crops were confiscated by the government and sent to the front, the men and boys who harvested them conscripted. By the end of the war, the once lush fields lay fallow due to lack of seeds or seedlings, many of the men and boys were gone forever, and everyone in Nishimi and on the farms left to starve.

Young Mori continued, his voice devoid of emotion. "Those of us who managed to cross the bridge didn't escape the enemy. Americans controlled the other side of the island. For two years, we traveled along narrow trails that crisscrossed the jungle, trying to avoid capture. Staying alive became our only objective."

Yoko sat back, her brows knitted together. She could not imagine Takeda in such conditions—her handsome, spoiled husband was not a man to suffer privation.

"Then one day, an airplane flew overhead and dropped leaflets. Some fell through the jungle canopy and fluttered to our feet. The leaflets informed us the Emperor had surrendered." He sighed and dropped his face into his hands, shaking his head as though still unable to believe the war was over, that he'd survived, that Japan had been defeated.

His father, sitting on the edge of the packing platform and examining a bowl, must have heard the story before. Still, his hands trembled and his eyes became glassy with tears. After his son left the factory and Asai, the factory's master potter, had led the others back to their work, he approached Yoko.

"I am glad my son and his wife have returned to Nishimi," he said. "But I am sorry if he upsets you with his stories. He is having a difficult time adjusting to the loss of his son and daughter in the earthquake and to our lives now—the lack of help from the government regarding food, the damage to his foot and not being able to return to his old job."

Yoko pulled at her earlobe. Her eyes narrowed in concentration. "Maybe there is something he can do here, once his foot has healed a bit."

"When his foot heals, he'll want to go back to forestry. For the present, I thought we might use him to help pack."

She nodded. "We aren't that busy right now, but there might be some work for him."

"Thank you, Yoko-san. It is not good for a man to have no work to support his family—even though that family is now only his wife."

Yoko nodded again, wishing there was something more she could do.

Months went by and still no Takeda. Yoko couldn't understand it.

"Maybe he is ashamed," young Mori said. He sat on the edge of the packing platform. A putrid smell arose from his injured foot, propped on a chair. He glanced at her from beneath his brows, then lowered his eyes. Several moments passed before he raised them. "Most believed your husband to be the one who set off the charges that took down the bridge."

Yoko stared, face blank, not speaking, not wanting to believe her husband would have done such a dishonorable thing. Her lips tightened on the knowledge that such a cowardly act by Takeda Yoshida was perfectly plausible. "No one accused him? Punished him?"

Young Mori shrugged. "After the bridge came down and we were on the other side of the chasm, the Army fell apart, breaking up into small groups. There were no clear lines of authority or communication. Takeda kept to himself, not joining any one group for long." He leaned over and gently rubbed his bandaged foot. "But he was alive at the end of the war. I saw him myself, boarding a ship in New Guinea. Just like the rest of us, he was skinny as a skeleton. But with his height, he was easy to recognize."

Yoko scowled. If Takeda had come back to Japan, where was he?

Ishihara was convinced he had the answer. "We are now a fourth-rate country," the old man said. "Like others, maybe Takeda has taken his own life rather than live with the shame of our defeat."

Yoko snorted at such an idea—suicide would be too noble a gesture for her husband. No. Ishihara was wrong. Young Mori was wrong, too. Takeda Yoshida wasn't dead and he wasn't staying away from the village out of remorse or guilt. He was somewhere feathering his nest, doubtless without regard to those he might be harming.

Fourteen months to the day after the war ended, the outside door shoved open. Studying a new order and estimating the amount of clay they would need to complete it, Yoko looked up, frowning at the interruption. She stiffened. Takeda— looking well fed and as handsome as ever. From his casual demeanor, one would think her husband had been out for a brief stroll, enjoying the fall colors. Damn the man.

She stood, dropping the order to the desk. "All the other village men, the few left, came home a year ago. What's taken you so long?" She clenched her fingers, wishing she hadn't asked. He would only use it against her.

"Why should you care, wife? I'm here now. Call Mori and Ishihara to me, then go get me something to eat.

I'm hungry." He dropped his large frame into her abandoned chair and reached for the accounts book.

Yoko fled to the door at the back of the office. Angry tears blurring her vision, she grasped the railing, worn smooth by the passage of two hundred years and a thousand hands, and made her way down the short flight of steps to the packed earth floor of the factory's production area.

In the drying room, Ishihara slid a plank laden with soba bowls onto a shelf.

"Where is Mori? My husband has returned. He wants both of you in the office."

Ishihara slapped his hands together to rid them of clay dust. "Hunh…has he said what has kept him?"

"No. Where is Mori?"

"Directing the loading of the kiln. I will fetch him."

"I'll get him." Yoko crossed to the open double doors at the back of the factory. Mori stood behind two workers bricking up a loaded chamber of the kiln. Other workers were loading the remaining chambers before those chambers, too, would be bricked shut. Firing was to begin the following morning. She called to Mori. "My husband has returned. He wants you in the office."

Surprise flickered across Mori's face. He bobbed his head in acknowledgement. Yoko didn't want to talk to him, nor did she have any desire to return to the office, where her husband now sat at her desk, going through her accounts. Instead, she hurried around the side of the factory toward her house.

What if she continued walking, past the Abi store, through Nishimi and down the mountain to Sakayama?

Once in the city, she could disappear. If she took the other direction, past the lane to Sanyo's pig farm, the new school, the Hara's farm and into the mountains, she could also disappear. Or maybe she should go up the track, past the burnt-out remains of the old Katsuragawa summer estate with its still-standing caretaker's house, to the craggy mountain peak beyond, and throw herself off.

Instead of disappearing or throwing herself off the mountain, she slid open the door of her house, kicked off her shoes and walked across the frayed tatami mat to the kitchen. There was little to eat, a couple of scoops of rice, a few slices of fried lotus root and two carrots. Even after all this time, over a year since the war ended, the nation still starved and the government, from the Emperor on down, did little to help. She put the rice and lotus root in a bowl along with one of the carrots. It would have to be enough. She ate the remaining carrot.

She returned to the factory. Her husband's lips turned down. "What is this? I told you I wanted food, not this pig shit." He struck the bowl from her hand.

Mori and Ishihara looked away.

"It is all we have, husband."

"Then go get something from the Abi store. What is the matter with you?"

Yoko's jaws clenched so tight, she could have broken another tooth.

Mori cleared his throat. "You do not understand, Takeda-san. Little is available at the store to purchase. Even though the war has been over for more than a year, it is only in the cities, in black markets, that food is plentiful."

Takeda scowled, but did not apologize. "Go do something useful," he told Yoko.

She stalked out, seething.

At least she could enjoy some revenge. As soon as the Emperor conceded defeat, she'd sworn Ishihara to secrecy and had him build a secret space in the back of a tonsu drawer, a hidden compartment large enough to hold the yen notes she later placed in it. She'd been careful with the bookkeeping, maximizing expenses, minimizing profits. After ten years of running the factory without him, she wasn't about to hand over everything now he'd returned. Her cursed husband could rail at her incompetence all he wanted, but there was no way for him to know she had a secret cache of money.

She went home and stared at the tonsu. Grim satisfaction soothed her anger, even brought her a modicum of comfort.

Fall gave way to winter. As the days and weeks passed, Yoko's resentment of Takeda's presence grew. Her husband did nothing at home but eat, drink whatever he could get his hands on, and use her in bed. At the pottery factory he sat at her desk, now his, and studied the accounts book. He made no attempt to learn how they had managed in his absence, the changes Yoko had been forced to make in order for them to survive. His only comment was that the factory being so unprofitable in his absence didn't surprise him. "It is well-known women can't manage on their own."

After too much sake one night, he revealed what had kept him from Nishimi for so many months after the war.

"The military stores were available for the taking." His words were slurred, but not enough that Yoko couldn't understand him. "The Army abandoned everything—equipment, tools, food."

"So where is it, this abandoned treasure?" Just as she'd supposed—feathering his nest.

He ignored her question. "A market exists for everything." He giggled and put his finger to the side his nose. "All I needed to do was find it."

Yoko didn't push for more details that night, but bit by bit, she learned he'd stolen food, blankets and medical supplies from unguarded military stockpiles and sold them on the black market. She didn't bother asking if, in addition to his profiteering, a woman had been involved with his delay. There was always a woman. With any luck, he'd find one in Nishimi, too.

2
KEIKO

Oregon

The half-empty train was newer than the one they'd traveled on to Idaho three years before. The toilets didn't reek and overflow. Also, there were no armed soldiers guarding them. But the eyes of their fellow passengers were fixed on Keiko and her father, some with curiosity, some with speculative looks, and others with hatred. Keiko wanted to stare back, but she knew that would be rude.

"People should have better manners," she whispered to her father. "You'd think we were animals in a zoo."

Her father leaned against the maroon upholstered seat back, his eyes closed. "Ignore them, daughter. They are only curious."

He was right that she should ignore them. The simply curious, she could. But ignoring the animosity in some eyes.... She would try.

"I'm anxious to get there. It seems so long since we left Portland." And so much had happened: their internment at Camp Minidoka after Japan attacked Pearl Harbor, her mother's death in that awful place, Tommy and Mako joining the 442nd and going to Europe to fight.

Her father, eyes still closed, said nothing.

Her chaotic thoughts shifted back to Mako. In his last letter, now folded and tucked into her handbag, he hinted at them getting married. She wanted to say yes. She loved him with all her heart. But she had plans that didn't include marriage, at least not now. Mako would need to wait…if he would.

The train racketed on. Out the window lay the harsh, barren landscape of eastern Oregon. Keiko couldn't help but compare it to her memory of green and mellow Portland. What would the city of her birth be like now? Would it welcome them or treat them as enemies? Earlier, when they'd boarded the train in Twin Falls, she'd been confident that she could handle whatever life threw her way—nothing could be worse than the three years she'd spent in Camp Minidoka. Now she wasn't so sure.

"Papa, what if the editor at *The Irrigator* was right and the Japanese Exclusion League has come to Portland?" The editor of the Camp Minidoka newspaper had shown her an article from a Seattle paper. He had speculated the organization might have traveled south, possibly as far south as California, which would include Portland.

Her father sighed and turned to her. "Keiko, you must stop borrowing trouble. Whatever comes, we will manage."

Keiko tried to put the rumors and the article from her mind, but by the time they reached Portland's Union Station the following morning, she stepped onto the platform unsure what to expect.

Keiko's father had reserved a room in a hotel they'd been told welcomed returning internees. The clerk, however, made no effort to hide his hostility. Hatred was in his eyes and in the downward pull of his lips. "You have to pay in advance. Thirty-two dollars a week, plus a thirty-two-dollar deposit."

Keiko's eyes widened. "That's ridiculous."

"Take it or leave it."

Her father paid the exorbitant sum and the man handed him a key.

Keiko and her father lugged their suitcases up three flights of stairs, stopping to rest on each landing, then down a narrow hall. Their room was even smaller than Keiko's old pre-war bedroom in Portland's Japan-Chinatown. No more than ten inches separated the two narrow beds. A chest-of-drawers with a lamp on it sat under the window. A chair was wedged between the chest-of-drawers and the wall. The lavatory was down the hall—she'd smelled it when they passed.

"It won't be for long," her father said, staring around the cramped room. He pushed the switch next to the door and a feeble light shone down from the fixture in the middle of the ceiling.

Its dimness reminded Keiko of the single bulb in their barrack space at Camp Minidoka. Anger surged through her. There seemed no end to the degradation the color of their skin and the shape of their eyes forced them to endure. Lips tight together, she crossed to the window and pulled back the curtains. Dust billowed. Beyond the dingy window was the side of a brick building.

"It won't be for long," her father repeated.

Keiko prayed he was right.

Standing beneath her umbrella in the drifting rain the following morning, Keiko hardly recognized 3rd Avenue. Mr. Takai's Newspaper and Magazine Shop, on the ground floor below her family's old apartment, now sold Chinese herbs and tonics. Next to it, in place of the Tanaka's photographic studio, a shop offered writing materials. Down the street, Wei Laundry and Dry-Cleaning Service replaced the Oki's laundry, and a fish market resided where Kashima's Grocery used to be.

Nothing was as Keiko remembered it. Worse, most windows held signs: *No Japs*. She trudged up the sidewalk to Burnside and took the bus back across the Willamette River to their hotel. Japan-Chinatown no longer existed. Now it was simply Chinatown.

The next three weeks she tramped the wet sidewalks hunting for an apartment for her family. From beneath umbrellas or hat brims, most of the people she passed glared at her, and just like in Chinatown, No Japs signs hung in the windows of stores and apartment buildings.

"I don't think there is anything for us here, Papa," she said after another futile day of searching. "Tommy will be returning from France soon. What are we going to do if we can't find a place to live before he gets here?"

Her brother would be discharged in two weeks. Mako also. She wondered if she'd even recognize Mako, or if he'd recognize her. She was no longer the innocent teenager happily playing the piano, dreaming of a career in music. What would he say of her intention to study law and become an attorney instead?

"We'll find something soon. Be patient, Keiko-san."

But Keiko was running out of what little patience she possessed. At least her father had been able to return to his old job at the University Club. They'd always liked her father and Keiko was glad they wanted him back to help members don their coats, hail cabs, and do whatever other odd jobs he could. He was happy and claimed not to care about the bus commute each day. "I write poetry in my head."

Then another good thing happened. One of the Club members had a client who owned an apartment building in Southeast Portland. The client agreed to rent to the Ugawa family.

The furnished apartment wasn't spacious, but Keiko threw herself on the bed, clasped her arms to her chest, and giggled aloud. She'd be sleeping in a real bedroom. One with real walls, not blankets suspended from ropes, like they'd used at Camp Minidoka. Ropes and blankets had been the only way they could have any privacy in the limited space each family was given.

One evening, footsteps sounded on the stairs followed by a loud knock on the door. Keiko's breath caught. Her frightened gaze flew to her father. It was just like the evening after Pearl Harbor, when the government men had come and taken him away. It had been dinnertime then, too.

"I'll get it," her father said.

When he opened the door, Keiko's heart nearly burst. "Tommy!"

Looking thin and tired, though quite resplendent in his dark green uniform, Tommy dropped his duffle-bag from his shoulder. Keiko rushed to him, but he already had their father enveloped in his arms.

Tommy claimed dinner was better than anything he'd eaten in two years, this despite Keiko's inexpertly cooked rice curry. Afterward, they sat around the table reminiscing about life before the war. They even found a few things about their time at Camp Minidoka to chuckle over, like when she and Tommy had snuck into the desert one night to get rocks for the garden area their father built next to their barracks. To the consternation of the camp administrator, gardens had flourished around most barracks, as many teens did the same for their parents.

"Good thing we found places to go over the barbed-wire where the guards couldn't spot us," Tommy said. "It wouldn't have been such a grand adventure if one of us had been shot."

"You've probably done things a lot more dangerous than that in Europe," Keiko said.

Her brother's eyes clouded.

Her father nudged her with his knee and she fell silent.

That night, a full moon shining through her bedroom window, Keiko lay wide-eyed for what seemed like hours. Tommy had said Mako was with his father in Nyssa, a small town on the Oregon side of the Idaho border. She wondered if he would remain there. Before the war, he and his family lived on a truck farm in California. Nyssa might suit him very well, as it, too, was a farm town. The weather was also similar. Her eyes smarted. Despite his letter and his hints of marriage, she might never see him again.

Soon after he arrived home, Tommy told Keiko about a new college opening in a place called Vanport. "It's because of all the returning veterans wanting to go to school on the GI

Bill. I guess there aren't enough schools to accommodate everyone."

Keiko put down her teacup. "Not enough jobs, either. Seems like feast or famine—not enough jobs or not enough people." She took a bite of toast. "Never just right. So where is Vanport, anyway? I've never even heard of it."

"Between Portland and the Columbia River. Henry Kaiser built it for all the folks who came here to work in the shipyards, his shipyards."

"Are you going to enroll there?"

"I plan to try. After two years, I'll transfer to the University of Oregon, assuming they'll take me."

"Before you got home, I applied to two schools in Portland, but each claimed to be full," Keiko said. She'd thought it was another case of discrimination. But maybe it wasn't. "No one mentioned this new school, though."

She decided to apply with Tommy, even though she'd yet to find a job and didn't know how she'd pay for it. Her father said they'd manage. At least her brother had the GI Bill to rely on.

With their Camp Minidoka High School diplomas in hand, she and Tommy took the bus to Vanport the following day. "Locals call it Kaiserville," Tommy said.

"Who lives there now the shipyards are mostly closed?"

"Over half of the residents have returned to wherever they lived before Kaiser recruited them—but that still leaves 20,000," he said. "Mostly Negroes."

"Where did you hear all this?"

Tommy shrugged. "Talking to people."

Before the war, Keiko had hardly ever seen a Negro in Portland. She supposed they weren't welcome until they were needed to help build America's ships—like Japanese-Americans weren't welcome until they were needed to save America's farmers.

When they stepped off the bus and looked around, Keiko was struck by Vanport's similarity to Camp Minidoka. It would have been built about the same time. Even though the Vanport buildings were more finished than Minidoka's barracks—they weren't covered with tarpaper, at least—they, too, had a temporary look. Several dark-skinned children were playing ball in an open space. A woman pushed a baby carriage along the uneven sidewalk.

It took some effort to locate the school in the maze of buildings, but when they did, Keiko and Tommy were accepted as students. A few days later, Keiko was hired to work in the school office. She couldn't stop smiling—finally, studying law was within her grasp.

That evening, Tommy sat at the dining room table, leafing through a new textbook. "What made you decide you wanted to become an attorney anyway? I thought you were sold on studying music."

"Camp Minidoka."

He gave her a perplexed look. "What do you mean?"

"What happened to us, how we got there. Everyone knew it was wrong, but few did anything besides rail about it. Mitsuye Endo was the only one who hired a lawyer and filed a lawsuit claiming that internment was unconstitutional. Although it took them three years to get around to it, the Supreme Court finally agreed. Unanimously. It was her standing up that forced President Roosevelt's administration to let us go." Keiko straightened her shoulders, as though preparing for an argument from Tommy. "Mitsuye Endo is my hero." She lifted her chin another fraction of an inch. "That's why I decided to study law. It will be through the legal system that we make sure nothing like that ever happens again. I plan to do my part."

Tommy gazed at her a moment before nodding. "Have you told Mako?"

She shook her head. "I only told him I planned to enroll in school when the war ended. He probably expects me to continue with my music, but Papa understands. Mako will need to as well. Besides, he might decide to stay in Nyssa, with his father. I might not even see him again." There, she'd finally given voice to her secret fear.

"I doubt that. You're all he ever talked about. Drove me crazy asking for stories about you." Tommy grinned. "I told him about the time you were playing on the monkey bars at school and that kid pulled on your skirt to get you off them."

Keiko's cheeks reddened, as if she was still hanging on the bars in her underpants, her skirt puddled on the ground below her dangling feet. She'd never been so embarrassed. "You didn't!"

"I did." He grinned again. "A few other things, too."

"Brat."

Keiko needn't have worried. Just before classes began, Mako appeared on their doorstep. When Tommy threw open the door, welcoming him, Keiko's heart thudded.

3

NOBUKO

Japan

After the war ended Nobuko continued to live in Sakayama, trying desperately to put the past several years behind her, forget about Masato Abi. Mrs. Mori never mentioned him in her letters, and Nobuko hadn't asked. If he'd died in New Guinea like so many others, she didn't want to know.

Fluent in English and Japanese, Nobuko worked for the Occupation Forces as an interpreter and special assistant to the unit's commanding officer. One evening following a particularly grueling day of talks between her boss, Colonel Anderson, and Sakayama's mayor over streetcar tracks repair, she'd returned to the house where she rented a room, wanting only a hot bath and bed. She was stunned to find Masato with her landlord.

"Forgive me for not coming to you sooner, Nobuko-san. Only today did I learn you hadn't returned to America as I thought."

"I was here," she said, when she could get the words out. "Waiting for you." Only as she said the words did she realize their truth. Waiting for him was exactly what she'd been doing. They were married three months later.

Not everyone in Nishimi welcomed Nobuko when Masato had brought her home to the mountain village as his bride two years before. Mrs. Abi, her mother-in-law, found ways each day to make clear that Nobuko was not the wife she'd wanted for her only son. Yoko Yoshida, making dire predictions of future misfortune, encouraged the villagers to shun her.

Masato, however, was perfect—everything she could want in a husband. He was a gentle and playful lover, an entertaining conversationalist—nothing escaped his fun-filled eyes and active imagination—and whenever possible, he acted as a buffer between Nobuko and his mother's acid tongue.

He also insisted a toilet be installed in their living quarters.

His mother objected. "A benjo inside? That is ridiculous. Why should we go to such an expense? Why should things be different because we have an American, a gaijin, living here?"

Although his tone remained courteous, Masato's eyes narrowed. "The times are changing, Mother. We do not need to cling to the old ways because they are familiar. We need to modernize—our living spaces, but also the way we do business." He strode around the store and pointed to stacks of dated merchandise. "This store is behind the times. Nishimi is behind the times." He came to stand in front of his mother. "A bus will soon run between here and Sakayama. You've seen how the government is widening and paving the road in preparation for it. If we do not update, people will take the bus and do their shopping in Sakayama. The stores there are open once again and filled with goods."

"Nonsense," Mrs. Abi said, scowling. "Going to Saka-yama, even on a bus, would take far too long. Besides, we have everything anyone would want right here." She gestured to the same piles of goods Masato had disparaged moments before.

That argument was the first of many on the subject. Timid Mr. Abi, whom Nobuko had always liked, stayed out of the fray. Nobuko knew Masato was right, change was inevitable, but like Mr. Abi, she made certain to busy herself elsewhere whenever the subject of the toilet came up. It took months for Masato's mother to give in, but if she understood the correctness of her son's opinion that they needed to update their home and the store, she gave no outward sign that Nobuko could discern.

The new toilet proved to be a success. Often shoppers requested to see this phenomenon. Before a week passed, Mrs. Abi acted as though its addition had been her idea. "You'll notice how easily the lever works and how the water quickly carries everything away. I believe a man from Nagoya came up with the idea."

Although the toilet was a welcome addition, it made their living spaces behind the store even more cramped.

And there was no privacy. Every conversation, every word spoken, could be heard throughout. Nobuko and Masato resorted to taking long walks in the surrounding woods, looking for secluded spots.

"When the snows come, we shall need to think of something else," Masato joked.

To Nobuko, their lack of privacy wasn't something to be jested about. Aside from craving the intimacy she and Masato shared in their mossy hideaways, she was eager to become pregnant. With both her parents dead and her brother an ocean away, she longed to surround herself with family. Four children would not be too many, but she would settle for one.

Her wish was not granted. Conception-less months piled up, one upon another, each one noted by Mrs. Abi. Nobuko didn't need her mother-in-law's sly innuendoes, suggesting her body was too small and boyish to conceive, to make her feel unworthy. She didn't need reminding she was lucky to have Masato, either.

"I can't imagine what my son was thinking," Mrs. Abi said one day when Masato had left the store to deliver some mail. "As handsome as he is, as well-educated…he could have had his pick of young women. Instead, he chose you, whose scarred face will no doubt frighten a child if you should ever have one."

Nobuko fingered the scar on her cheek, wondering if it would ever fade. Despite her mother-in-law's frequent references, the mark that went from just below her right eye to an inch above her lip didn't distress her. That slight disfigurement was nothing compared to what so many others had suffered.

Masato often kissed the scar, calling it visible proof of her courage and selflessness. "When Mrs. Mori told me how you flew down the mountain during the earthquake, without concern for your own safety, and single-handedly tried to push away the massive boulders that buried the school, I knew you were a woman to treasure. I believe that's when I decided to marry you."

Nobuko fingered the scar again, thinking of the children who'd been killed. The memory of the small bodies laid out on the rough ground made her chest tightened and tears sting her eyes.

Nine years had passed since that terrible day. She'd come to Nishimi for what had been intended as a short visit with Mori, her father's cousin, Mrs. Mori, their daughter-in-law and grandchildren. The earthquake happened the very next day. She closed her eyes, remembering everything—not only the loss of so many village children when a large granite outcropping had sheared off and crushed the school in the clearing below it, but all that followed the earthquake, the aftershocks, the unremitting grief, and then the war and the hunger. So often during those years she'd felt God had forsaken her.

Now, Mr. Mori, who'd become ill a few months before, was dying. Just as her father had died when he was released from Camp Minidoka, the internment camp in Idaho where her parents and her brother had been sent after Pearl Harbor. Her mother had died while they still lived at the camp.

All the years of the war, Nobuko had thought her family safe on their truck farm in California. Instead they'd been surrounded by barbed wire and armed guards in watchtowers. Often, when she'd been most troubled—when the villagers turned against her, when Masato was conscripted, when old Mr. and Mrs. Hara died of starvation and left her with young Kensai to care for—she'd dreamed she felt her mother's comforting presence, as though her mother's arms enfolded her. Since death had released her mother's spirit, maybe that was so.

At least with her 'Japan father', as Mr. Mori called himself, when the time came, she would be at his side. But the time came long before Nobuko was ready. Mori's daughter-in-law rushed into the store on a blustery February morning, snow glistening on the scarf covering her head and shoulders. "You must come. He is leaving us. He wants to see you before he goes."

Minutes later, Nobuko knelt beside Mori's futon, rubbing one cold hand between her own. Mrs. Mori knelt across from her, holding his other hand. Unable to settle in one place, young Mori, whose foot had failed to heal and had been removed, clomped in and out of the room on his crutches. His wife trailed after him, trying to offer comfort.

Mori's breathing was low and raspy. He opened his eyes and looked at Nobuko. "Who would have thought you would remain in Japan, Nobuko-san?" he whispered. "But you did, and you've come back to us."

Nobuko nodded, unable to speak.

"You have Masato now. The two of you can grow old together, like us." He looked over at Mrs. Mori and smiled before turning back. "Be strong, my American daughter. Don't let the petty views of Yoko Yoshida and some of the villagers wear you down."

Nobuko swallowed. "I won't, Mori-san. I promise."

"Or your mother-in-law's."

She tried to smile. Unchecked tears cascaded down her cheeks.

Mori sighed and once again closed his eyes. Nobuko remained beside him, across from Mrs. Mori. Both wept softly. Mori's son and daughter-in-law came to join them, heads bent.

Late in the afternoon, while the wind whistled outside and a thin, wintery sun shone through the frost on the window, dust motes floating in the beam of light above him, Mori took his final breath and let it out on a long sigh.

That night, Nobuko lay next to Masato, her head on his shoulder, their down-filled quilt pulled up to their chins. She had no tears left. "I'll never forget his kindness to me, even when others considered me a gaijin, an outsider and an enemy."

"He was a good man," Masato said. "But how do you suppose he tolerated working for Yoko all those years? Or worse, Takeda."

"That man is evil," Nobuko said. She linked her fingers through Masato's. "Everyone in the village knows how he treats Yoko, yet no one does anything—even though they owe her a great deal. She kept this village going while her husband fought in the war. The pottery factory is the heart of Nishimi—without it, Nishimi would disappear. I asked your mother why no one goes to Yoko's defense. She said I should mind my own business. Mrs. Mori says it's just the way things are."

Masato shifted his head on the pillow, reached over and smoothed Nobuko's hair, his fingers trailing across her cheek. "In a way, they are both right. When there are difficulties between a husband and wife, the law is most often on the husband's side. The villagers know there is little they can do."

"I'm afraid men have the advantage in America, too," Nobuko said. Although in America, she thought, women could at least own property and run for political office. They'd been voting since 1920, too. In Japan, women hadn't been allowed to vote until MacArthur forced a new constitution on the country. A smile came to Nobuko's lips as she imagined her mother-in-law, speechless for once, at the news she was to cast a ballot.

"No matter what the law says, Takeda's behavior is not right. He frightens the village children, too."

"He frightens me," Masato said, laughing without humor. "I have no idea what that man is capable of."

Nobuko shivered.

4

VIRGINIA

Idaho

Although Virginia's daughter willingly called him Papa, Bella knew John Sato wasn't her father. She knew because she went to Seattle with Virginia to get him.

In the fall of 1942, Virginia, pregnant and unmarried, had moved back to the family farm, ostensibly to care for her brother Marc and their cruel father, by then too weak to be of concern, but also too weak to be of much help to Marc.

In the spring, with labor scarce, Marc suggested that they make use of Japanese internees from nearby Camp Minidoka. Virginia had been dead set against it, worried they'd be set upon by spies, or worse, murdered in their beds. Her father had railed against it, too, but he'd railed against most everything.

How foolish she'd been. John came that first summer. Keiko Ugawa came, too. They arrived the week before Bella was born. What a night that had been. Marc had been no help, other than to get Keiko, who knew even less about childbirth than Virginia. But they'd managed. And she'd gotten her beautiful Bella.

While she regained her strength, Keiko took over preparing meals for the workers. Virginia chuckled at that memory. Poor Keiko. Everyone complained about her lack of cooking skills. Virginia was almost forced to get back on her feet before the men quit and returned to Camp Minidoka.

Over the summer, Virginia grew infatuated with John Sato's good looks, his golden skin. And she couldn't get over his friendliness, his kindness to her and Bella, his wry humor, and his intelligence—what a difference he was from Bella's biological father, whom Virginia hoped she'd never see again.

When the war started, Japanese-American men had been classified as enemy aliens, even though they'd been born in America and were U.S. citizens. But as the need for fighting men grew, that policy was voided, and in the spring of 1944, John was drafted. Although Virginia had tried to keep her feelings hidden, even from herself, she'd been heartsick the day she and Keiko came upon him waiting to board the Army bus that would take him away from Camp Minidoka.

A soft smile curled her lips when she recalled how pleased she'd been to find his first letter in the mailbox, shortly after he'd left for training at Camp Shelby. She still had it, along with all his others, tied up with yellow yarn. After that first one, they wrote to each other every week while John was in training, but after he shipped out, his letters were sporadic. Neither of them expressed their feelings directly, but Virginia soon knew she'd grown to love John Sato. She was pretty certain he felt the same about her, too.

Then the war ended. She waited and waited for John to contact her, racing down the lane to the mailbox each day, searching through the mail for an envelope with his familiar handwriting on the front. A letter never came.

She'd nearly given up hope when Reverend Greene came to the house. He and John had once been friends. "I have news of John Sato I believe you should know," he said.

Virginia tensed. "He's well?"

Reverend Greene nodded.

Virginia's shoulders relaxed. "I was so afraid he was hurt. He has no next-of-kin here, no one the government would have notified." She knew she rambled. "Where is he? Why didn't he come back to Idaho?" Come back to me, she meant.

Reverend Greene gazed at her, unsmiling, but with understanding in his eyes. "John thought a relationship between the two of you—a white woman and a Japanese-American man—would be unfair to you, especially in these times. He's looking for work in Seattle."

Before he left, Reverend Greene gave Virginia John's address. She didn't hesitate. The moment the door shut behind him, she ran upstairs and pulled her suitcase off the closet shelf. The next day she and Bella boarded a Seattle-bound bus.

The address Reverend Greene had given her was a tall Victorian-style house with flaking paint, flanked on either side by similarly aging houses. Next to the front door, there were several names and apartment numbers, including John's. She pulled open the heavy door and she and Bella entered a dimly lit hall. She would have run up the dingy, narrow stairs, but couldn't because of her four-year-old daughter's short legs. With each slow step, Virginia's heart beat faster.

Finally, they came to the top of the stairs. Virginia paused in front of John's door. She knocked, her hands sweating and the vein in her temple throbbing. Footsteps sounded within. John opened the door. Virginia stood, unable to utter a sound.

Their eyes, his obsidian, hers navy-blue, locked for several seconds. John drew a deep breath. "I love you, you know."

Virginia nodded, her throat so tight she feared she might choke. Warm tears filled her eyes. A minute seemed to expand into an hour, and still they gazed at one another.

Bella tugged on her hand. "Mama…are we going to have a papa now?"

Virginia looked from her daughter to John, her eyebrows raised. Would they? Her heart thudded, waiting for his answer.

He gazed back at her. "Do I have a choice?"

She shook her head and whispered, "No."

John now joked that he'd been given no option but to return to Idaho. "I was kidnapped by two impossible-to-resist beauties."

Virginia slid her hand over to John's side of the bed. It was already cold. She wished he was still there, wished she could cuddle up next to him and they could both forget all the things they needed to do that day and every day. But he was already out in the fields where, for days, he and Marc had been plowing, from four in the morning until nearly ten at night, their tractors' headlights blazing trail, poking through the dark. When they finished one field, they moved on to the next.

Leo, her and Marc's eldest brother, should have been helping, but he seemed less and less capable of doing anything since he'd returned from the war.

With a sigh, Virginia threw the covers back and put her feet over the side of the bed, searching for her slippers. The thin carpet covering the hardwood floor did little to prevent the cold from stabbing into her feet. She wasted no time climbing into her clothes, thrown over the end of the bed the night before.

Down the hall, five-month-old Neil still slept soundly in his crib. In her bed by the window, Bella was buried beneath the covers and only a bit of her blonde hair was visible, cascading over the pillow. Virginia closed their bedroom door and went downstairs, where she slipped into an old corduroy jacket and her barn boots.

Outside, her breath came in puffs of white as she crossed the yard. The peak of the barn and the cottonwood tree beside it reached into a leaden sky. From behind the barn came impatient lowing. Poor Bessie. Virginia knew just how the animal felt—her own breasts were full and soon would be leaking.

She leaned into the heavy door and slid it open.

Her hand clapped over her mouth, stifling a scream.

Leo lay sprawled on a bale of hay, their father's old shotgun beside him, blood everywhere.

She fell against the door frame. Her brother had no face. A lone fly buzzed around where it had been. Loud ringing filled Virginia's ears. Her stomach convulsed and she spewed green bile into the dirt.

My God, my God. Leo. What have you done?

She yanked the barn door closed, shutting off the gruesome scene, and staggered across the yard to the side of the house. Head reeling, she stumbled against the wooden post where the brass farm bell was mounted. Over and over she pulled the rope, ringing the bell, until finally John and Marc arrived on their tractors.

Both jumped down and rushed to her side.

"What is it?"

"It's Leo. Dear God, Marc. Our brother has killed him -self."

"Where? Where is he?"

She pointed. "In there."

Marc ran for the barn.

John stayed with Virginia. She collapsed into him. "I knew he was unhappy—I should have guessed he might do something terrible." Her tears soon soaked his worn jacket. She drew back slightly when she heard the kitchen door open. Bella.

John's arms tightened. "Go back inside, sweetheart. Mommy and I will be there in a minute."

"Neil is crying."

Their son's distressed wails floated out the open door. Virginia struggled to control her own sobbing and wiped her eyes and nose on the sleeve of her corduroy jacket. "I need to get him. I need to get Bella ready for school. The cow still needs milking, too. And breakfast." Her shoulders sank. Tears flooded her eyes once again. "I don't know what to do."

Ashen-faced, Marc came out of the barn and started toward them. As always when he was under stress, his limp, the result of a childhood leap out of the loft and a poorly set break, was more pronounced. "I'll call the sheriff."

Virginia's shoulders tensed. John's arm slid around her waist and she leaned into him as he gently urged her and Bella into the house. Marc's hushed voice came from the hall, where the telephone hung on the wall.

Virginia drew a deep breath and straightened her shoulders. "I need to get the baby."

"Papa, why was Mommy ringing the bell and crying?"

"Something's happened to Uncle Leo. Mommy needed Uncle Marc and me to come in from the fields."

"Oh."

Virginia left her husband and daughter and went upstairs to Neil. She tried to hold him close, comfort him and herself, but he flung his body backward, almost out of her grasp. His arms outstretched, he flailed his anger.

Several minutes later, his face red and blotchy and smeared with mucous, his breath still coming in quivering sighs, she carried him downstairs.

In the hall, Marc hung up the phone.

Bella sat at the kitchen table while John filled her bowl with Wheaties and milk. Her daughter didn't like Wheaties, but she made no complaint. She rarely did. Such an easy child, Virginia thought. It was already clear, even at five months, Neil would be nothing like his big sister.

"What did the sheriff say?" John asked Marc.

"He'll be here shortly, along with the coroner."

They both came, but neither stayed long. The sheriff asked if they'd heard the gunshot, but they each said no. "He must have done it this morning, after John and Marc left for the fields," Virginia said. She swallowed. "I was asleep."

They later told folks Leo accidentally shot himself, but everyone knew it was no accident. Virginia's brother was just one more victim of the war.

The following day, Paul and Suki arrived by train from Palo Alto. Not Irene. When Virginia was finally able to reach her sister, she claimed she couldn't take time off from her new job.

Leo's funeral was held in Reverend Greene's church, the church where Suki and Paul had married two years before. When the war ended, instead of returning to Seattle and the church he'd left in 1943 to follow his congregation to Idaho, Reverend Greene remained in Twin Falls. Some former internees had settled there as well. With their homes and businesses gone, many saw no point in returning to the various towns and cities on the West Coast from which they'd been rounded up after Pearl Harbor. Others returned to Idaho when they found they weren't welcome in those towns and cities.

Reverend Greene didn't say much about Leo. Instead, he spoke about Magic Valley and all the young men who'd left it to fight in the war. He spoke about how some hadn't come home and how some came home changed forever. Some, like Leo, came home broken. He also spoke about hope and a future without war.

Virginia frowned at the last bit. She didn't think such a thing was possible. Hadn't the Great War been the war to end all wars? People should have learned something from that. For one thing, that the defeated couldn't be punished forever. From what she'd read and what John pointed out to her, the Allies, led by America and Great Britain, were repeating that mistake with Japan. It seemed the world blamed Hitler for the war and exonerated the German people. In Japan it was the opposite. The Emperor was held exempt and the people were being punished.

But how could the German people not have known what was happening in those death camps, the ones Leo and his unit had come upon near the end of the war? She'd seen pictures of the broken, skeletal bodies of the dead, the starving faces and empty eyes of the survivors. The pictures were horrible enough. How much worse it must have been to see them in person.

Leo had always been emotionally fragile. He'd taken the worst of their father's brutish behavior, too. She was almost glad the old man had been dead and gone before Leo came home from the war. Thin as a rail, his eyes sunken and haunted, Leo had claimed all he wanted to do was forget the war and help Marc and John on the farm. Then he began drinking and in the end was no help at all—to himself or anyone.

The organ startled Virginia out of her thoughts. Slightly off-key, Mrs. Greene sang the opening lines of Nearer My God to Thee. They all joined in. Later, after another brief service at the cemetery, they returned to the farm.

Paul said he was going to his and Suki's room. Virginia's eyes followed her brother as he slowly climbed the stairs, his hand gripping the banister. Her brother clearly didn't want his family's company. Virginia looked at Suki, who silently shook her head.

When they'd arrived the day before, Paul had said he didn't want the downstairs bedroom, the one their father had occupied, even though it was bigger. Perhaps it was as well he and Suki stayed in the bedroom Paul had grown up in and had returned to after he was invalided out of the Navy. The bed in his room was small for two people, but nothing had been changed. Paul knew how many steps from the door to the bed, to the bathroom down the hall, the stairs. He wouldn't have moved around so confidently in their father's old room.

Virginia sighed and took a sleeping Neil upstairs to put him down for a nap. He'd cried most of the way home, refusing the bottle she tried to give him. He didn't stop crying until they turned into the lane.

"Maybe we'll get an hour or two of peace," John said when she returned to the living room. Both he and Marc looked like they wanted to be somewhere else. With all of them gathered together, Virginia was surprised no one commented on Irene's absence.

Suki, in the chair by the window, picked up a magazine with a tractor on its front, then set it down. "Marc," she said. "What do you think it will take for Paul to forgive your father?"

"Forgive him for what, being a curmudgeon? The old man was a bastard, all right, but Paul didn't have it any worse than the rest of us."

Suki frowned and bit her lower lip. She looked as though she might say something more. She didn't, leaving Virginia to wonder if there'd been something between their father and Paul she didn't know about.

After a few minutes of puzzling that question, she suggested Suki help her fix dinner. Suki stood, looking grateful for something to do.

"Guess I'll get changed and go check the animals in the barn," Marc said, and left the room. John picked up the magazine Suki had earlier discarded and was quickly engrossed.

Suki smiled. "Obviously he finds crop rotation more compelling than I do."

The two women went into the kitchen. Virginia was about to ask Suki what she had meant with her question to Marc, but Neil's cries interrupted her. She rolled her eyes heavenward. "That child will be the death of me. I can't get him to take the bottle and I have no more milk myself. Emotional strain, I guess. I just dried up."

Suki put an understanding hand on Virginia's arm. "Emotional strain for him, too."

"You're right." Virginia sighed. It seemed that was all she did these days.

"Neil cries a lot," said Bella, who'd followed the two women into the kitchen.

Suki, always the mediator, tried to explain. "Some babies are like that. My little cousin was the same. I slept in her bedroom, too, before we were sent to Camp Minidoka."

"Did she cry at night and keep you awake?"

"She did. She finally got over it, though."

"I hope Neil does."

"He will."

Bella nodded, but didn't appear to have much confidence in such an outcome.

Unsure she did either, Virginia went upstairs to get her son.

A few days after Leo's funeral, Virginia and Suki sat in the kitchen, Virginia feeding a hungry Neil. He'd finally accepted the bottle and was now urgently making up for what he'd missed.

"I wish we could stay longer, but Paul needs to get back. He can't miss any more school." Paul was upstairs, napping again.

Sleep was the buffer Virginia's brother appeared to have chosen to put between himself and his family. "It's not good for him, you know, all this napping."

"I know. But I'm at a loss what to do about it."

"Suki, is there something Paul never told any of us about? Something between him and Dad?"

Suki was quiet for a moment. "You need to ask him." Virginia frowned, wanting her sister-in-law to say more, but Suki shook her head. "I can't. It's for Paul to tell you."

Paul had always been hard to understand, though Virginia remembered him as more pliable when he was a boy. When had that changed? While he was in the Navy? "I suppose he has terrible memories of that plane crashing into his ship and so many of his shipmates being killed. That would be enough to give anyone nightmares."

"Yes, but he won't talk about it. Whenever I push, he tells me it's over and to forget it."

"But he obviously can't." Virginia took the nipple from Neil's mouth. The baby gasped and yelled his displeasure. She put him against her shoulder and patted his back until he let out a loud, echoing burp.

Suki laughed.

When Virginia gave Neil the bottle again, he attached himself with ferocious eagerness. "I wish you were staying longer, too. If Keiko were with us, it would be almost like old times."

Suki nodded.

Suki and Keiko had never been on the farm this late in the year, though. In the fall, after harvest, they'd returned to Camp Minidoka and the barracks, Keiko with her father, Suki with her aunt and uncle and their three children, crowded into a narrow space partitioned with ropes and blankets, a single bulb hanging from the ceiling, and a pot-bellied stove against one wall. Virginia's lips tightened, thinking again how miserable they all must have been—nearly ten-thousand people crammed into that awful place. The pathways between the buildings had turned to mud whenever it rained, or when the snow melted. The walls had no insulation. In this part of Idaho, the heat could climb to well over a hundred degrees, and in the winter, it could plummet to below zero. Unbearable. And the wind was a constant.

Suki broke into her thoughts. "I wonder how Keiko is doing in school."

"You know how she is when she puts her mind to something—I'm sure she's doing well."

Virginia didn't have the opportunity to talk privately with Paul before he and Suki left, returning to Palo Alto and school. Paul was in Wallace Stegner's writing department at Stanford. Suki attended classes with him, took his notes, typed his papers. Virginia could only imagine what an odd couple they must appear on campus—her tall blind brother with his nearly white blond hair, accompanied by tiny, dark-haired Suki.

It took several weeks for life on the farm to find its new normal. Virginia often looked out the kitchen or bedroom window, expecting to see Leo walking out of the barn or into the prove-up shack—he'd kept bottles of liquor hidden in both. Then she'd catch herself and remember. When she wasn't grieving for Leo, doing barn chores, or taking care of her family, she thought about Paul. What had happened to set him against his own family?

In the spring, Irene, turned up…sans husband number two. Her sister waltzed in like nothing had happened, as though their brother Leo had never existed. She took over their father's old room, tossing her clothes over the chair and bed, kicking off her shoes wherever she felt like. In the bathroom, her cosmetics were on the back of the sink and the top of the toilet tank, her wet nylons hung from the bathtub curtain rod. Virginia wanted to hit her.

"Dad's room reeks of her perfume," she told John and Marc. "He'd be having a hissy-fit…say the place smelled like a brothel."

John patted her hand. "Maybe you could at least get her to hang her wet nylons somewhere else—I'm tired of fighting my way through them to get to the bathtub."

Marc laughed, but with little amusement. "Don't worry. She won't be here long."

Marc was right. Less than a week after Irene arrived, off she went again. No 'thank you,' no 'goodbye.' The only thing she left behind was a tube of ruby red lipstick called 'Cherish Me.' Bella found it and tried it on herself and Neil.

5

CHEIKO

Chieko swallowed hard, trying to hold back the bile rising in her throat. *How can my parents, who claim they love me, consider such a match? He is an old man. I'll be a widow by the time I am thirty.* Fighting the urge to turn and flee, she sat with what she knew was unseemly haste. She would not bring shame or embarrassment to her family, but a stone as big as a melon formed in the pit of her stomach.

While her parents and the matchmaker drank tea, and exchanged gossip and pleasantries in the private meeting room of a hotel near her father's medical clinic, Chieko sat mute, her head bowed, taking only an occasional sip of tea. She didn't touch the pink, bean-filled pastry on the square, bamboo mat next to her cup. Now and again she lifted her head long enough for a sidelong glance at the stern countenance of the man they intended for her.

He appeared broad and powerful through the chest and arms, although the formal black kimono he wore, made it difficult to be certain. When he stood at their intro-duction, their eyes were nearly level. She couldn't forget those obsidian eyes. They made her feel like a schoolgirl and not a twenty-year-old woman ready for marriage.

When the ordeal finally ended, Chieko and her parents returned home in a taxi. Her father left her and her mother at the entry to their house before hurrying on to the neighborhood bathhouse.

"He will soon be boasting to his friends of the fine catch he's made for his daughter," her mother said as she slid open the door.

Fingers clenched, Chieko followed her mother into the entry hall. "I don't care how old and noble his family is, there is nothing fine about Hirotaka Katsuragawa."

Her mother motioned her to be quiet while a maid knelt on the rough floor and helped remove their outdoor shoes. The maid then assisted them up the step to the polished wood floor of the gallery, where two pairs of navy blue felt slippers waited.

Slipping her feet into one pair, Chieko ignored her mother's frown and the maid's presence. "How can you and my father do this to me?"

The maid moved away on silent, tabi-clad feet, giving no indication that she'd heard Chieko's words.

"I know your doubts and questions, daughter," her mother said, laying a gentle hand on Chieko's arm. "I reacted much the same when I understood I was to marry your father."

Chieko scowled, her dark eyes flashing. "That was different. You were raised together. You knew everything about him."

Her mother shook her head. "Not as different as you might think. He was fifteen when he joined our family and I was little more than a baby. Then he went away to school."

"If you know how I feel, why are you doing the same to me?"

"Because your father and I understand what is best for you, the same as my parents understood what was best for me." Her mother smiled, but it didn't take the sting from her words. "You are not to argue about this, Chieko-san. Your father and I have chosen well for you. In time, you will appreciate our efforts."

Chieko briefly closed her eyes, wishing for some alternative. Finding none, she heaved a tiny sigh and retreated to her room. Kneeling in front of her mirror, she smoothed her hair with trembling hands and studied her features, the straight lines of her upward-tilted brows, her almond-shaped dark eyes, her small, cupid's bow mouth. Pretty in a traditional way, but not beautiful enough to capture a man's interest. What had he seen in her, and why had he asked the matchmaker to approach her parents? Because of the family's wealth?

She'd always understood that when the time came for her to marry, her parents would select her mate. Much was invested in the process. At seventeen, she began the lessons to prepare her for the role of homemaker and wife. She learned carriage and posture and how to behave in every situation. She'd been enrolled in classes for cooking, flower arranging, and tea ceremony. Her mother talked to her of the responsibilities of being a wife and certain aspects of the marriage bed. She was prepared to be a good wife.

She accepted that her parents were responsible for arranging her marriage. But why couldn't her future husband be a handsome young man with fine long legs? Why must he look like a short, bow-legged toad?

That evening, while her mother remained in the kitchen directing preparations for the evening meal, Chieko brought her father his tea. Earlier, she'd heard her mother tell him of her unhappiness with their choice.

"Hirotaka Katsuragawa is from a fine old family," her father said when Chieko put the tray on the floor next to the cushion where he sat, the evening newspaper on his lap.

Chieko avoided his eyes and said nothing.

"His ancestors were *samurai;* they served this region's *daimyo.*"

She remained silent, as though she hadn't heard him. From a small, long-handled clay pot, she poured the fragrant, steaming tea into a matching teacup and placed the cup close to him.

He picked it up and blew on the tea. "He has given two brothers to his Emperor and fought with honor in New Guinea." He took a sip from the cup.

As far as her father was concerned, Chieko knew that honor took precedence over everything. As an orphan of a good family, but one without monetary means, her mother's parents had adopted him to carry on both the family name and the family tradition in medicine. It was a common custom when there was no male heir. Even so, Chieko could not keep quiet.

"His family is old, Father, but he is old as well."

"He is a respected artist, daughter. Already they call him *sensei.*"

"But, Father. He is almost forty."

"You exaggerate. He is only a year past thirty. But that he is older than you, means he is experienced and wise—a good counterpoint to your youth and inexperience. He is doing our family a great honor with this marriage, daughter. We expect you to bring honor to your family and behave with dignity. You will marry him."

"Yes, Father," Chieko whispered as she bowed her head. A tear trembled on her lower lid and slid onto her cheek.

Five months later, dressed in her wedding finery and escorted by her family, Chieko approached the shrine where she would be wed to the man she'd neither seen nor spoken to since the day they were introduced.

That morning, her mother had given her a mild sedative -laced tea, but the inner terror that had gripped Chieko for weeks, preventing her from making such simple decisions as which obi to wear, wouldn't go away. She hid her shaking hands in the folds of the brocaded sleeves of her wedding kimono. She hoped the heavy make-up she wore hid the panic she felt certain would otherwise be reflected on her face.

Her mother, along with the matchmaker and two female cousins, escorted her to a special room and instructed her to await a signal. Chieko tried to smile assurance to her mother, but the smile quickly fell. Her mother patted her hand and gave Chieko a consoling look. Then everyone bowed and backed from the room.

After what seemed like an eternity, the awaited signal came in the form of a door sliding open. Chieko's heart thudded in her ears and her hands shook harder than ever as she stepped through the door. Drum and flute music played. She looked at her intended husband, facing her from three meters away, in front of another sliding door. They walked toward one another while attendants waved sacred tree branches tied with paper streamers above their heads.

Her feet in high geta, Chieko concentrated on not tripping. She swallowed repeatedly when she and her intended arrived in front of the priest, turned and faced him. A high-pitched noise sounded in her ears. She feared she might swoon. She drew a restorative breath and the sound faded.

Family members and the matchmaker looked on with varying degrees of pride on their faces while the priest said the words that would bind her forever to the stranger at her side. Only long years of vigilance by her parents and teachers kept Chieko's back straight and her head bowed in acceptance of her fate.

"You may stand now, wife," her new husband murmured in her ear. The ceremony had ended.

Chieko rose in the single fluid motion she'd been taught years before. Moments later, as though in a trance, she was led out of the shrine to the nearby banquet hall. For the next hour, she stood mute as the photographer posed the wedding party for picture after picture. Like a puppet whose strings were being pulled by strangers, she was posed first to the right and then to the left, her head tilted one way then another, her hands clasped or at her sides. She wondered if her new husband, standing silently beside her, felt frightened and alone, as uncertain as she about the future.

6

NOBUKO

Japan

Guests filled the large banquet hall, the men in dark, western -style suits and ties, the women in silk kimonos with elaborate obis. All were chattering and exclaiming. Exotic flower arrangements in shades of purple, yellow and salmon stood in every corner of the room and spilled from baskets scattered along tabletops. Lavish gifts were at each guest's place—a set of fragile demitasse cups for the women, an onyx tie clip and cuff-links for the men. Nobuko had never witnessed anything so splendid.

At their table near the front of the hall, Masato leaned close and murmured to Nobuko. "A little grander than our wedding, is it not?"

The corners of Nobuko's mouth turned up at her husband's words. Their much smaller ceremony had been attended by her aunt and uncle, her two cousins, and Colonel Anderson, her old boss. In addition to his reluctant and disapproving parents, Masato had been attended by his friend, the new groom now sitting at the table facing them.

"I feel sorry for the bride," Nobuko whispered. "Look how frightened she is."

"She has nothing to fear from Hirotaka."

"No, but she doesn't understand that."

Like many arranged marriages, the bride and groom had not met since the time the matchmaker introduced them—months in which Hirotaka's bride would have worried and wondered about her intended husband and about their future together. As the two had walked toward each other at the beginning of the wedding ceremony, Nobuko easily imagined the young woman's inner turmoil.

"She will soon learn." Masato spoke the words with confidence.

Nobuko wondered if her husband was right. Since Hirotaka often came to their quarters to visit or play a game of chess, she'd become better acquainted with her husband's good friend. He considered himself to be nothing more than a humble artist and a part of the village. But Hirotaka had been raised the son of a wealthy nobleman, and there was an aloofness about him that held him apart from others. She thought it might take some time for his young bride to discover his many fine qualities.

She stopped musing and turned her attention to the spectacle of the multiple courses being delivered to each table by a flock of attendants. Whole fish appeared to leap from platters; slices of lotus root and sweet potato, lightly battered and crisply fried, were served with tender bits of roasted pork; boiled lobster tails were sectioned and arranged to look like peonies; tender young spinach, steamed and mixed with soy sauce and rice wine, was served with pickled ginger, salted baby eggplant, and sweetened white rice stuffed into seared tofu.

The bride's father rose and went to the microphone. He tapped it before he spoke. "I am very humbled you have come here today to help celebrate my daughter's marriage to Hirotaka Katsuragawa. As you are all aware, my new son-in-law is from a fine old family, revered by each of us. They served their Emperor and Nippon well. Hirotaka most recently during the war in the Pacific, where he endured three brutal years on an island in New Guinea. It is a tragic loss to us that this great family has dwindled to one—but you will be happy to hear that my daughter is eager to do her part to increase that number."

Most laughed at the bride's obvious discomfort. Despite shoulders held rigid and straight, attempting to mask her distress, Nobuko saw the pain in the young woman's eyes. *Poor child—she must think she is living her worst nightmare.*

While the speakers droned on, each trying to outdo the other, Nobuko shifted her attention once again to the man seated to the bride's left. The day she and Masato had married, Hirotaka had thanked her for her help. When Nobuko worked for the Occupation Forces after the war, their major task had been transferring property ownership from the hands of the aristocracy, where it had resided for centuries, to the common people. Unlike most, Hirotaka had not resisted. In return for his easy acquiescence, he was granted the Nishimi property where his family's summer estate had once stood.

During the war, lightning had struck the roof of the huge main house. The whole village had rushed to the site and tried to put out the resulting inferno, forming a line and throwing bucket after bucket of water from the koi pond on the blaze. But their efforts failed; the house and everything in it had burned to the ground.

"Thanks to you and Colonel Anderson, I'm now living in the caretaker's house, just as I planned," Hirotaka said.

Hirotaka still lived in the caretaker's house, where he would take his bride following their brief honeymoon in Kyoto. She hoped Chieko was ready for Nishimi. The lavishness of the wedding showed the extent of her family's wealth—it was rumored they lived in a large house, with multiple servants to cater to their every need.

Although Hirotaka's reputation was growing as both painter and teacher—people called him sensei, honored teacher, and his work was shown in a new and popular Sakayama art gallery—there was no way he would be able to offer Chieko the comfort she enjoyed in her father's home. There would need to be adjustments and compromises by both.

How lucky she was to have Masato. If only they could have a baby. Maybe soon. Mrs. Mori had given her some herbs and told her to steep them in a pot of tea, which Masato and she were to share. Nobuko meant to give the herbs a try. They couldn't hurt, and they might help, although she didn't put much stock in the words Mrs. Mori told her to chant while preparing the tea.

"Let us go offer our congratulations to the bride and groom," Masato said, bringing her back to the present. The toasts were over.

When they reached the head of the line of well-wishers, Nobuko bowed her congratulations to Hirotaka. She then turned to Hirotaka's bride, who was quite beautiful, though up close looked even younger and more nervous, despite the traditional and heavy makeup she wore. Nobuko smiled reassurance. "We must support each other and become friends. I, too, am an outsider to Nishimi."

The bride mumbled a few polite words before looking down at the toes of her *geta*-clad feet, all that could be seen below the hem of her elaborately brocaded wedding kimono—so weighty Nobuko thought her shoulders must ache from supporting it.

After congratulating the bride's parents, Nobuko followed Masato outside, into the afternoon sunshine. The shrine and the new banquet hall were near the Nishimi River, not far from where her aunt and uncle lived.

"Do you want to visit them before we return to Nishimi?" Masato asked.

"I think I would prefer going home now. I will see my aunt another time." Nobuko still had little use for her uncle. She couldn't forgive how he'd ordered her to kneel next to his prized radio and listen to the war news each night, following Japan's attack on Pearl Harbor and her unexpected return to Sakayama.

"We are invincible," he'd crowed, and for a while, as Japan smashed through the Pacific and Southeast Asia, Nobuko feared he must be right. After her uncle was conscripted, her aunt and her cousins moved to a smaller house, one with no room for Nobuko. She had happily returned to Nishimi to live with the Moris. Her aunt had insisted Nobuko take her uncle's radio with her—a significant act of defiance by her aunt. It had soon become a nightly ritual for the villagers to gather at Mori's house to listen to news of the war. Unlike her uncle, the villagers didn't gloat when Japan won a battle. Nor did they storm when the Allies won. Their only thoughts were for the wellbeing of their husbands or sons.

Public transportation now existed between the city of Sakayama and the village of Nishimi, but the bus didn't run on weekends. Masato had arranged for them to travel up the mountain in a farmer's truck. Dressed in her best kimono and patent-leather pumps, Nobuko stepped up on the running board of the clattering vehicle and slid onto the seat, smiling thanks to the farmer, who had laid down a cloth for her to sit upon. Masato climbed in after.

She was reminded of her first trip to Nishimi, when she'd traveled up the mountain in a farmer's cart, pulled by a giant ox with feet the size of pie tins. This farmer was unlike her first escort, however, who'd said nothing the entire trip beyond a mumbled greeting when she'd climbed over the cart's wheel and sat on the wooden bench next to him. This one talked non-stop about everything from the warm August weather to the latest news and the economy.

"Things are better now America has so many of its soldier boys and sailor boys here," he said. "Now that our government isn't taking all our crops to feed the army, we are no longer starving."

Nobuko made no comment, but she shuddered, not wanting to remember those years.

Masato, however, nodded. "You're right—and it's nothing like the first couple of years after the war ended, either, when America and the Allies were only interested in punishing us."

The farmer frowned, his mouth turned down. "That was a bad time. With the fighting over, everyone thought things would be better."

They started up the mountain, the truck's engine straining. While Masato and the farmer talked on about politics, Nobuko gazed at the fields of rice and millet they passed on the mountain's lower elevations, at the men and women toiling side-by-side, even on Sunday. The scene reminded her of working in the rice paddy on the Hara farm during the last two years of the war.

Hirotaka once told Masato that his parents died of broken hearts. They'd lost two sons and feared Hirotaka dead as well. Like old Mr. and Mrs. Hara, who'd died because they had nothing to eat and nothing to live for, Hirotaka's parents, too, were victims of the war. Just as her own parents, who'd died an ocean away from her, had been its victims.

Nobuko sighed. This was meant to be a happy day. She put sad thoughts aside and instead tried to envision the caretaker's home, where Hirotaka was about to take his bride. Rough, small and remote, it was nothing like his bride was accustomed to. How would she adapt to her changed circumstances? Growing up in the hustle and bustle of Sakayama, she was bound to feel isolated in a mountain village. Had Hirotaka thought of that?

The farmer swerved the truck to avoid a large rock fallen onto the road, and Nobuko was thrown against Masato. He chuckled and helped her straighten. She smoothed her kimono.

"Sorry," the farmer said, then made another comment to Masato. "It was because America needed us when they were fighting in Korea. They needed a place to stage their men and supplies."

"I think their change in attitude was more than Korea," Masato said. "They realized we could be a strategic and well-placed partner. All we needed was help in rebuilding our economy."

The farmer shrugged. "Well, you may be right. All I can say is, it's good we aren't starving any longer. They may have been our enemies then, but they're our friends now. If not for America and General MacArthur, I wouldn't own my own farm. I'd still be leasing it from the Katsuragawa family."

Nobuko nodded, a pleased smile crossing her lips. She once again recalled how eager Hirotaka had been to be rid of his family's tenant farms. It was nice to know at least one farmer appreciated it.

When they entered Nishimi, she was struck anew by the changes to the village. When she first arrived, she'd been unprepared for anything so primitive—the unpainted shacks, the lack of shops and other amenities. Worst of all was the smell rising above the garbage-filled ditch running alongside the main street, often used by children as a toilet.

Many of those old shacks were gone, replaced by more modern homes. And the women who'd once appeared so hostile, were her friends. Well, with the major exception of Yoko Yoshida.

The sun was setting when the farmer brought the truck to a stop in front of the Abi store. Nobuko was glad the long day was nearing its end.

The next afternoon, Nobuko's mother-in-law handed her a letter. Seeing it was from her brother, Nobuko ripped the envelope open, her eyes eagerly scanning Mako's near-illegible hand. Her lips parted on an intake of breath. "Mako is getting married." She still thought of her younger brother as she'd last seen him, his hair slicked down and parted in the middle, standing next to their parents on the dock in San Francisco, waving goodbye. He'd been sixteen to her twenty. He would be twenty-nine now. How he must have changed.

Masato looked up from studying an invoice. "Who is he marrying? Someone you know?"

"No, a woman he met at the internment camp where he and my parents were sent. Her name is Keiko Ugawa. She is soon to graduate from a law school in Portland, Oregon." Nobuko frowned. "The war must have changed things in America, too. I never heard of a Japanese woman becoming an attorney, not even one born in America."

"When is the wedding?"

Nobuko looked back to the letter, deciphering a few more lines. "June, he says."

Masato moved to her side. "Would you like to go? We'll need to get passports—we can get them now."

It felt as though the air was sucked out of Nobuko's chest. She didn't trust herself to speak. America imprisoned her family behind barbed wire. It rejected her when she'd been desperate to return home. How could she even think of going back now?

Masato covered her hand with his. "We'll talk of it later."

7

CHIEKO

Japan

Chieko stared at her surroundings, trying to think of something to say. No words came to her, but tears filled her eyes and questions filled her heart. This was where she was to live the rest of her life—this hovel? It was not a quarter, not even an eighth the size of her parent's home in Sakayama. It stank of turpentine, linseed oil and paint. Finished paintings, of people and places she didn't know or understand, leaned against one wall. A half-finished painting of an arched bridge and teahouse was positioned on an easel in front of the only window in the room. There were no comfortable cushions scattered about, no scroll on the wall, no small table for an ikebana arrangement in the recessed space of the tokonoma—nothing in the entire house to make it feel like a home.

The man who was now her husband showed her the small kitchen, the pots, the cabinet where she would find rice, though little else to make a meal. Again, she stared, unsure what to do. His frown was so fierce, she feared he might strike her.

"Rice will do for tonight, wife. Tomorrow you can shop for whatever else we need."

"Where?"

"At the Abi's store in Nishimi. It isn't far."

"Oh."

"Call me when you have prepared the rice."

That night, she swallowed her sobs. Next to her on the futon, her husband slept undisturbed. He hadn't bedded her since the second night of their brief honeymoon in Kyoto. How he must hate her, hate her youth, her inexperience, hate everything about her. Why wouldn't he? She couldn't even cook rice properly.

Chieko woke to the sounds of muffled, feminine giggles. She resisted the urge to bury her head beneath the quilt and return to the sweet oblivion of sleep. Though reluctant to face the world she now inhabited, she forced herself to rise and slip on a robe.

In the kitchen, she found two young women. Instead of kimonos, they wore Western-style blouses and loose pants gathered at the ankle. Kerchiefs covered their hair. One was scrubbing rice from the pot Chieko had burned the night before. The other was taking dishes from a cupboard.

They stopped what they were doing and bobbed their heads in unison. "Ohiyo gozaimasu, Katsuragawa-san."

"Good morning," Chieko said, returning their greeting. She hesitated, staring first at the young women, then at the pot and dishes. She returned her gaze to the women, a frown knotting her forehead. "Who are you?"

They giggled and told her their names.

"Your honored husband came to Nishimi this morning, on his way to Sakayama," Ichiko said. "He told us to come here. We are to clean the house and make it more pleasant."

"He said we are to do just as you tell us," the other young woman, Tomiko, said.

Chieko's eyes widened. Thoughts swirled through her head. Was it even possible to make this place pleasant? Would they really do everything she told them? The kitchen was so small, it wouldn't take long to clean and organize. What should she have them do next?

She nodded. "I will be back shortly."

She returned to the room she'd shared with her husband the previous night. It was separated from the main room by a row of sliding rice-paper shoji screens, all of which needed cleaning or replacing. From her trunk, still waiting to be unpacked, she took out a summer kimono of dark blue, flowered cotton, and a white apron with sleeves and a ruffled edge. While donning these serviceable garments and tying a kerchief over her hair, she planned out what to do.

The night before, her new husband had pointed to a steep and narrow stairway leading from the kitchen. "A storage loft," he'd said. Chieko now climbed the stairs and looked around. There wasn't much to see. At one end, a large window overlooked the crumbling foundation of what once had been a large building. At the other end of the loft, a smaller window revealed a steep embankment. A few boxes were stacked under the eaves. The rest of the space was bare.

After lunch, which the young women fortunately brought with them that morning, Chieko left them to finish cleaning and refreshing the tatami mats. Following their directions, she traveled down the track leading to the village of Nishimi. As promised, it wasn't far, taking her little more than twenty minutes to walk the short distance.

She easily found the Abi store, the only commercial establishment in Nishimi other than what appeared to be a pottery factory. There were pots stacked on a bench in front, and piled high under a covered space next to it. Behind the factory, a tunnel-shaped object of brick and earth flowed six meters or more down the mountainside. A kiln, she decided.

Fewer than a half-a-dozen modern houses lined the street, along with a dozen that were little more than unpainted shacks. No one was about, only three small children playing in the street, and a black and white dog, it's tongue lolling as it loped in a circle around them. She supposed the older children were at school, although she could see nothing that might serve as one.

A bell tinkled when Chieko entered the store. From behind a waist-high wooden counter, Nobuko, the wife of her husband's friend, counted out change to a customer. Nobuko looked over and smiled a welcome, at the same time handing a bundle wrapped in brown paper and tied with a string to the customer. "Thank you for your purchase, Tanaka-san."

The diminutive customer, who looked to be nearly one hundred, bobbed her head and turned to leave. When she saw Chieko, she paused and twitched her nose, then bobbed her head again and scurried out of the store. Chieko imagined a thin tail extending from beneath her kimono.

"Who is she? She looks like a mouse."

"Mrs. Tanaka," Nobuko said, smiling. "She is the official town crier. You will be the talk of Nishimi within the next ten minutes. She considers it her job to keep us all informed."

Chieko froze inside at the thought of strangers talking about her.

Nobuko came from behind the counter. "Don't worry, the villagers won't intrude, and you will soon get to know them. Your husband stopped here this morning. He said you would be coming to shop. Can I help you find something?"

Chieko hesitated. "I need everything."

Nobuko's eyebrows went up. "Everything?"

"There is only rice." Chieko felt her cheeks flush with the admission.

Nobuko laughed. "Now isn't that just like a bachelor? Well, let us begin. I see you brought a large basket. Good."

"There is no refrigerator in the house and limited storage, so I need things that will keep."

As well as food, Nobuko helped Chieko gather dish-towels, dishrags, bathing towels, soap flakes, washing powder and hand soap, all of which they piled on the counter.

"You can leave some of the things for Hirotaka to carry home," Nobuko said.

"That's a good idea. I don't think I could carry all that. He sent two young women to clean. Fortunately, they brought the buckets, soap and scrub brushes they needed."

"I'm sorry the caretaker's house isn't what you are used to."

Chieko's cheeks reddened again—she didn't want Nobuko to think she was complaining or disloyal. "I will manage." She hid her embarrassment by examining a pile of silk cushions. She selected two, one the color of a ripened persimmon, the other of a newly unfurled leaf. She fingered the silky material a moment. "I have money. I will pay for these and take them with me, along with the food for our dinner tonight. The rest I will leave for my husband to pay for and carry."

Ten minutes later, Chieko left the store, her chin up, half expecting an onslaught of questions from strangers. None came, although she felt many hidden eyes upon her as she walked through the village with her filled shopping basket over her arm.

By the time she returned to the house, Tomiko and Ichiko had accomplished what Chieko had asked of them. The living spaces, the kitchen, and the loft above it were thoroughly cleaned and smelled of soap and pine. After putting away the items she'd purchased, the three began carrying out Chieko's plan.

Tomiko and Ichiko had gone. Dinner was prepared, and all ready for her husband's return from the weekly classes he taught in Sakayama. Chieko's hands trembled when she heard his footsteps on the gravel path outside the house. No longer confident, she feared what he would say to all her changes. She knelt on the persimmon-colored cushion, holding her breath as the door slid open and he entered, carrying the items from the Abi's store in a lumpy-looking duffle bag slung over one shoulder.

Chieko's eyes held his for only a moment then fell to a spot on the freshened tatami mat at his feet.

Silence.

She lifted her eyes to see him staring around the room and through the opened screens to the room beyond.

"My paintings? My easel? My paints and brushes?"

Chieko bowed her head once again and answered, her voice a mere whisper. "In the loft, husband." She swallowed. The easel was heavy and awkward. It had required all their efforts to get it up the stairs, Tomiko above, pulling, Ichiko and Chieko below, pushing.

Her husband dropped the duffle bag, the items inside clunking together, and rushed to the kitchen and the stairs leading to the loft. Chieko rose and hurried after, reaching the kitchen in time to see his feet disappear through the opening. Above her head, footsteps sounded. She waited for him to descend, unsure if he would be furious or pleased. Perhaps she would be beaten. Worse yet, she might be sent home in disgrace. She swallowed.

After several minutes, he climbed down the steep steps. His back to her, Chieko couldn't see his expression until he turned.

He nodded. "It will do. I will take my bath before I eat."

Chieko drew a relieved breath as her heartbeat returned to normal. "The ofuro is heated and ready for you, husband."

Ichiko and Tomiko returned the next day. The house in order, they turned their energies to the derelict garden, pulling weeds, hoeing, and turning the clay soil. They'd brought seeds—carrots, peas, cabbage, soy beans—though it was rather late in the year to plant.

For hours they labored, pulling down part of the foundation of the ruins Chieko had observed from the loft window, using the stones to build up a falling wall next to the garden. When she brought the women lunch, they explained the foundations had been part of the Katsuragawa summer estate.

"Their main residence was in Sakayama," Tomiko said.

From Tomiko's and Ichiko's descriptions, Chieko believed the estate was now a city park and museum. As the young women talked, she learned all the things her husband hadn't told her about his childhood and his family, his imperious father, his graceful mother, his two brothers.

"The oldest son, Shunsuki, was the father's favorite. He died in China of cholera," Ichiko said. "My mother told me Shunsuki could do no wrong in his father's eyes, while Hirotaka could do nothing right. The middle brother—I forget his name—was fun-loving and easy-going, but his plane crashed into the ocean during the war."

"His name was Kinya. He liked jazz," said Tomiko. "His father hated it."

"They say your husband's mother made his father relent and allow him to study art instead of the economics classes he disliked," said Ichiko.

Chieko nodded. While they were in Kyoto, her husband took her to visit the famous Kyoto School of Painting where he had once studied.

"His mother was renowned for her beauty and grace," Tomiko said, taking another rice ball. "Those who served her, my aunt included, loved her. But they were afraid of the father."

"This place must have been very beautiful, too," Chieko said, taking in the vista spread before her. Stands of cedar and pine edged with cherry and dogwood alternated with fields of millet, rice paddies and lotus ponds, the whole dotted with farms that clung like barnacles to the side of the mountain. The Katsuragawa family had chosen well in locating their summer estate. She looked over her shoulder to the rugged tor looming above the house. Once again, she wondered what it would be like here in winter.

Tomiko and Ichiko appeared not to notice the land-scape beyond the ruined estate, probably because they'd grown up in Nishimi and saw this view every day.

"On the other side of the foundations, you can see where there were gardens and a koi pond," Tomiko said.

"Oh?"

"Would you like to see them?"

Chieko followed the two, scrambling over vines and broken foundation to the former site of gardens and pond. Trees and shrubs, no doubt hand-pruned and trained for decades, were now grown out of control. Part of an earthen wall stood upright, a wooden gate in the center hanging on one leather hinge. Before them, an undulating empty trough stretched nearly a dozen meters. A graceful bridge, un-broken, arched above it.

"There is a stream beyond that wall," Tomiko said. "They must have used it to fill the pond."

Chieko nodded, trying to picture the beauty that once had been. She imagined graveled pathways where Hirotaka's mother would have strolled, stooping occasionally to trail her hand in the water. She pictured her, beautifully dressed in a silken kimono, crossing the bridge, stopping midway to drop breadcrumbs to the fish swimming below. Perhaps there'd even been a pavilion for tea ceremony, she thought, imagining a wisteria-covered platform set to embrace the view of rockeries, shrubs, and koi pond. The picture on Hirotaka's easel.

With a sigh, she turned her back on the forlorn remnants of a life that no longer existed, and followed Tomiko and Ichiko to the new garden.

She helped Ichiko carry the lunch things into the house. Ichiko returned to help Tomiko in the garden. Chieko washed the few dishes and thought about the garden and the abandoned koi pond and Hirotaka's beautiful mother. How could she ever compete with such a gilded memory?

Once the garden was in and the house no longer looked abandoned, Ichiko and Tomiko came only one day a week. Even then, there was little for them to do. Chieko missed their lively chatter. At home in Sakayama, there'd always been activities to fill her days. Her many classes, but also shopping, visiting with friends, and occasionally going to the movies, a pastime her father frowned upon.

"American cinema is nothing you should be wasting your time on," he'd claimed. "Either they are about fools and women with no morals, or they are about gangsters."

But Chieko had often enjoyed watching Cary Grant, so handsome, Lana Turner, so sophisticated. And Esther Williams—if only she could swim like Esther Williams, and look so beautiful in a swimming suit. She blushed at where that thought led her.

Winter came and was even harsher than Chieko had imagined. When not traveling to Sakayama to teach, Hirotaka spent most of it in the loft, painting. Sometimes,

Chieko pulled out one of the boxes from under the eaves, sat on it and watched him, but she sensed he preferred being alone, so didn't do that often. She was relieved when spring arrived.

With little to occupy her time besides her daily grocery-shopping trips and the brief visits with Nobuko Abi, Chieko brightened when a couple came to the door.

"I am Takeda Yoshida," the man said. He did not introduce the woman behind him, who carried a large bundle. Only later did Chieko learn the woman was Yoko Yoshida, Takeda's wife.

She invited them in and offered tea.

When her husband returned home that evening, she told him about the visit. As soon as she uttered the name Yoshida, Hirotaka's shoulders stiffened.

"Have I done something wrong, husband?"

His voice remained calm, but his eyes nearly pinned her to the wall. "Tell me what happened."

"They brought us a wedding gift." A vase, burnished red in color, tall and gracefully narrow at the top. Chieko admired its beauty. Her husband only glanced at it before turning back to her.

"What else did he say?" He didn't appear interested in Yoko, only Takeda.

"Nothing of importance. They didn't stay for tea. They left when they found you weren't here." Chieko didn't add that the man had made her uneasy. Takeda Yoshida was very handsome, but the way his eyes darted like the beady eyes of a crow, coupled with his easy assurance, gave her a dislike of him. His wife had said nothing, only scowled at Chieko for the length of their brief visit.

"If he comes again, don't let him in. He is not to be trusted. And get rid of that." He pointed to the vase. "I don't want it in my house."

Chieko lowered her eyes. "Yes, husband."

Chieko was disappointed about the vase. It would have been perfect to display in the tokonoma, perhaps containing a single flower and a graceful branch, a scroll on the wall behind it.

Her husband said nothing more, merely nodded. After she served him his evening meal, he went to the loft and painted until long after she retired for the night. The next time he went to Sakayama, two days later, he came home with a lovely celadon vase.

Chieko clapped her hands together, delighted that he thought to bring her a gift. "It is lovely. Thank you, husband."

It wasn't until later that she wondered about the cost of the vase and whether they could afford it. Perhaps that was the reason the house contained so little, why everything in the grounds had been left to deteriorate.

Without stopping to think, Chieko wrote to her mother and explained what they lacked. A week later, a small, three-wheeled truck appeared on the track leading to the house. Chieko's eyes lit with anticipation.

When her husband returned that evening, he took one look at the newly decorated house before turning and walking out the door, firmly sliding it closed behind him. Two hours went by, two hours in which Chieko paced and worried, before he returned and called her to him.

"I realize things were lacking, wife. Things you have been accustomed to. I'm sorry I didn't see how much you missed your old life."

Chieko caught her breath, fearful of what he would say next.

"I would have gotten these things, perhaps not right away, but eventually." He gazed at her, pityingly she thought, as though he couldn't understand her youthful impatience.

She bowed her head, hiding the tears trembling on her lashes. "I will return everything."

"That is not necessary, Chieko-san. It is my fault. I shouldn't have taken a wife until I could afford one."

Oh no, he was going to send her home.

"However, we are married, and we must make do. These things your parents have sent will make our lives more comfortable. I will write and thank them."

Chieko closed her eyes. Her lips trembled as she tried to apologize for her ignorance and thank him for his understanding and forgiveness.

He brushed her apologies aside. "We won't speak of it again. But I am hungry, and I would like my dinner served on this fine new table."

"A little slice of human existence."
TONI MORGAN
TRILOGY
ECHOES
from a falling bridge
A NOVEL

TONI MORGAN
TRILOGY
HARVEST
the wind
A NOVEL
"Clear and lucid writing."

TONI MORGAN
TRILOGY
LOTUS
blossom unfurling
A NOVEL
"Terrific and surprising storylines."

8

KEIKO

Oregon

Keiko woke to the sound of rain slapping against her bedroom window. It had been coming down non-stop for days—a wet spring, even by Portland standards. Noises came from Tommy's room. She threw back the covers and hurried to beat him to the bathroom.

Dressed and ready for school, she was relieved to see her father's rain gear still hanging on a hook next to their apartment door. He'd been even later than usual getting home the night before. He was nearing sixty and she worried about him, especially with his extended hours and long commute.

"I often sleep another hour after you and Tommy leave for school," he'd said the last time she'd scolded him about working so late. "I don't need to be at the University Club until ten-thirty."

"But, Papa. You don't get home until after ten, or even later some nights. You're working nine or ten hours a day, six days a week."

"I am fine, Keiko-san. You worry about you."

Still, she fretted. On the bus that morning, she and Tommy discussed their father's long hours, but neither of them had a solution. If their father didn't work his assigned hours, there were plenty of others to take his place. Keiko frowned and stared unseeing out the bus window.

"Look at Johnson Creek," Tommy said, pointing to what should have been a narrow stream. "Those houses are going to be flooded if it doesn't stop raining."

Muddy water swirled half-way up the trunks of the willow, cottonwood, and maple trees lining the creek's banks. "On the radio last night, the newscaster said it's been so warm, the snowpack in the mountains is melting faster than normal," Tommy continued. "Rivers are spilling over their banks everywhere."

The rain still bucketed down when they reached their stop. Tommy ducked his head into his collar and darted off to his first class. From beneath her umbrella, Keiko eyed the grass-covered railroad berm separating the Columbia River from much of Vanport, imagining a rivulet of water forcing its way through the dirt, the berm suddenly erupting, water crashing through. Rain splatted against her umbrella with such force the handle vibrated in her hand. She tore her gaze from the still intact berm and hurried after Tommy.

Later, she met him in the cafeteria. "My professor said if it doesn't stop raining, there could be flooding along the Columbia and the Willamette. Do you suppose we'll have class next week?"

"It shouldn't be a problem—long as the berm holds. Come on, don't tell me you're scared you'll miss a couple of classes." As usual, Tommy tried to tease Keiko out of her concerns. "It's practically the end of the term. Stop being a worrywart."

"We're transferring to four-year schools next year... I don't want anything to mess that up." The man at the

University Club who'd helped them find their apartment had recommended Keiko to the dean of Northwest School of Law. She could hardly believe her good fortune when she received a letter telling her she was accepted and would be enrolled in the fall—assuming she completed the term at Vanport College. What would happen if she didn't get to finish? There were still exams to take.

"Relax," Tommy said. "Nothing's going to come between you and that law degree you're after. Is Mako coming for dinner tonight?"

She shook her head, still thinking about the rising river. "Tomorrow night. He has a class this evening."

"I don't know what that guy is thinking of, still wanting to marry you after eating your cooking."

"Ha-ha. Very funny."

Tommy was right, though. Usually, Keiko accomplished whatever she set out to do, but try as she might, she was not an accomplished cook. The night before, she'd used her mother's recipe for breaded veal cutlets, but instead of being melt-in-the-mouth tender, they were leather-like slabs. She'd helped Virginia cook at the farm, but Virginia had done most of the main courses. Keiko could whip out an excellent pot of oatmeal if she could make enough to feed ten hard-working laborers. Cooking for three or four defeated her.

They finished lunch, then separated for their afternoon classes. To Keiko's surprise, her fun-loving, baseball-playing brother had decided to major in education and history. He planned to get a job teaching high school kids about what leads up to war. She guessed they were both determined to do whatever they could to make sure history didn't repeat itself.

When she opened the door for Mako the next evening, raindrops glistened on the shoulders of his jacket and on his hair. He smiled and held out a bouquet of daffodils. "I stole them from Mrs. Smith's garden. There are so many, she'll never notice these few are missing."

Mako had started a landscaping business the previous summer. Three evenings a week, he took business administration classes at Vanport College. Keiko had tried to get him to take a full course-load. "Why not, since the government will pay for all of it?" He'd earned that, the same as Tommy, Paul Franconi and the hundreds of thousands of other men who'd fought in the war. But Mako insisted he couldn't afford to delay getting his business started. He had big plans.

Keiko filled a vase with water and stuck in the daffodils. "Tommy has already headed over to a friend's, and Papa isn't home from work yet." She gave the flowers a critical look, thinking of the amazing arrangements her mother had made with just two or three flowers. She shrugged and put the vase in the middle of the table, where, with luck, it would detract from the gooey rice and vegetables she'd prepared. When she once cried to Mako about her lack of skill in the kitchen, he'd only laughed and told her not to worry. "We'll hire a cook."

The radio was turned low while they ate. Then Vaughn Monroe's dreamy baritone voice, crooning about cool, cool water, was interrupted with a special news bulletin warning of more flooding in the area.

Keiko put down her fork. "Tommy says Vanport will be okay as long as the railroad berm holds."

"He's probably right. The Housing Authority says it'll hold." He rubbed the back of his neck. "The Columbia is pretty high, though. It makes me think of California's Sacramento River—it flooded every spring when I was a kid."

Keiko's father came in just then, shaking water from his coat and hat. Outside, heavy raindrops hit the window like marbles.

"You're early, Papa. Is something wrong?"

"They sent everyone home because the lights kept going out. Many streets are flooded."

"Sit down. I'll get you something to eat."

He shook his head. "I already ate. But I would enjoy a cup of that tea," he added, nodding toward the teapot on the table.

He looked tired, refueling Keiko's worries for his health. She blinked away the sudden threat of tears. If she lost him, too…. She stood and went to the kitchen. A few minutes later, she returned with another cup. "Here you are, Papa. I bought some tea cakes today. The kind you like."

After his tea and a pink, coconut covered teacake, her father excused himself and went to bed, reminding Keiko of how he used to retire behind his curtain at Camp Minidoka whenever Mako came to visit.

"I'd better go home, too," Mako said. "I have some studying to do. Tomorrow I'm going to draw up some plans for a new brochure advertising my services."

"But tomorrow is Memorial Day."

"I don't think it's going to stop raining. And I have no graves here to decorate."

"We will be visiting the graves of my mother and her parents."

"What time are you going?"

"Not until around two. You'll have the morning to work on your brochures."

"Okay."

"Bring an umbrella," Keiko called as he hurried down the stairs.

The next morning, there was another announcement from the Housing Authority telling everyone that the dikes in the area were safe and that there would be plenty of time to evacuate homes if that became necessary. Relieved, Keiko returned to her history text and comparing the administration of Theodore Roosevelt to that of Franklin Roosevelt.

Most people knew about Franklin Roosevelt's polio, though he tried to hide it from the public, but she was surprised to learn that Theodore Roosevelt had been a sickly child, suffering with severe asthma. By force of will, he survived and beat the disease back.

Keiko bit a stray lock of hair. If only her mother had been able to do the same. But the dust, cold and wind in Idaho during the winter, plus her weakened heart and the dreadful living conditions, were too much for her. Keiko's jaw tightened. It always did when she thought about the government putting them in that place, remembering how her mother had to gasp and struggle to breathe. It wasn't right. She could do nothing now to change what had happened or what might happen again. One day....

With renewed determination, she returned to reading her history text.

They took the bus to the cemetery where Keiko's mother and grandparents were buried. They were immediately swept up in a stream of umbrella-wielding visitors filing along the walkways. Another stream passed them, heading toward the bus stop.

"My grandfather worked as a landscaper, too," Keiko told Mako. They trailed after her father and Tommy. "For a rich family on Council Crest—probably near where your Mrs. Smith lives with her daffodils. My grandmother was the family's maid."

Keiko knew Mako had no intention of being the kind of landscaper her grandfather had been, working at one house, basically a groundskeeper and maintenance man. Mako planned something much bigger and grander—he wanted to design gardens and parks, raise his own nursery stock. He was already saving for a few acres of land east of Portland. She admired his ambition, though she was concerned he might be disappointed, fearing no one would hire him to design a park.

She had the same worry for her own future. Once she had her law degree, what firm in Portland would hire her? What client?

When they reached the spot where her mother's and grandparents' graves lay, she squished through the soggy grass and arranged the flowers they'd brought, placing a damp and bedraggled bouquet on each grave.

She missed the simple, white column that marked her mother's grave at Camp Minidoka—one of her father's poems carved into it:

Flowers bloom
She treads among them
Their fragrance
Lifting her spirit aloft
Heavenward
To God

When the government exhumed all the graves at the camp, sending the remains to wherever relatives wished them permanently interred, the coffin with her mother's remains was sent to Portland for reburial, but the marker wasn't included. Keiko's stomach burned at the memory.

"Don't worry," her father had said. "I'll have a new one made in stone."

He did, but it wasn't the same.

They returned home late. Keiko needed to shop for groceries and Tommy needed new sneakers for gym class. Mako, who'd left them earlier in the afternoon, waited at their door. His face told Keiko something bad had happened.

"What is it?"

"The dike broke. Flooding is everywhere."

Keiko gasped. "But just this morning we heard it was safe."

Her father unlocked the door. In a jumble of wet umbrellas and dripping coats and jackets, everyone trooped inside. Tommy turned on the radio. As the announcer spoke, sirens sounded in the background.

"At or around 4:17 PM, the Spokane, Portland and Seattle Railroad berm burst. A ten-foot wave of water flooded through it, west of Vanport, near Vanport College. Immediate flooding of Vanport was delayed slightly because of all the sloughs, backwaters and creeks in the area, allowing residents more time to get out of their apartments." The announcer was breathless as he spoke, his distress easy to hear. *"Fortunately, many were away, because of the holiday. Also fortunate, school was not in session. But oh my, folks! The devastation! Buildings*

have been swept off their foundation, cars flipped and bobbing in the water like toys, people running for their very lives."

Keiko clutched the tabletop. So often over the last two years, she'd seen young children playing or walking with their mothers, older children walking home from school, teen-aged boys shooting basketballs on one of Vanport's several courts. All those children—their parents' too. From what the radio announcer described, lives had to have been lost—children were without parents and parents without children.

In the days and weeks that followed, the Vanport Flood was all over the national news reports on the radio and in newsreels—Oregon's second largest city had been obliterated in one afternoon. Fifteen people lost their lives, but many more lives would be forever changed.

Keiko was grateful to learn she would still be accepted at law school, but she couldn't stop worrying about the people who'd made homes for themselves in Vanport. In many ways, Portland was more southern than western, and she wondered if, like her and her family and so many other returning Japanese-Americans after the war, those people, Negroes mostly, would face difficulties finding places to live. She determined to talk to her father—convince him they could share their apartment with a displaced family until permanent lodging was found. It was the least they could do.

9

VIRGINIA

Idaho

Virginia pressed four-year-old Neil's hand against her rounded belly. "Do you feel that? That's your little brother or sister."

Neil's eyes widened. "How did it get in there? Can it get out?"

Bella, now going on ten, rolled her eyes.

Virginia chuckled at them both. "How it got in there is a miracle. I'll be going to the hospital soon to get it out."

"Can I come?"

"You need to stay home. Papa and Bella and Uncle Marc will need your help."

Neil's almond-shaped gray eyes filled with tears. "But I want to come with you."

Virginia cupped her son's cheek in her hand. How like John he looked, especially that firm little mouth. "Papa needs you. I won't be gone long, just a few days. Then I'll come home with your new baby brother or sister."

"I don't want a baby brother or a baby sister. Only Bella."

Virginia sighed and closed her eyes. This was not going as she'd planned—with Neil, things rarely did. The baby would be arriving soon—in less than a month. She didn't want to leave John with an inconsolable son to worry about.

Her husband had too many other things on his mind. They'd religiously followed the business plan he and Marc had worked out after the war: buying up property whenever it became available. Since the war and the migration to the city by many young men, many farms had gone up for sale. As a result, they'd become rich in land and equipment, but poor in cash. Worse yet, they were having trouble finding the labor they needed. The Bracero Program, the government program bringing in Mexican and other Spanish-speaking workers, helped, but it wasn't enough.

So similar to the labor shortage at the start of the war, when all able-bodied workers were either enlisting in the army or working in munitions plants or other war-related industries. That's when the government started issuing work permits to internees at Camp Minidoka. There were plenty of volunteers, as they could earn more money on the farms than at Camp—Marc paid going wages then, just as he and John did now with the Braceros.

The Korean War was causing the same problem. A shiver ran through her, remembering how terrified she'd been that John would be called up again. They'd talked about the possibility. In a way, she thought he might want to go—he might have been staged in Japan, where he could have tried to find his parents. He'd written to them after the war ended, after he returned to Idaho, but he never heard back.

Although he rarely spoke of his parents, Virginia was sure he often thought of them, wondered if they'd survived the war. She'd suggested he see if the Red Cross could locate them, but he shook his head. "When they returned to Japan, it was to a village where my father and his family lived when he was a boy. That's where I wrote them. If they aren't there, they're nowhere."

At least they didn't have the entire farm planted in sugar beets, like during the war. She'd had no idea sugar could be used in making munitions and synthetic rubber, that is until the man from the government came and told Marc about it. All the farmers in the area were encouraged to help with the war effort by growing sugar beets. Although the same push wasn't being made now, many of the neighboring farmers still grew them.

Sugar beets were so labor intensive, though. She was glad Marc and John mostly raised corn, wheat, and potatoes. They still needed help to keep the irrigation ditches clear. During planting and harvest they needed extra people, too.

She rubbed her hands across her stomach, feeling her hardened uterus. She had no answer—Marc and John needed to worry about it. She had her hands full with a clinging son, who now had visions of his mother abandoning him. She sighed and stroked her son's cheek again. He reacted by trying to pull himself onto the bed, nearly oversetting the tin of talcum powder and the lamp on the nightstand.

Bella came to her rescue. "Come on, Neil, let Mama rest. Let's go see the baby kittens in the barn."

Neil quickly acquiesced. They left her bedroom, Neil scrambling to be first, and clattered down the stairs. Her daughter, so grown up for her age, seemed to have been born knowing how to be a big sister. Virginia leaned her head against the pillow and thought of Bella's father. *How could someone so cruel and selfish have sired a child so beautiful and kind?*

The pains that had been mild in the morning were in full swing by noon. "You need to ring the bell for Papa," Virginia told Bella, while holding both hands to her stomach. Moments later, the same bell that had brought Marc and John when Leo shot himself, the bell that had rung years earlier when the letter came informing her and Marc of Paul's war injuries, his blindness, and again when Bella's father descended on them, rang once more. At least this time, it was for a good reason.

Mrs. Perez, a widow and a parishioner of Reverend Greene, had agreed to housekeep and help with the children for several weeks. She waited for them in front of the small house she shared with her niece, her niece's husband and their three young children, where she would keep Bella and Neil while John took Virginia to the hospital. Bella hopped out of the car without a fuss, but Neil cried, refusing to get out. He grabbed the back of Virginia's seat. "I want to go with you."

Virginia gritted her teeth against another contraction and a wave of nausea.

Mrs. Perez reached into the car and removed a kicking and screaming Neil. "Don't worry," she said above his cries. "He will be fine. You go."

John didn't hesitate. As soon as Bella slammed the rear door, cutting off Neil's howls, he drove away from the curb. "After the baby comes, I'll pick them all up and take them home," he said.

Virginia nodded, unable to speak. John reached across the front seat and covered her clenched hand with his.

They named the baby Amanda, which Neil soon shortened to Manda and then Mandy. Right away, Virginia knew this baby's temperament would be closer to Bella's than to Neil's, even though she looked almost identical to her brother when he'd been a newborn. The same almond-shaped eyes and golden skin. Her fine straight hair was a shade darker, but other than that, they could have been twins.

It seemed Neil had grown in the short time she was in the hospital. The hands that five days before had looked so small and pudgy, so babyish, appeared huge compared to his baby sister's. His behavior seemed to have changed as well. Virginia didn't know whether to put that down to Mrs. Perez's calming influence or to him taking on the role of big brother. Either way, she was relieved his tantrums had subsided.

John and Marc noticed his improved behavior, too.

Virginia had long before taken to serving Bella and Neil dinner early—getting Neil to eat a balanced meal was often a battle. Even so, it was a rare evening the three adults could eat without interruption. John was partially responsible. Tired as Virginia knew him to be, he would soon give in to Neil's whining and allow their son to climb up on his lap and pick through his dinner.

She scolded and Marc shook his head, but John said to let him be. "He'll get over it."

Marc snorted. "Yeah, and when he does, he'll be so big you'll need to sit on his lap."

The first night Virginia came home from the hospital, Mrs. Perez took Neil by the hand and forcibly removed him from the dining room. She did the same thing the second night. At first, he protested, but after a week he went with her willingly.

Marc watched the two of them disappear through the doorway, into the kitchen. "That woman is a miracle worker."

John agreed.

Virginia frowned, offended they might think her inadequate, unable to properly care for a four-year-old. "You two don't know what a handful he can be."

"Oh yeah, we do," Marc said.

John took another bite of his roast beef. "I wonder if we can get Mrs. Perez to stay on."

Virginia set down her fork and stared at him. "Can we afford it?"

Marc scratched his chin. "Can we afford not to might be a better question."

Virginia readily admitted it would be a relief to have Mrs. Perez's help with the children and in the kitchen. "Especially since we'll soon need to bring on extra workers for the corn." Even field corn needed to be chopped and hauled.

"Potatoes, too. They'll be ready to dig in a few more weeks."

Virginia took the first opportunity to ask Mrs. Perez to stay on. Tears in her eyes, Mrs. Perez agreed.

Recalling the size of the house she'd lived in with her niece's family, Virginia wasn't surprised. It was a shame Mrs. Perez and her husband, who'd died several years before, had no children, as she was a born mother. Unlike me, Virginia thought, climbing into bed and pulling the covers up.

"It's not that I don't adore my children," Virginia told John. "I do. But caring for them non-stop, disciplining them when they need it…it isn't instinctive with me, not like it is with Mrs. Perez."

John took off his reading glasses and put them, along with the newly arrived Farm Journal, on his nightstand. "You're a great mom."

Although Virginia smiled and turned off the light, she still thought about Mrs. Perez and how unkind fate could be.

★

The following fall, when Mandy was nearly a year old, Virginia received a letter from Keiko containing an announcement and a surprising request—she would be graduating from law school in the spring and she and Mako were getting married. She wanted to have the wedding at the farm.

Mako and I met in Idaho. And it holds some wonderful memories—you and Bella, Marc, the farm. And I've missed those long talks about ethics and politics with John. I hope Suki and Paul will come as well.

It's more than that, though. Others might think I'm crazy, but I know you and Suki will understand. Mama's body may be buried in Portland now, but to me, her spirit is still at Camp Minidoka. I need to be near her when I get married.

If it's okay with you, John, and Marc.

I hope you'll say yes. If so, I'll write to Reverend Greene and ask him to do the honors. I've invited Mako's sister and her husband to the wedding and she's going to come. Mako doesn't know. I'm keeping it a surprise.

Papa says hello.

Your friend,

Keiko Ugawa

Although Virginia couldn't help wondering how Keiko was going to keep from Mako the secret of his sister coming from Japan, she quickly wrote that of course it was okay for the wedding to be at the farm. The timing would be perfect. Most of the spring planting would already be done. Paul would be out of school, too. She would insist he and Suki come. It would be a happy time, happy enough to erase some of the sorrow of their last visit—Leo's funeral.

10
YOKO

Sprawled on the futon next to her, Yoko's husband lay spent, breathing hard and reeking of sake. She had hoped he'd find another woman to satisfy his needs. Maybe a war widow—there were plenty of them around. Perhaps he had, but he still insisted he would get Yoko with child, even though gray now laced her hair and her cheeks were sunken due to the many teeth she'd lost over the years.

Every month her flow came, Takeda berated her. "Worthless whore. Why can't you do anything right?"

Her flows were erratic now and would soon stop altogether. Maybe then he'd leave her alone.

At the factory, she'd been forced to stand by while he'd gotten rid of all the women workers, even Asai. When all able-bodied men were gone from the village, fighting first in China and then in New Guinea, Asai had served as the factory's master potter. She had done the work well. Without a word of warning, Takeda fired her and hired a man from Shikoku in her place. He also got rid of young Mori, claiming they didn't need a cripple getting in their way. Yoko was glad Masato Abi had taken the man on to do odd jobs.

Takeda also insisted they return to the chemicals they'd once used, before the war made chemicals nearly impossible to acquire.

"People have grown to like the patterns made by the paddles and incising," Yoko said.

Takeda gave a dismissive snort. "A waste of time. Colors derived from chemicals are faster. This is a production factory, not an art studio."

The changes, the insults and the physical and verbal blows inflicted by her husband weren't what made Yoko's jaw tighten and blood pound in her ears, however. It was being reduced to dusting and serving tea. After a decade of successfully managing the factory, a decade in which economic depression and war made everything more difficult, dusting and serving tea were her reward.

Ishihara gave her sidelong, sympathetic glances, just as Mori had done before his death the year before. Yoko ignored him. She didn't need the tepid pity of a coward.

They were all cowards, including her pig of a husband. Every night, she plotted new ways she would rid the world of him. Maybe some night, when he was in another of his drunken stupors, she would drown him in the ofuro. Or with a club or a knife, she would lay him open and hide his body in the woods. Let wild animals tear apart his limbs. If neither of those methods worked, there was always poison.

The Fates had not finished making her life miserable, either. Oh, no. They must also bring Nobuko Ito back to Nishimi, bring her back as Masato Abi's wife.

Mrs. Abi claimed to be no happier than Yoko about her son's choice. "After he came home from the war, I told old

Mori's nosy wife that Masato no longer had an interest in the gaijin. I said she shouldn't mention my son in any of her letters, as it would be sure to break the woman's heart."

Mrs. Abi soon made clear the reason for her antagonism toward her daughter-in-law. "My dearest friend married and moved away from Nishimi when she was fifteen, but we have corresponded over the years. Her daughter would have been perfect for my son…had he but considered her."

For two years Masato's mother had managed to keep her son ignorant of the gaijin's presence in Sakayama. Too bad his ignorance hadn't lasted, Yoko thought.

Four years had passed since Masato brought the woman back to Nishimi, and still people fawned over her: "She's so brave," or "She's so kind." Yoko scoffed at their idiot behavior. Soon enough, they would realize Nobuko Abi brought misfortune. Hadn't she caused the earthquake that killed so many village children, including Yoko's two daughters, her beautiful daughters? Didn't she bring the lightning strike that burned the Katsuragawa summer estate to the ground?

★

Several times a week, Yoko saw Hirotaka Katsuragawa waiting for the bus to Sakayama, a heavy-looking satchel in hand.

"The satchel contains his art supplies," Ishihara said. "He goes to Sakayama to teach."

An image of a long-ago summer morning popped into Yoko's head. "Remember when he helped you and Mori fire the kiln?"

Ishihara nodded. "And stayed throughout—hauling wood, adding it to the fire, bringing Mori water whenever he asked for it, stretching out on the ground, next to one of the other workers, to grab a few minutes of sleep. For those three days, he was part of the village."

"And then his father appeared and Hirotaka changed before our eyes." Yoko shook her head thinking of the long look the two had exchanged—like two stags about to clash. Without his father having to say a word, Hirotaka dropped his challenge and followed the old man out of the factory, never looking back. "A year later, he was in New Guinea." Somewhere in those jungles, that boy, the son of a nobleman, who expected most everyone to bow to his demands, had disappeared. In his place a humble artist had returned.

On more than one occasion, Yoko's husband approached Hirotaka. He wanted something, but each time he approached, Hirotaka shook his head and moved on, leaving Takeda to stare after him. Yoko had given up asking her husband what he wanted. His answer was always the same, a snarl.

Then one morning when Hirotaka boarded the bus, Takeda climbed on as well.

Yoko stood in the factory doorway until the bus disappeared around a bend. Why was Takeda going to Sakayama—to continue trying to convince Hirotaka of whatever it was he wanted? Or was there some other reason? Stop wasting time, she told herself, and stomped back into the factory to continue her battle with clay dust.

That evening, as he always did, Hirotaka returned to Nishimi. Takeda did not.

Yoko ate a solitary dinner and went to bed, only to wake the next morning wondering why Takeda hadn't returned. Maybe he couldn't. Maybe she wouldn't have to kill him after all. Maybe Hirotaka, or someone else, had done it for her. In the following days, she held that comforting thought close, turning it over in her mind as she dusted, swept, and served tea.

Takeda returned the following week, swinging down from the bus as though he did it every day. Like a heavy stone, disappointment filled Yoko's belly. A smug smile was all she got when she asked where he'd been.

That disappearance was the first of many. Sometimes her husband remained away for a few days, sometimes a week or two. He never said when he was going or how long he'd be away.

Ogawa, the man Takeda had hired to replace Asai, was an incompetent fool. How much his incompetence was affecting their business grew more apparent to Yoko with each passing month. The reputation they had worked so hard for, she had worked so hard for, was being thrown away. She couldn't let that happen.

Takeda was on one of his mysterious trips when two large orders arrived in the morning mail. "We should fill this first," Yoko said, handing an order to Ishihara. "A new customer—let us impress them with our prompt response."

When she later checked the inventory, she discovered they were low on certain chemicals. "You'd better order more," she told Ogawa. He gave her a disdainful glance, but otherwise paid her no heed. She wasn't surprised when their meager supply ran out. She ordered the chemicals herself, telling the supplier to rush them. Even so, the order wasn't completed and shipped in the short amount of time she'd imagined.

Her brief period of influence ended when Takeda returned, and she reverted to dusting the office and showroom and serving tea to the workers at break time. Ogawa made no effort to hide his pleasure at seeing her so reduced. This back and forth sparring went on throughout the summer and fall as Takeda kept disappearing. To hide her frustration with Ogawa and with her husband's indifference to the pottery factory, his heritage, Yoko took up the habit of tobacco. She also avoided Mrs. Mori and twitchy Mrs. Tanaka—they would be sure to ask Takeda's whereabouts when he was gone, and where he'd been when he returned. Her single solace remained her secret cache of money.

Winter set in and, for the most part, Takeda remained in Nishimi. The village was no longer cut off from the rest of the world by the snow. A large truck with a blade on its front, along with a team of workers, kept the road between the village and Sakayama clear. Unlike the war years and the years immediately after, goods filled the shelves in the Abi store.

In the factory's storeroom, rectangular blocks of clay, dug by the workers, were wrapped in damp burlap, and stacked in row upon row. The supply of clay would need to last until the ground thawed and more could be dug.

Yoko skimmed over the desk with a feather duster and wiggled her freezing toes inside her felt boots.

"Where is the order from the Moritani Department Store, the one we got last week?"

Startled at the intrusion into her dreams of balmy weather, Yoko glanced at her husband and shrugged.

"You must have seen it." He slapped the desk in front of her. "I put it right here this morning."

"Maybe you put it in the file."

"Don't be stupid, woman. If I'd put it in the file, I'd know where it was."

"I haven't seen it."

"You're lying. Who else would have taken it? Tell me what you've done with it."

He hit her before she could duck. She fell, striking her head on the kerosene stove that filled the area between the office and showroom. When she returned to consciousness, the room was empty. She struggled to her feet, her senses whirling, her head pounding. She clutched at the desk to keep from falling. The Moritani file lay open upon it, with the order dated the week before on top.

Yoko put her hand to the side of her head, fingering a lump the size of a pigeon's egg. Blood oozed from it. She closed her eyes. Her head spun and her stomach churned. Her mouth tasted like she'd swallowed something rotten. Staggering to the door, she barely got through it before everything she'd eaten at breakfast came up. She leaned against the doorframe to steady herself.

Masato Abi hurried toward her. "Yoko-san, are you all right? You look pale. You shouldn't be outside without a coat in this bitter weather." He drew closer and stared at the side of her head. "You're hurt."

"It is nothing." Yoko grabbed the mail from his hand and went inside, sliding the door shut with a bang. Masato Abi's concern was the last thing she wanted.

When spring at last arrived, Takeda once again disappeared. Yoko was happy to put off telling him he'd gotten his wish: she was pregnant.

It would soon be Obon. Once again, Yoko would be forced to pretend she believed the nonsense that her daughters would come back to her in spirit form. She didn't want them in spirit, she wanted them in the flesh. That would never be, though, thanks to Nobuko Abi. Her girls were dead, gone forever, crushed by the mountain. She sighed and put her hand over her stomach. Perhaps this child would dull memories of the past, fill her with new ones.

When Takeda returned from wherever he'd gone, he saw right away that she was pregnant. The smugness of his smile set her teeth on edge, but at least he quit bothering her in bed.

A few days after his return, he insisted she go with him to Hirotaka Katsuragawa's house to present the artist with one of the factory's finest pieces of pottery, a piece made by Yoko's father-in-law fifty years before. It was nonsense, of course. Takeda knew Hirotaka would not be at home—they'd both seen the man leave on the Sakayama bus that morning. He also knew Hirotaka would not keep the grand gesture, so it came as no surprise when the wife returned it, flushing with embarrassment, and saying they couldn't accept such an important gift. Yoko wondered what kind of game Takeda was playing at.

Now he was gone again. "Don't worry," he said the morning he left. "I'll be back in time for the birth of my son." Yoko didn't want to think of what he'd do if the child she carried was another girl.

She was going through some old orders when Ogawa slid open the door from the factory. "It is time for our tea. What are you doing, woman, dawdling and day-dreaming?"

His insolence made the muscles in her shoulders tense. "Mind your manners, boy. You'll have your tea when I get around to fixing it."

His chin pulled in. He frowned, but said nothing. A moment later, the door slid shut behind him. Yoko waited another fifteen minutes before arranging the tea things, wishing she had something lethal to put in Ogawa's.

After the men left the factory that evening, Yoko stayed behind. Takeda and Ogawa had taken to keeping the accounts book locked in the bottom drawer of the desk. With the tip of a tool used for cutting through clay, she managed to unlock the drawer. She pulled out the book and studied it.

Over the last eighteen months, the factory had remained busy, but there wasn't as much work as there should have been, nor as much profit. As she'd already noted, the Moritani Department Store's orders no longer came with regularity. Nor did she find the names of two of the restaurants that had once been steady customers. Had the restaurants gone out of business, or had Takeda managed to lose them with his frequent absences? Several times while Takeda was away, people had called for him on the factory's new telephone. Although Yoko left him notes of who had wanted to speak with him, Takeda seldom called back.

She closed the book and returned it to the desk drawer. It was just as she'd thought—they were losing business. Takeda owed it to the child she carried to keep the factory thriving. Instead, he was off somewhere frittering away his heritage—the factory that had been started two-hundred years before by an ancestor who had traveled to Korea to learn the art of pottery making.

Maybe he was still involved with black marketeering. Although food was no longer scarce, other things were. If the stockpile of medicines and goods he'd stolen after the war still existed, he might be selling them. If so, where was the money?

Disgusted, Yoko turned out the light and went home.

The night was warm and humid. Far off, thunder rumbled. A storm was coming. She hoped the weather would clear before they needed to fire the kiln. Maybe Takeda would be back by then…or maybe he'd be struck by lightning.

★

Yoko sat on the tatami-covered platform in the showroom and packed sake sets for shipment. She placed each item in a partitioned wooden box, each section filled with a protective nest of shaved wood. The boxes had been built to hold each set. When Takeda walked in, with his usual indifference to whatever might have transpired in his absence, Yoko didn't acknowledge him. He ignored her and went to the door at the back of the room. He called for Ogawa to come up to the office.

Eyes glittering, Ogawa entered the room and sent Yoko a sly grin. Yoko ignored the look. What a weasel the man was—why would she care what he told Takeda about her?

"Is the kiln ready to fire?" Takeda asked.

"The chambers are loaded. We will finish bricking the last one closed this afternoon." Ogawa said this as if it was him and not Yoko who had overseen the loading and bricking of the chambers.

"What about wood?"

"There is plenty—enough for several days." Again, the man omitted that Yoko had been the one to arrange with the forester for wood and kindling. Disgusted, she shook her head at Ogawa's feeble attempts to parade his importance, and her husband's inability to see through him. Bah! They were both idiots.

The following morning, Yoko stood well back from the kiln, observing the tradition that called for women to remain fifteen feet from a lit kiln. Back when all the men were away fighting, how irate old Ishihara had been when forced to use women to manage the firing.

"You don't know how the kiln-kami will repay us for such an outrage," Ishihara had claimed.

Yoko smiled at the memory, surprised to admit she missed the old fool, now he was gone. Old Mori, too.

Takeda lit a fagot and thrust it into the oven at the bottom of the kiln. The wood caught. Before long, the fire leaped over the oven wall, into the first chamber. Ogawa called out for wood to be thrown into that chamber's stoking window. Soon, the fire leaped to the second chamber and wood was thrown into its stoking window. Then the third chamber and the fourth. Smoke came out of the chimney at the top of the kiln, seven meters up the hill from the oven at its lower end. The smoke was a trickle at first, then a steady stream. A sigh went up from the crowd of villagers and workers who'd gathered to observe. The firing of the kiln was still an event.

Takeda must have felt his job was complete. He returned to the cool of the factory. Yoko remained behind to ensure the wood was thrown at the correct angle. A badly thrown stick of wood might knock over a shelf-full of the pots, vases, bowls, and platters lining each chamber.

She glanced over her shoulder to the collection of broken and misshapen vessels two-hundred years in the making. More would no doubt be added at the end of this firing. There always was. She would do her best, however, to make sure that number was kept at a minimum. Ogawa was so cocky—left to his own, there was no telling how much damage he would do.

After three days, the firing was completed, the chambers opened and allowed to cool. Two days after that, they began the task of unloading the kiln.

All morning, Yoko had carried boxes of fired pots up the hill, through the factory and up the steps to the showroom, where she placed them on the packing platform. Now she stopped and straightened, pressing her hand to her dome-shaped stomach. The child inside rolled over, pressing hard on her bladder.

Takeda, sitting in the desk chair, glanced at her and frowned. "What do you think you're doing you foolish woman—trying to lose my son? Sit down. Let the apprentices carry the boxes from the kiln. You can unpack them."

Although reluctant to do anything Takeda ordered, for the sake of her unborn child, Yoko sat and began unloading the box. She took out a tall vase and studied it. No wonder they were losing customers. Ogawa's work was nowhere near as fine as Asai's had been, the walls of the vase not nearly as thin.

Takeda was a good potter, but he didn't work at the wheel unless they had a larger order than normal, which had become rare. When he was in Nishimi, he seldom did anything, in fact, other than write in his books and bedevil her—to her great displeasure, he now said he planned to remain in the village until the baby was born. She sighed and started unloading another box.

"It is time for our tea break," Takeda said. "Stop what you're doing and fix it."

Yoko lumbered to her feet, her spine stiff with resentment. Someday, he would regret how he treated her.

11

NOBUKO

Japan

Nobuko approached the Buddhist shrine through a grove of gingko trees, her feet crunching on the gravel path. Moving from the shade into bright sunlight, she shielded her eyes and mounted the stone steps. The spicy scent of incense filling her nostrils, she stepped from her shoes and entered the shrine's cavernous main room.

She dropped a coin through the wooden grate of the cash box. *Please let me become pregnant.* The coin made a dull thump when it hit the bottom. She rang the bell and bowed from her waist. *Please let me become pregnant.* Straightening, she clapped twice to awaken the god, bowed again, and backed away. *Please let me become pregnant.*

Finished, she slipped into her shoes and retraced her course down the stairs, onto the gravel path.

Nobuko had been raised a Christian, but her prayers for the miracle of conception had gone unanswered. Mrs. Mori's herbs had done no good, either. Perhaps Buddha would intercede. She hoped God would understand, and forgive her desperation.

It would be best, she decided on her way back along the path, not to tell Masato of her visit to the shrine. He would only worry about her and blame himself for her inability to get pregnant.

That evening, a loud knocking sounded from the front of the closed store. Masato's parents were already asleep. Nobuko followed close behind Masato, who hurried to unlock the door.

"Who can it be?" she whispered.

Masato opened the door and Hirotaka Katsuragawa surged inside.

Moments later, Nobuko and Masato sat in the two western-style chairs Masato had bought and placed next to the stove in the center of the store. In front of them, Hirotaka paced.

"What is troubling you, Hirotaka-san?" Masato finally asked.

Hirotaka stopped pacing and frowned. "When I came home this evening, I found a changed house."

Nobuko tilted her head to one side. "A changed house?"

"Chieko wrote to her mother and told her all the things our home lacked. In return, my mother-in-law and father-in-law sent a truck loaded with boxes and furniture—as if I hadn't intended to provide those things myself one day."

"What did they send?"

"What they didn't send might be easier to answer. Tables, scrolls for the tokonoma, vases, silk cushions of every size and color, a small refrigerator, and more dishware than Chieko will ever find room for, more than we could require in a lifetime."

He scowled and paced more. "She'd already rearranged the house—with the help of the two women I hired when I first brought Chieko to Nishimi. They even moved my easel and painting things into the loft. Don't ask how they managed the easel—it weighs as much as me."

When he finished outlining all the changes Chieko had made to his well-ordered life, Hirotaka shook his head.

Nobuko turned away to hide her smile. She'd been right—adjustments were called for.

Hirotaka sighed. "She's so very young.   I shouldn't have married her, especially when I couldn't afford her."

"Why did you?" The question, which had long puzzled Nobuko, popped out of her mouth.

Masato flashed her a warning glance, but Hirotaka didn't appear to mind her nosiness.

"She came to my gallery in Sakayama one day with a group of friends," he said. "Though I'm sure she doesn't remember. From the moment I saw her, I wanted her for my wife. I used her father's desire for a noble connection to make sure he would agree to the match."

Masato frowned. "But you never take advantage of your noble birth."

"To my shame, this time I did. When the matchmaker introduced us, I even wore a formal kimono with the family crest, intending to impress her and her parents."

The first day Chieko came to the store, she'd been shy and unsure. When Nobuko asked her what she needed, she'd replied everything. They had since both laughed over that first shopping trip. Nobuko enjoyed Chieko's daily visits, enjoyed seeing the young woman gain confidence. She hoped their friendship would continue to grow.

"She is young, Hirotaka-san. In some ways, younger than her years. She may have been spoiled and indulged by her parents, but she is trying to learn how you would like her to behave, how to be your wife. She will make mistakes, as will you."

After a few more lamentations, Hirotaka went home to his Chieko. Nobuko and Masato returned to their futon, chuckling and feeling wise.

Nobuko was on her own, stacking tea towels one afternoon, when Mrs. Mori entered the store. Nobuko still missed old Mori. She smiled a welcome to his widow.

"Do you have time for tea?"

Mrs. Mori perched in one of the chairs, her feet dangling. "Tea would be very nice."

Nobuko pushed the stool Masato had placed between the two chairs closer. She was glad the Mori's son and daughter-in-law had returned to Nishimi before old Mori died, knowing how much comfort Mrs. Mori had drawn from their presence. She opened a tin with a picture of Mount Fuji and cherry blossoms on its side and sprinkled tea leaves in the bottom of a clay teapot burnished by years of service.

"Real tea, not what we had to drink during the war," Mrs. Mori said as Nobuko poured in hot water from the kettle that resided on the stove in all seasons but full summer. It was something the old woman often remarked on.

"I remember," Nobuko said. "Terrible."

Mrs. Mori settled into her chair, preparing for a long visit. "I saw Toshio Hara come into the store the other day."

Nobuko nodded and lowered herself into the second chair. Like Mrs. Mori, only her toes reached the floor. She propped her feet on the stool next to her friend's.

"I didn't see Kensai with him. Did he say how his son does?"

"Not even when I asked. Just picked out what he needed, paid for it and left."

Mrs. Hara sighed. "He is a strange man."

Nobuko closed her eyes, for a moment overcome with memories of those years on the Hara farm. At first, she'd taken pleasure working in the fields and the rice paddy, even though the work was the hardest she'd ever done. But then the government confiscated most of the crops, claiming everything needed to go to the front for the war effort. Even the ox was forfeit when they had nothing left to feed it. Every night, poor little Kensai, hungry, cried himself to sleep.

Just before the war ended, Kensai's grandparents died. With nothing and no one left for them on the farm, Nobuko took the little boy to Nishimi. She couldn't remain there herself—the villagers insisted she brought bad luck. Heartbroken, she'd left Kensai with Mr. and Mrs. Mori, even though they had little, if anything, to spare. Setting out on foot the next morning for Sakayama, with no idea what she would do if her aunt refused her room, she'd never felt so desolate, so abandoned.

"I'll never forget when I first saw Toshio Hara after the war, after he was released from that prisoner-of-war camp in Australia," Mrs. Mori said, bringing Nobuko back to the present.

Nobuko had heard the story many times, but let her friend tell it again.

"Kensai played on the floor, spinning a yellow top that once belonged to Jiro. I still have it." Her voice cracked and Nobuko knew she was thinking of her grandson, killed in the earthquake along with his sister and so many other village children.

After a moment, Mrs. Mori went on. "Kensai gasped and grabbed for the top. I followed his gaze to the door, and I also gasped. A man stood framed there. He was so thin, his uniform hung off his frame like clothes on a rack. He wasn't the first soldier to come to the door begging after the war ended, but his appearance still startled me and I took care to place myself between him and Kensai. Then the man gave me his name."

Tears filled Mrs. Mori's eyes.

Nobuko poured more tea into their cups.

"Thank you, Nobuko-san. I don't mean to be a foolish old woman, but it was so sad, you see. Toshio told me he'd come to take the boy home. Kensai started to cry, but Toshio told him to quit being a baby." She gave a feeble smile and took another sip of her tea. "He was only six. He hadn't seen his father in five years. What was he supposed to do?"

Nobuko shook her head in sympathy, but could do little to bring comfort. She embraced her own memories of the funny little boy, with his big ears and crooked smile.

Mrs. Mori went on with her story. "I had no choice but to let Toshio take him. It broke my heart. My husband's too. Even though he'd been with us just a few months, we'd both come to love the child."

Nobuko's throat thickened. Kensai must be nearing fifteen now. He'd been such a dear little boy. "I'm afraid his life hasn't been easy—his mother died when he was little more than a baby, his father away in the war. Then starving on the farm…seeing his grandparents die." Once again, Nobuko pictured the old couple on their futon, eyes closed as if in sleep. "Growing up with Toshio for his only company can't be much fun, either."

Every time she saw Toshio Hara, she wondered why he was so angry with the world—one had only to look at him, look into his eyes, to see that was so. Had his Australian jailers been so cruel? Was it something else that had happened during the war? Or was it the deaths of his wife and parents? But wouldn't having Kensai mitigate some of that pain?

Mrs. Mori nodded. "You're right. That man never talks. Mrs. Sato is the same way. Whenever I meet her on the street and try to strike up a conversation, she just shakes her head and hurries on. What do you suppose happened to her husband after the police took him?"

Nobuko shrugged and took a sip of her cooled tea, thinking of the woman.

"When they first came to the village, her husband said they had lived in the state of Washington for many years. Their two sons were born there. The youngest son died in a logging accident. Bereft, they decided to return to Japan, but the older son refused, saying he was American, so it was just Mr. and Mrs. Sato who came to live in Nishimi."

"I feel sorry for her, losing not one but two sons in the end. Then her husband being taken off by the police and never returning. She must feel God has forsaken her." Nobuko recalled similar feelings and gave a little shake.

"The villagers think he was a spy," said Mrs. Mori.

"The villagers thought I brought bad luck—some still do. We both know how crazy that is."

"The war has been over for eight years. If Mr. Sato was coming back, he would have done so by now, don't you think?"

"Probably."

Mrs. Mori put her cup and saucer aside. "Yoko Yoshida is due to deliver her baby soon."

Nobuko frowned. Since Yoko avoided her, making sure not to come to the store in the mornings, when Nobuko was the one serving customers, she hadn't seen the woman in some time. "I would think she is too old to be giving birth—it is bound to be hard for her." Her hand went to her stomach, above her own empty womb.

Mrs. Mori shook her head. "True. But despite that and Takeda's crowing to all Nishimi, she must be excited. It's been too long since she lost her daughters."

Self-pity rose in Nobuko's throat. Everyone but her could conceive. Chieko Katsuragawa, married less than a year, was already rounded with child, as was Mrs. Mori's daughter-in-law. And Yoko. Nobuko was glad for them, but sad for herself and Masato. When would their turn come?

Mrs. Mori stood. "Well, I must leave you. It is time for me to go to the shrine." Every afternoon, Mrs. Mori offered coins to the spirits of her husband and her grandchildren.

As they prepared for bed that evening, Masato put his arm around Nobuko's shoulders. "Why are you so sad? You haven't said a word all evening."

Nobuko shrugged and ducked her head, ashamed of her foolishness.

"Something is wrong. What is it?"

When she finally confessed that she was jealous of others' happiness, Masato held her as she wept.

A few days later, he handed her a packet. "You are not to quibble that we can't afford it. We can."

The packet held steamer tickets. They were going to America.

12

NOBUKO

Japan and Oregon

Nobuko stood on the Kobe dock for the first time since the cold December day fourteen years before, when the Osaka Maru came steaming back into the port just twenty days after they'd left. With Masato now beside her on the crowded pier, she gazed at the ship they were about to board. Her heart pounded as memories of that aborted trip swept over her.

"Maybe we should have flown," Masato said. "They say the service takes less than twenty-four hours. I thought this would be more relaxing."

Nobuko swallowed, still staring at the ship. "It was raining that day. Both days, actually—the day we left and the day we returned. No one was on the docks to see us off, and when we came back, only the military police waited. They took away all the Occidental passengers."

"Were there many?"

"They filled the backs of three trucks." Nobuko drew a steadying breath. "I always wondered what happened to them."

While waiting for the signal to board, people pointed to various parts of the ship, and said goodbye to friends and family. They'd all been told their suitcases would be waiting for them in their staterooms.

How different from that cold, drizzly day when Nobuko, dragging her heavy suitcase, had huddled with the other passengers on the *Osaka Maru's* deck, and questioned why her parents had insisted she return to America. *Right away,* her father's letter had said. An hour passed before she and the others had been allowed to go below and find their cabins—she'd shared a small, windowless one with three middle-aged nuns.

The ship's whistle sounded, signaling they should board.

"Ready?" Masato said, his eyes still filled with concern.

Nobuko drew a quivering breath and nodded.

Nobuko's fears were soon set aside. Instead of a cramped cabin shared with strangers, she and Masato enjoyed a private stateroom. Every crewmember, from the young man who cleaned their cabin to the waiters in the dining room, attended them with quiet efficiency. During the day, they played shuffleboard, or lazed in the sun. In the evenings, after dinner—which Nobuko enjoyed dressing for—they danced in the ballroom or enjoyed a musical show. Time passed in a happy blur.

They were a day out from Honolulu. The ocean spread from horizon to horizon and the ship's effervescent wake streamed behind them. Masato sat in a deck chair next to Nobuko's, his eyes closed beneath the shade of a straw hat.

"You were right," Nobuko said. "This is relaxing." He answered with a smile.

Then, as if from nowhere, the memory of being in nearly the same balmy waters intruded, shaking her from her tranquil state; the day when the *Osaka Maru* made its abrupt change in course. She'd been dozing in a deck chair, enjoying the sunshine, and letting go the tensions that had steadily mounted after receiving her father's letter. Then the woman in the chair next to hers shook her arm.

"Look, we're turning."

Nobuko had struggled upright, blinking away the fog of sleep; the ship's wake was in the shape of a large U.

"Maybe someone has gone overboard," the woman said. They rushed to the railing but spotted nothing that looked like a rescue attempt.

Nobuko gathered with other passengers, in small groups, debating the reason for the course change. Several were elected to ask crew members, but their questions were met with stony silence. It wasn't until late the following day that they found out why the *Osaka Maru* had turned: on the morning of December 7, Japan had attacked Pearl Harbor. The United States, the country of Nobuko's birth, and Japan, the country she had grown to love, were at war.

To avoid being hit by a torpedo, the *Osaka Maru* had zig-zagged its way back across the Pacific to Kobe harbor. Nobuko had been terrified of what would happen to her, if she'd end up in a prisoner of war camp, or worse, begging on the street.

Instead of either of those dire fears coming to fruition, she'd returned to her aunt's house in Sakayama. The moment she entered, however, her uncle greeted her with the information that she was to be the family maid. "In return for food and a place to sleep, you will clean and cook, and you will do the family laundry," he'd said. "And it will be done to my satisfaction."

At least scrubbing the toilet and floors, cooking meals, cleaning tatami mats and airing all the family's bedding had kept her from worrying about her parents and how they must have felt when her ship failed to arrive in San Francisco.

Then her uncle was conscripted and her aunt and cousins moved to a smaller house. "I'm sorry," her aunt had said. "There will be no room for you, Nobuko-san."

Even though she feared she would get them in trouble with the police, as her uncle had warned, Nobuko wrote to Mr. and Mrs. Mori in Nishimi, her Japan parents, as Mr. Mori call himself and his wife. They'd welcomed her, and she'd been happy for a time—until the villagers had turned against her.

Her stomach roiled. She glanced again at Masato, who, eyes still closed, seemed to be in perfect peace with the world. She closed her own eyes, but the oblivion of sleep evaded her.

★

Nobuko and Masato were among the many passengers lining the ship's rails, waving goodbye, shouting aloha, and throwing leis. A band played and native girls in grass skirts danced barefoot on the dock. As their ship pulled away, Nobuko vowed to put unpleasant memories aside and enjoy the remainder of their trip.

"Would you like to visit here one day?" Masato asked.

Nobuko looked up at the clear sky then down again at the dancing girls. "The weather is perfect. The people seem friendly, too."

"Maybe we should plan to celebrate our twenty-fifth wedding anniversary here."

Although she laughingly agreed, Nobuko couldn't see so far into the future. What would the world be like then? Things had changed so much since the summer of 1939, when she'd traveled to Japan to learn the culture of her ancestors—things were bound to change again, just as she and Masato would change.

Four days later, a swirling fog dissipating in the sunshine, the air damp and cool, they sailed under the Golden Gate Bridge and into San Francisco Bay. Nobuko's breath caught as she recalled the day she'd left California for Japan, her family waving farewell, her promise to write every day, seals barking, seagulls wheeling overhead. Throughout the war, she'd drawn comfort by picturing them at work on the farm near Fresno, picking apricots and strawberries, and waiting for her to return home.

But in reality, that home had been gone. Instead of waiting for her at the farm, her parents and brother had been sent to an internment camp. Her mother had died there, without Nobuko at her side. In Idaho. Where she and Masato would be in another ten days, witnessing her brother's marriage to a woman she didn't know. She wondered how much her brother had changed, if they'd even recognize each other when she and Masato arrived in Portland.

Her pensiveness was soon driven away by Masato's obvious delight in San Francisco—its sidewalks crowded with pedestrians, car horns blaring, cable cars, with people hanging off them, clanging their way up and down the steep hills. Their taxi driver drove much too fast for Nobuko's comfort, however, and when he pulled up to the curb outside the train station in Oakland, she stepped out of the cab on shaking legs.

"You're going to see your brother in less than twenty-four hours," Masato said when their north-bound train was well underway. "Excited?"

"Of course. A little nervous, too."

"Nervous? Why?"

"I'm not sure, really. It's just that so much has happened to the two of us—he fought the Germans in France and Italy while I survived the war in Japan."

"Don't forget, I fought the Americans in New Guinea."

"Maybe they'll hate us."

"They will not hate you. It wasn't your fault you couldn't get home. Me? That might be a different story."

"Now I'm beginning to think we shouldn't have come."

Masato took her hand. "Relax. Everything is going to be fine. Look out the window now and enjoy the scenery. This farmland is so different from anything I've seen before. The fields are enormous and it's all as flat as the ocean."

"I remember how miniscule the fields seemed when I first arrived in Japan," Nobuko said. "I felt like Gulliver, traveling in a miniaturized world."

The flat lands soon gave way to rolling hills. Late in the evening, the train climbed into the Siskiyou Mountains, marking the border between California and Oregon.

On Portland's Union Station platform, surrounded by a surging sea of strangers, Nobuko and Mako stared at one another for the first time after so many years. Her brother had changed and yet he hadn't. There was the same boyish gleam in his eye, the same stubborn cowlick at the back of his head…he used to try to tame it with something called Brylcream. Nobuko wondered what he thought when he looked at her, if he saw how much she'd altered, inside as well as out. She bowed, but then she could hold back no longer and threw her arms around him.

When they separated, Mako held her at arms' length, his eyes taking her in from head to toe. "I can't believe you're here."

"Sailing into San Francisco Bay brought back a lot of memories," Nobuko said with a wistful smile. "I kept remembering you, Mama, and Papa standing on the dock and waving goodbye. I was so overwhelmed, thinking I'd be gone for three whole years. Instead, it's been nearly sixteen."

Her brother squeezed her arm, and they both blinked back tears. A beautiful young woman hovered a foot or two behind Mako. He turned and took the woman's elbow. "My fiancé, Keiko Ugawa. Keiko, this is my long-lost sister, Nobuko."

Keiko smiled and held out her hand. "I've wanted to meet you since Mako first told me he had a sister—when we were both at Camp Minidoka. I'm so happy you could come for our wedding. It wouldn't be complete without you."

Nobuko's pulse beat faster when Keiko said the words 'Camp Minidoka,' which she could only associate with her mother's death. In an attempt to hide her discomfort, she turned to Masato. She'd been teaching him English, but he wasn't yet adept enough to follow long conversations. After interpreting Keiko's and Mako's words, she introduced him.

Masato paused only a moment before taking Keiko's proffered hand. Nobuko smiled at his hesitation, remembering how shocked Mrs. Mori was with the idea of a man and woman shaking hands. *"It is not done, Nobuko-san. You would be considered an immoral woman."*

Mako's apartment wasn't large enough for her and Masato to stay with him and it wouldn't be appropriate for them to stay with the Ugawa family, whose apartment was also crowded. Instead, they took a room in a downtown hotel. The hotel was quite luxurious. When she questioned Masato about the cost, he dismissed her concerns.

"This is a special trip. You are not to worry about money. You are to enjoy yourself."

Although guests from all over the world stayed in the hotel, Nobuko intercepted harsh stares whenever she and Masato spoke together in Japanese. Masato appeared to ignore them. And he claimed to enjoy walking along Portland's wide sidewalks, even when showers threatened.

"I can't get over the differences in the people here," he said. "Yellow hair, red hair and every variety of brown. The same with their skin—from white to yellow to black. Their eyes, too, every shade of blue, green and brown. It's truly amazing."

"It is said that America is a melting pot. That may be so among white nationalities, but I don't think there is much melding between white and black or white and yellow."

Nobuko had yet to meet Virginia and John Sato, friends of Mako and Keiko, who would be their hosts in Idaho. Mako had told her a bit about Virginia Franconi Sato, a white woman of Italian descent. John Sato was Japanese-American. Nobuko considered their marriage to be an exception.

Their last day in Portland, before driving to Idaho for the wedding, Keiko's father hosted a dinner for them at a place called The University Club, where he worked. Keiko explained that it was very unusual for an employee to dine there with guests. "They have always liked my father, though. They even gave him his old job back when we returned to Portland after the war. I'm not sure what we would have done without it. Many people in Portland hated the Japanese then."

"I wondered about that," Nobuko said. "I've seen some hostile looks."

Keiko sighed. "It's better now, but those attitudes linger."

Nobuko and Masato arrived at The University Club a few minutes before seven. Mr. Ugawa met them at the door. He bowed and escorted them to the dining room, his shoulders back, his head held high. It was easy to see how proud he was of the establishment and of his position.

Mako, Keiko and Keiko's brother Tomiyuki, or Tommy as everyone called him, were already seated.

Masato gazed upward at the high ceilings and large crystal chandeliers. "I've never seen anything to compare," he whispered to Nobuko. "I believe it is even grander than our hotel."

Mr. Ugawa overheard Masato. "It is modeled after the very famous Yale University Club and has been a Portland institution for over a hundred years," he said in Japanese. "Everyone of any importance in this city is a member."

Like Nobuko before she traveled to Japan, her brother spoke very little Japanese. Growing up, their parents always insisted they speak English at home. "You American. You speak American." From their blank looks, it was obvious Keiko and Tommy didn't understand their father's words, either.

A waiter handed each a large menu, and then filled their glasses with water. Mr. Ugawa translated the menu for Masato.

Nobuko turned to Keiko. "Your father is very kind. And I can see how the people here respect him."

Keiko nodded, smiling her pleasure. "He is a special man. Tommy and I are lucky."

When they'd all ordered their meal, there was a momentary pause in conversation.

"Why are they being allowed to eat here?" said a woman two tables away. She had been staring at them since Mr. Ugawa led Nobuko and Masato into the dining room. "He's nothing but a glorified doorman." The woman's carrying voice grated on Nobuko's ears.

The man at the table with the woman, presumably her husband, tried to quiet her. "It's to celebrate his daughter's wedding next week. The members said it was okay."

"I don't care what it's for. They shouldn't be here. This is for members only, not a bunch of Jap riff-raff."

"Muriel, please. They'll hear you. You're causing a scene."

"I'll cause a scene if I want. They killed my brother."

Like a rock cast into a pool of water, silence spread across the dining room. People stared at the woman and at the Ugawa table. Mr. Ugawa appeared stricken, red mounting his cheeks. Keiko reached for her father's hand. Tommy turned in his chair and glared at the woman.

Even Masato understood what the woman said. He stood. "I believe it best we leave."

Nobuko and the others rose and they quietly filed out of the dining room. Behind them, the silence broke, the sounds of ice clinking in crystal glasses, silverware on china, and voices raised in conversation resumed. It was as if, with their departure, they'd ceased to exist.

Nobuko's brother took them to a family-run restaurant not far from Nabuko's and Masato's hotel. They crowded around a small table and enjoyed a pleasant meal. No one spoke of what had just occurred except Mr. Ugawa, who kept trying to apologize. He wasn't allowed to finish.

Although they didn't discuss it, the scene played out again and again in Nobuko's mind. She hoped there'd be no repercussions when Mr. Ugawa returned to work after the wedding. It wasn't his fault. Maybe it wasn't the woman named Muriel's fault either. Her brother had died in the war, at the hands of the Japanese. How would she feel if it had been her brother killed by the enemy? Or Masato?

The next morning, without further reference to the previous evening, they crowded into Tommy's car and Mako's work truck to begin their journey to Idaho.

13

NOBUKO

Idaho

Nobuko stood at the window. After a night of heavy rain, the landscape shimmered. Above the ragged peaks on the eastern horizon, below the gray clouds, was a strip of the purest blue, just wide enough to allow sunlight to slip through and gild the fields. She hoped the weather would hold for her brother's wedding on Saturday. It seemed so strange to think of him as old enough to take a wife. But he was nearly thirty now and no longer her pesky little brother.

"Why are you up so early?" Masato said from the bed behind her. "Come back to bed." He patted the mattress.

"It's going to be a beautiful day," she said.

"You haven't told me about your visit to Camp Minidoka."

Nobuko had gone to the camp the day before with her future sister-in-law. As Keiko had pointed out, they'd both lost their mothers to that place. Torn between an impulse to decline and the desire to see where her parents and brother had been interned, Nobuko reluctantly agreed.

The highway they traveled passed through field after field of wheat, corn and potatoes. Keiko, driving her brother's car with a seeming detachment, finally turned onto a narrow, graveled road before coming to a stop. "This is it," she said.

Nobuko climbed out of the car and looked around: a building with glassless windows and a wide-open door that slapped against the outside wall; a weed-filled path led nowhere; a canal filled with dark, rushing water, cattails climbing its banks; a hawk circling overhead. She had hoped to get a sense of her parents but felt nothing. She could not imagine nearly ten-thousand people, surrounded by barbed-wire fences and watchtowers, living in the vast and windblown emptiness.

Keiko's mother, whose health Keiko said had been poor to start with, had died soon after arriving at Camp Minidoka. She'd been unable to survive the bitter cold and dry winter. Nobuko's mother, already worried about Nobuko, had lost her will to live after Mako was drafted. A letter stating that the truck farm that had been their home for twenty-five years had been sold to a stranger was the final straw. Thoughts of her mother's despair at not knowing if either of her children was alive, and then receiving word their home in California was gone, brought tears to Nobuko's eyes.

"It was hard to imagine all those people living there," she told Masato, taking a seat on the edge of the bed. She drew a deep breath, trying again to imagine the rows of barracks, the heat and dust, the rain that turned the dust into the muddy quagmires Keiko had described. And through it all, Keiko had said, no matter the season, summer or winter, hot or cold, there was the unrelenting wind— tumbleweeds, and anything else that wasn't nailed down blasting along with it.

"She said there was a hospital and schools, along with pig and poultry farms and seven hundred acres of irrigated fields. Now, the canals remain, but all the buildings are gone. It is like they were never there."

Masato stroked her arm.

Still seated on the edge of the bed, Nobuko glance down and gave him a slight smile. "Despite how awful it must have been, they survived that place. They raised potatoes and corn and other vegetables, enough to send to some of the other camps. With virtually no help, under armed guards and behind barbed wire fences, they created a place to live. They planted gardens around the barracks, built furniture from greasewood found on the desert, sewn and hung curtains in their barracks for privacy, made crepe-paper flowers to decorate, formed baseball and basketball teams."

She finally stretched out on the bed and rested her head on Masato's shoulder.

"They proved themselves to be better than those who put them there," he said.

After breakfast, John Sato and Virginia's brother, Marc, returned to what seemed their endless plowing. The little boy, Neil, captured Masato, taking his hand and leading him out to the barn to see a litter of kittens. Nobuko smile tenderly at the sight—what a wonderful father Masato would be.

Upstairs, the little girl, Mandy, slept. Many of the adults, led by Keiko, went back out to Camp Minidoka. Keiko's father was off birdwatching, something which apparently had kept him sane while interned at the camp. Virginia's daughter, Bella, who'd stuck to Nobuko like glue all morning, chattered away about the new school she would be attending in the fall.

From the corner of her eye, Nobuko saw Virginia head upstairs to where her brother, Paul Franconi, had gone shortly after breakfast. Several minutes later, Nobuko heard their raised voices. She wondered what troubled him, why his harsh features never softened. When she looked at his lined face, his blind eyes, she saw pain. It was as if he carried a terrible and heavy burden known only to him. Might he share it? If he did, perhaps the burden wouldn't be so heavy. She determined to make the opportunity to see him alone. Perhaps she could get him to drop his guard and confide in her.

The opportunity arose less than an hour later, when Virginia took Masato and the baby into the nearby town of Jerome to shop. Paul descended the stairs, carefully grasping the hand rail.

"Paul-san, even though it is a warm day, would you like a cup of tea?" To Nobuko, a cup of soothing, hot tea always made a problem lighter.

Paul turned at the sound of her voice. "Nobuko? Yes, please, I would like a cup of tea." He moved into the kitchen. "Where is everyone?"

Nobuko explained that his sister had taken Masato and the baby to Jerome to shop for groceries. "Most of the adults have gone to Camp Minidoka. I believe Bella is in her room, reading a book, and Neil is still in the barn, playing with a litter of kittens."

Paul's face softened and the edges of his lips crept up in a smile. "I remember doing the same when I was his age. He'd better watch for Mama Cat. She might not care for him disturbing her babies."

"We had a barn cat, too. Mako and I were always trying to lure her into the house, but she'd have no part of it."

"When my sister Irene was little, I remember her dressing one of the cats in her doll's clothes. The cat was patient up to a point, but when he tired of it, he'd streak off, doll clothes littering the ground behind him. I'd often see him later, a big orange mouser, trying to smooth out the fur rearranged by Irene's ministrations."

Nobuko placed the cup and saucer on the kitchen table, where Paul had taken a seat. "Be careful. It's hot," she said. She got her own cup of tea and sat across from him. "This area makes me think of California—we had a truck farm near Fresno. Even the irrigation canals here seem familiar to me."

Virginia's brother's face lit with interest. "Before our ship headed for the Marshall Islands, we visited San Francisco and Los Angeles, but I've never been to the middle part of California, the Central Valley."

"It gets hot, like here, but I loved it."

"Suki and Keiko met at Camp Minidoka—I've never seen the place. It wasn't built before I left home, and when I got back…"

He left the sentence unfinished, but Nobuko understood what he meant. When he got back home, he couldn't see anything.

Paul took a sip of tea. Holding the saucer in place with his scarred right hand, he returned the cup to it. "Suki has told me what happened to you, how you got trapped in Japan by the war. She met your parents at the camp, I believe."

"Yes, she said as much." Nobuko felt she had waited long enough. Paul looked at ease, his long legs stretched out on the floor and crossed at the ankle. He might be ready to confide in her. "You seem very unhappy here in your old home, Paul-san. Is there anything you would like to share with me? I'm not being nosy. Speaking to someone who is a stranger, or a near one, can sometimes help. They say in Japan that a shared burden contains half the weight."

A silence fell between them. Paul drummed his fingers on the table top, but Nobuko remained patient. Finally, he spoke. "I doubt Virginia has spoken to you about our father. He was a violent man and a terrible father. Keiko could tell you. She knew him. Suki, too."

Nobuko thought of her uncle in Japan. He was also a heartless and terrible man.

"None of us escaped his tongue or his fists," Paul said. "Mom included."

Nobuko said nothing, letting Paul tell the story at his own pace.

He shifted in his seat. His legs uncrossed and he sat up straighter. A deep line formed between his brows, and his blind eyes actually seemed to protrude.

Nobuko drew back. Her fingers tightened.

Paul took a breath and let it out, his face gentling somewhat. Nobuko sensed he was letting go of something he'd been holding tight to his chest.

"Virginia had already left the farm, kicked the Idaho dirt off her feet as soon as she could. I didn't blame her. If I'd been a few years older, I would have done the same. But I was only fourteen." The breath he drew was shaky. "One day I went with Dad into Eden—he liked to drink beer with some of his buddies on Saturday afternoons." Paul's mouth screwed with distaste on the word buddies. "When he'd had enough, I was supposed to drive him home. In the meantime, I planned to look up one of my friends."

Nobuko's heart fluttered with a sense of foreboding, but she did nothing to stop Paul from talking. She tried to swallow her unease.

"They were sitting on the sidewalk in front of the barbershop, complaining about the government, the price of corn, or whatever else came to mind. I was getting ready to go find my friend when these people came walking toward us on the street. They were Oriental—Chinese, Japanese…I wasn't sure what. A man and a woman and their two kids, one a baby, the other, a little boy, maybe three or four. They were dusty, the kids were crying. Their car had broken down, the man said."

Nobuko's fingertips went to her lips.

"Dad and the others said they'd help. They told the couple and their kids to get in the back of one man's old rattletrap truck. The woman looked worried, but they got in. Dad hollered for me to follow in our truck, then he and one of his cronies hopped in with the family. The Asian man tried to stand, pointing in the opposite direction. But Dad and the other man pulled him down. The woman and the little boy started to cry. I followed them a mile or so out of town, then they took off across the desert—heading toward a place called Lizard Butte, a large outcropping of granite near here that looks like a lizard sunning itself. I didn't know what was going to happen, but I followed." Paul clutched at the edge of the table with his good hand. "God help me, Nobuko. I was excited." He fell silent.

Nobuko's stomach clenched. It seemed as though the earth's rotation was slowly coming to a stop. In the hall, the clock chimed eleven. "What happened, Paul?" She barely got the words out, her voice a hoarse whisper.

Paul's answer, when it came, was delivered in an emotionless monotone. "They beat up the man first, then they went after the woman. One of the men knocked the little boy against the base of the outcropping." He stopped speaking and drew a breath.

Nobuko thought of Virginia's little boy, Neil. Blood pounded in her ears. She tugged at the collar of her blouse.

When Paul began to speak again, his voice shook. "He'd just been trying to help his mother." He shook his head, as though to dislodge a memory. "I keep seeing his body, so small and fragile, lying crumpled on the hard ground." Paul's shoulders slumped and tears flowed down his lined cheeks and dripped off his chin. "I tried to stop them, tried to pull the man off the woman, but he was too far gone in his bloodlust. I ran into the desert, ran until I fell and couldn't get up." He hung his head for a moment and then straightened. "The next morning, I went back. Even from a distance, I could see the trucks were gone. Ours, too. I went closer, thinking maybe the family was still there and I could help. But they were all dead. Before my father and the other men had left, they'd poured gasoline on the bodies and lit them on fire."

Nobuko gasped. Her hands trembled. She swallowed. "Did you go to the sheriff?"

Paul wearily shook his head. "I was afraid to. I thought they'd arrest me and lock me up."

Tears flooded Nobuko's eyes. "I am so sorry, Paul-san. I can't begin to comprehend how you must have felt. How those terrified those poor people must have felt. And you've lived with this ever since." She swallowed again. "But what happened? Weren't the people missed? Did anyone come around asking questions?"

"I went back a week later. I couldn't keep away. But there was no trace anyone had been there. Even the burnt remains of the bodies were gone. I imagine someone disposed of their car, too. It was like they'd never been, never existed. Sometimes I think I must have imagined the whole thing—but what kind of sick mind would imagine something like that?"

"There was hatred for Japanese and Chinese in California at that time, too. And when people are in groups and have been drinking—well...."

Paul drew a deep breath. "He was a bastard, our father. Marc, Virginia and I have his genes. Irene, too. We're part of him."

Nobuko stared at Paul. He was right."Do they know?"

"I think Marc might have heard my father and me arguing—Dad kept trying to deny he'd been part of it—but I didn't tell him." Paul drew a shaky breath. "I did tell our oldest brother, Leo. I think that may have been part of the reason he killed himself."

"Keiko said he could never get over what he saw in the war. The German labor camps."

Paul shrugged. "Maybe."

"What about your wife, Suki? Does she know?"

"I told her before we got married. She needed to know what kind of family she was getting into."

Nobuko nodded. "I see."

"You probably wish I hadn't told you. I thank you, though, for listening, for not leaving in disgust."

Nobuko covered Paul's hand with her own, willing him to know she felt only sympathy for the young boy he'd been. Not disgust. "Is there anything you can do now? Should you go to the sheriff?"

Paul shook his head. "They're all dead, so I don't see how going to the sheriff at this late date would do any good."

"But those people would have had family, someone who missed them."

"It's too late. I should have gone to the sheriff when it happened, but I was too much of a coward."

Nobuko's hand on Paul's tightened. "Paul-san, you must not be so hard on yourself. You were only fourteen."

Paul didn't answer.

Nobuko watched him, biting her lip, her stomach roiling, thinking of what he'd told her. How could men do such things? Mob mentality. Or was it possible that Paul really had imagined the whole thing?

Virginia and Masato returned from the store. The baby had fallen asleep in her carrier. Virginia took her upstairs while Masato brought bags of groceries inside. Paul had already returned to his bedroom. Nobuko hoped that telling her had lightened his load, at least a bit. She wondered if she should tell Virginia or Marc, and then decided that would betray Paul's trust.

She went out to the truck to help Masato unload. They carried the last few bags inside. Behind them, Nobuko heard a car approach. She turned and saw a maroon sedan driving down the lane. Two men sat in the car's front seat.

14

VIRGINIA

Idaho

Mako's sister, who had intrigued Virginia since she'd first learned about her, wasn't anything like she had imagined. Instead of being hardened by all she'd endured after her ship returned to Japan following Pearl Harbor, Nobuko Abi appeared both self-possessed and shy. She would have been beautiful if not for the long scar on her cheek. Her husband didn't speak English very well, but Virginia sensed that he was the perfect mate for Nobuko. He had a ready smile, and humor danced in his eyes, eyes that seemed to embrace everything. Neil had taken a great liking to him. It amused her how they seemed to communicate without words.

She put a bag of rice on the pantry shelf and reached into the grocery bag for the cans of olives. Hearing the sound of a car approaching, she peered out the kitchen window. A dusty maroon sedan, with two strange men in the front seat. Still shaken from her fruitless discussion with Paul that morning, she straightened her shoulders, nodded briefly to Nobuko and Masato as they entered the house with the last bags of groceries, and went outside to see if the men were lost.

The driver stepped out of the car. He was short and had a fringe of gingery hair around a shiny, bald dome. "Are you Mrs. Sato?"

"Yes." She frowned. The other man, a head taller and with black hair, stepped out on the passenger side. They both wore dark suits, white shirts, and ties. There was something ominous about them. Virginia's heart thudded in her ears. Who were they and what did they want?

"FBI," the dark-haired man said. "I'm Jim Danvers and this is my partner, Ken Lawrence." They showed their ID cards but put them back in their pockets too quickly for her to read. "We'd like to speak with your husband."

"He's in the field right now." Her heart thudded even harder.

They gazed at her, unspeaking.

"I'll ring the bell. It will take a few minutes for him to get back."

"We've got time," said Danvers

Virginia pulled the bell rope just as Mr. Ugawa and Neil came out of the barn—no doubt her son had been showing off those kittens that so intrigued him. Both looked hard at the men and their car. Mr. Ugawa urged a reluctant Neil into the house. Her son didn't go without a struggle, pulling back on Mr. Ugawa's hand and staring over his shoulder at the two men.

Virginia returned to where the two men stood. She pushed a strand of windblown hair behind her ear, trying to still the trembling of her hand. "Is there something I can help you with?"

"We'll wait for your husband, thanks."

Virginia grew increasingly nervous as the minutes passed. She shifted her weight as a rock pressed against the side of her sandaled foot. A gust of wind rattled the branches of the cottonwood tree next to the old prove-up shack. Still, no one spoke. Finally, the sound of approaching tractors. All three turned as one.

Marc was in the lead tractor, John close behind. Both men kept their eyes locked on the two men with Virginia. John stopped his tractor and hopped down first. "What's going on?"

"These men are with the government. They want to talk with you."

"FBI,"Danvers said after introducing himself and Lawrence. "We're here in regards to your father."

"My father?"

"The Japanese Government contacted the State Department about him." Danvers said, his eyes unwavering. "Is there somewhere we can speak privately?"

"In the house," John said. "But there's nothing Virginia and Marc can't hear. Or anyone else, for that matter."

They filed inside, John leading the way to the living room. He invited the two men to sit but didn't suggest refreshments. "So, what is it you think I can help you with?"

Danvers spoke first. "We have information your father is being held in a gulag, a forced-labor camp in Russia. He was captured in Manchuria when the war ended and sent there. Thousands of others were as well."

John frowned. "Manchuria? What was he doing in Manchuria?"

"Working in the mines."

"That makes no sense. He never worked in a mine before, and he would have been too old to learn. They must have him confused with someone else."

Virginia stared at John. Was that wishful thinking on his part? A muscle in his cheek twitched, but he gave no other outward sign of agitation.

Danvers ignored John's comment "We're looking for subversives, foreign or domestic." He looked at his partner and then back to John, suspicion behind the veneer of FBI imperturbability. "Your father has been there a long time. The Japanese Government wants to repatriate all their men—but not if they're going to make trouble. Not if they've been brainwashed, like the Koreans did to our boys. We don't want communists in Japan. We don't want them here, either."

John's earlier frown deepened into a scowl.

Danvers went on. "You no doubt are aware your mother is still living in the town of Nishimi, Japan, where your parents moved after leaving the States in 1938. I suppose it's where they were originally from?"

John nodded. "My father was born there. I wrote them several times, but I never got a response—I thought they must have died during the war." He paused and rubbed his hand on the back of his neck. "We have visitors from Nishimi here with us now. Mr. and Mrs. Abi. I just learned from them two days ago that my mother is still alive."

Danvers and Lawrence stared at one another. "Are you serious?" Lawrence asked. "From Nishimi? What are they doing here?"

"They're here for a wedding. Mrs. Abi's brother is getting married tomorrow."

"And they are acquainted with your mother?"

"Nishimi is a village." John stood. "I'll get them. They can tell you themselves."

Virginia's puzzled gaze followed John. He seemed so calm, but the news that his father was alive and being held by the Soviets had to be a terrible shock to him. She looked back to the two men. "You are going to try to get his father back, aren't you? What is it you need from John?"

Neither man answered her questions. Danvers' eyes drilled into hers. "Who are these people from Nishimi? Friends of your husband's family?"

Virginia disliked the man, and she liked his inference even less. "It's only by chance they're here. The Ugawa family were interned near here, at Camp Minidoka. You've heard of it?" Her question was meant to be sarcastic. At their nod, she continued. "Keiko Ugawa worked for us during the war. She met her fiancé, Mrs. Abi's brother, in the camp. Mrs. Abi is from California. She traveled to Japan before the war and was trapped there. After the war, she wasn't allowed to come home. The U.S. changed its policy, but by then both her parents had died, she was settled and decided to remain in Japan." Virginia lifted her chin, staring back at both men. *They'd better not read anything sinister into this.* "She worked for the U.S. Army for two years following the war, as an interpreter with the Occupation Forces."

Both men nodded but continued to look doubtful. Virginia didn't really blame them—she still couldn't get over how John's mother lived in the same town as the Abis.

Marc, who'd remained quiet until then, cleared his throat. "It's not such a coincidence as you might think. We're told a lot of Japanese immigrants are from that same area. The U.S. was wrong to intern those living on the West

Coast—many were legal immigrants, others were born here and American citizens the same as you and me." He eyed the two men, as though daring them to disagree. "Those people saved this farm and most of the farms around here during the war. We owe them. The country owes them. My brother-in-law served in the 442nd. He's a decorated soldier. I hope you'll do everything you can to get his father out of Russia and back to his wife in Nishimi."

Virginia smiled her thanks. Marc didn't usually make speeches.

John came back to the living room with Nobuko and Masato. He pulled the piano bench over for them.

Virginia hoped Mako's sister and brother-in-law wouldn't feel as intimidated by these two men as she had been.

Mrs. Perez's voice, speaking quietly to Neil and Mandy, came from the direction of the kitchen. At least most of the others were gone. No need to involve them with all this. Unless John wanted them involved, of course.

After introductions were made, John looked at Danvers and Lawrence. "Tell me everything you know, and what you want from me."

Danvers began. "By the end of the war, there were anywhere from 500,000 to 750,000 Japanese POWs in the Soviet Union—the Soviets didn't repatriate them as they were supposed to. All the other Allies did. Like your father, many of those captured were sent to work in mines or on farms in Siberia. Others were used to build a railroad across Siberia to the Pacific Ocean. Over time, some were released, most perhaps. The Soviets deny it, but we think they're still holding another three-thousand, maybe more."

"And my father may be one of them? Why has no one told me this before?"

"We didn't know, Mr. Sato. His identity only recently came to light."

John leaned forward, his elbows on his knees. "How so?"

"Someone, a returnee, said your father was there." Danvers paused before continuing. "He also said your father has joined the Communist Party and has worked to recruit other Japanese POWs as well."

On the couch next to Virginia, John reared back. "I don't believe it."

"We're not sure how much we trust the person who said this. He's a petty crook. Evidently, he thought he could trade information for his freedom. The Japanese police passed what he said on to their government and knowing you're an American, they passed it on to us to look into."

Virginia's heart sank further. John still hadn't looked at her. She bit her lower lip. Tears pricked behind her eyes.

"No," John said. "You've got it wrong. My father wouldn't work for the Russians—he hated them. He had no use for communism, either. Whoever said that was either lying or talking about someone else." Virginia took his hand and squeezed it. He didn't respond.

"We can't say how we've come to know these things, Mr. Sato. What we've already said must remain in confidence. But we think, if it's true...and you may be right, it might not be true...but if it is, we think your father will contact you or your mother."

"How would he contact my husband?" Virginia said, her voice sharp. "His father can have no idea where John is now—it's been years since his parents returned to Japan."

"You'd be surprised, Mrs. Sato. Someone with the information may well have told him."

Virginia looked at John and shook her head. What they were saying couldn't be possible.

"If any of this is true, and I doubt that it is, it's more likely he'd try to contact my mother," John said, his narrowed gaze traveling from one man to the other. "He and I didn't part on the best of terms."

Virginia's brows drew together slightly. John had told her how guilty his father had felt over the death of John's younger brother in the lumber mill, but he'd never said that he and his father had quarreled before his parents returned to Japan.

Lawrence nodded. "You're probably right, which makes it convenient Mr. and Mrs. Abi are here." He turned to them. "Would you be willing to help us?"

Throughout the conversation, Nobuko's eyes had traveled from one speaker to the other, while quietly speaking to Masato—simultaneously listening and translating. Virginia's admiration for the woman grew. But would they help? They were virtual strangers to John and certainly didn't owe him anything. Besides, what could they do?

"To be clear, what, exactly, do you want from us?" Nobuko asked.

"Only that you befriend Mrs. Sato and ask her if she's aware that her husband is in Siberia, and what, if anything, she's heard from him."

Nobuko spoke to Masato, who pursed his lips before replying. Nobuko nodded and swung around to face Danvers and Lawrence. "If John agrees, we will try."

Everyone's eyes swiftly turned to focus on John. He frowned at his hands, now dangling between his knees. He looked up to stare once again at the two government men. "So, my father is a traitor to both Japan and America…and you want my friends here," he nodded to Nobuko and Masato, "to help you catch him if he returns to Japan. That is what you're suggesting, isn't it? Why can't you just wait and talk to him when and if he gets there?"

Lawrence and Danvers looked at each other. Lawrence answered, his blue eyes glinting under thick black brows. "You're right, Mr. Sato. We could simply wait, and that may be what we'll end up doing. But what if he gets back to Japan and we don't know about it, the Japanese government doesn't know about it? What if he acts as an agent for the Soviets? There's no telling what kind of harm he could do."

Virginia had heard enough. "Why is everyone so afraid of the Soviets and Communism? They have a different political philosophy to ours, but so what? Democracy works better. We all know that."

The sound of Neil's laugher floating in from the kitchen made Virginia feel even more empowered. She took a deep breath. "I don't want my children growing up in fear."

"Okay," John said. Still not looking at Virginia, he turned to Masato and Nobuko. "I appreciate your help, but please don't do anything to cause yourself or anyone else harm. Only let my mother know I'm doing well and that she has three beautiful grandchildren. Maybe she'll talk to you, maybe she won't."

After the two government men left, everyone remained in the living room, staring at one another without speaking. Finally, John stood and nodded to Marc. "Guess that field isn't going to plow itself." Virginia reached for her husband's hand as he passed, but he brushed past it.

Later that night, Virginia waited for John to come to bed. All afternoon, she'd pretended interest in planning the wedding with Suki and Keiko, she'd taken care of the children, helped Mrs. Perez prepare dinner—she'd done all the things she normally did. Underneath and whenever she had a moment to herself, she worried about John. He already considered himself only half-American—even after fighting for his country and getting wounded in the process.

She tossed and turned for nearly two hours before his footsteps sounded on the stairs.

"John?" she whispered when the door clicked closed behind him.

"Not now, Virginia. I don't want to talk about it just yet."

"Okay. But soon?"

"Soon."

"It's never going to end, is it?"

"What?"

"War. It goes on and on. I'm worried Neil will grow up and have to go away to fight another one."

Keiko's and Mako's garden wedding was perfect, the weather fine. The roses surrounding them filled the air with their fragrance. Virginia tried to be happy for them, but her thoughts kept straying to John.

After the newlyweds left for their honeymoon in Seattle, the others soon followed. Mr. Ugawa and Tommy to Portland, the Abis for San Francisco and their ship. Virginia was pleased that Paul seemed more relaxed when he and Suki departed, even holding her hand for an extra moment and saying thank you, as though he really meant it. She frowned as their taxi pulled away, wondering what might have caused the lightening of his spirits.

She sighed and returned to the house. Paul might have lightened up, but John hadn't. He still held to his stubborn silence regarding his parents.

15

YOKO

Japan

She had a son. Every spare moment Yoko wasn't dusting or serving tea in the factory or fixing Takeda's meals or cleaning up after him at home, she gazed at this child, unable to believe her good fortune.

Takeda bragged to everyone how he'd sired a son, as if he alone was responsible for Kazuhiro. "He'll be the best potter in the country if I have anything to say about it, which I do," he often claimed.

Yoko was sure that as soon as the novelty wore off, her husband would take another one of his unexplained trips. Since she was not alone in experiencing the rough edge of his tongue or his quick fist, she suspected the entire village shared her hope that Takeda would soon be gone. Even the children feared him.

For generations, children had played on the pile of broken pottery below the kiln. They chased after the small animals that made their homes in the heap, played king of the hill and other games on it—this despite their parents' warnings that someone would get hurt. Takeda yelled and cursed at the children, chasing them off whenever he saw them, cuffing those not fast enough to get out of his way. Like mice, they squealed and ran in every direction.

Whenever Takeda went on one of his periodic trips, the children migrated back. Yoko never bothered to chase them away. Why should she, when they did no harm?

So much had changed since the war ended, Takeda returned, and old Mori died—Mori, whom she'd depended upon and sparred with. Old Ishihara, too. He'd soon followed his lifelong friend into the afterlife. Besides Ogawa, Takeda had hired other new and younger workers. All men, of course, and mostly untrained.

In the old times, Mori had managed the kiln, while Ishihara had overseen the apprentices, teaching the new ones how to wedge the clay before it went to the potters to throw. After his death, that responsibility fell to Yoko. The skill, taught her by her mother-in-law when Yoko first came to Nishimi as a bride, soon returned—enough, at least, so that she could give proper instruction. She tried to follow Ishihara's example of patience. Patience produced better results than her mother-in-law's insults.

Yoko began instructions by taking new apprentices on a tour of the pile of broken crockery behind the factory, the most impressive way to explain the importance of pressing all the air-bubbles from the clay. "You have only to examine the shards to see what can result with poorly wedged clay."

The next step was inside at the wedging table, where she demonstrated how to place the hands on a large rectangular block of clay, and set the block in motion. Her body swayed as the block, moving clock-wise, became rounded on its bottom and soon formed small pleats on top. After a while, it took on the shape of a large bullet, ready to place on the wheel.

"Now you try it," she'd tell each new apprentice. Without fail, the apprentice would apply too much pressure, treating the clay like mochi—rice that was pounded into a rubbery paste and served at the New Year. She would then repeat the demonstration, often several times, until the apprentice caught on.

In addition to her responsibility for the apprentices' wedging skills and some other duties, most of which she liked, Yoko still served tea and dusted.

As time passed, Ogawa and the two potters he'd brought with him from Shikoku, had grown bolder in showing contempt for her. Like the morning when one of them had purposely spilled his tea and then ordered her to mop it up. The other two jeered. This while her husband sat to one side, his face showing no sign of censure. And when they again ran out of a needed chemical, Takeda blamed Yoko.

"How am I to know when to order this chemical or that?" she said.

"Ogawa claims he told you."

"Bah! He is a liar."

For weeks she carried the bruise that answer brought.

Yoko returned to studying her son. Kazuhiro's black eyes stared back at her. He already had the look of his father. His shoulders, broader than most babies', would one day grow into a potter's shoulders. Like his father, her son would be handsome. And tall.

Despite his inherited good looks and admirable height, Yoko vowed she would do her best to raise her son to be as different from his father as it was possible to be. Her husband might be an excellent, even a great potter when he made the effort, but Yoko knew how to run the factory. She would teach her son how to be the factory owner and manager his father was not. She would also teach him to respect women.

It was afternoon tea break. Those who weren't outside playing catch, were seated in folding metal chairs or on the edge of the packing platform next to the office. Yoko stood beside the desk, an empty plate in her hand, her mind wandering.

The gaijin and Masato Abi had returned from their trip to America. From what Mrs. Mori told Yoko, the trip was a success, the gaijin's brother properly wed. To a lawyer. Whoever heard of a woman lawyer? Not that a woman couldn't do anything as well as a man, but who would hire her? Hunh. Yoko had no time for such gossip and speculation, although Mrs. Mori also hinted the gaijin was pregnant. Which was about time. How long had she and Masato been married? Five or six years at least.

Yoko had thought the woman must be barren, but apparently not. As with Kazuhiro, it happened when it happened. Mrs. Abi hadn't stopped complaining about her daughter-in-law, whose barrenness had added fuel to the flames of her dislike. It would be interesting to hear what the smug old crone would have to say now.

Takeda grabbed Yoko's shoulder, interrupting her ruminations. "Stop daydreaming, wife. Pour me more tea." Ogawa smiled into his teacup. His compatriots elbowed one another. Yoko glared at the three of them.

Just as Yoko anticipated, several days later, Takeda boarded the morning bus for Sakayama. She had spotted a spider in the bedroom that morning. Takeda going to Sakayama must be the good fortune the spider promised.

He remained away for a fortnight, though Yoko enjoyed little satisfaction. Ogawa and his henchmen used every method at their disposal to keep her in her place.

"Bring us tea."

"That apprentice isn't doing the job right. You'd better wedge the clay yourself."

"Where is the order from Tomo's restaurant?" On and on they went, sending Yoko skittering from one end of the factory to the other.

She suspected Ogawa, in addition to being sly as a skunk, was also dishonest. Perhaps she could catch him out in something. In the meantime, she must do the bidding of he and his friends, or Takeda would hear about it the minute he returned. Even though her husband's blows were less potent and more from habit now, she'd sooner avoid them.

At least she had her son to keep her company and give her solace. That and the cache of money in the back of the tonsu. She thought back to the days when she dreamed of murdering Takeda. If only she'd followed through with her plans. But then there would be no Kazuhiro.

16
NOBUKO

After the wedding, Nobuko had been ready to leave Idaho behind. She was glad Masato had insisted they make the trip, especially when she realized that the anger she'd harbored for years against her birth country had subsided. She'd loved seeing what a fine man her brother had become, she liked his new wife and her family, but Nishimi was her home now and she was eager to get back to it.

Best of all was the miracle she'd been savoring for the past two weeks. When they boarded their ship, in the privacy of their stateroom, she shared her news with Masato. God or Buddha or Mother Nature had answered her prayers and pleas. She was pregnant.

When their ship finally reached Osaka, she couldn't wait to be on solid ground. She'd enjoyed the ship's gentle rolling motion on the journey to America, but the same motion on their return trip often caused her to feel ill. The trip on the Inland Sea steamer and the three-hour train trip from Hiroshima to Sakayama were worse. Masato insisted they spend the night in Sakayama so that she could rest before traveling up the mountain to Nishimi.

They stayed in a small inn, a two-hundred-year-old structure on a quiet side street. After a light meal of miso soup and mackerel, they enjoyed a stroll through the garden. "I cannot believe that in less than eight months we will be parents," Masato said.

"We will be good parents, won't we? I keep fearing something might happen. Don't you? The world keeps changing and we have no control."

"We will be excellent parents, and our child will have all the love we have to give. Do not doubt it for a minute."

With Masato's arms around her and his reassuring words ringing in her ears, Nobuko enjoyed a restful night. Unfortunately, her queasiness, which had abated once they'd stepped off the train the previous afternoon, returned tenfold as their Nishimi-bound bus lumbered around curves, past rice paddies and wheat fields, through stands of cedar and rock outcroppings. She tried to think about pleasant things, like how nice it would be to see her friends in Nishimi once again, the baby growing inside of her. She felt better for a few minutes, until the bus swerved around a big pothole, and a wave of nausea rolled over her. Sweat popped out on her forehead.

She tugged Masato's sleeve. "I'm afraid I'm going to be sick."

Masato stood, bracing his hip on the seat in front of them. "I'll open the window. Maybe that will help."

Nobuko gulped the fresh air, and instantly felt better. She leaned back in the seat once more and smiled her thanks. She returned to thinking about the baby. "Before long, I will begin to show," she whispered to Masato, and felt overcome with excited giddiness.

When they entered the village, Nobuko peered out the window, thrilling at the familiar sights of home. It was a warm day and in nearly every house, windows were open and bedding was hung over the sills to air. Dogs barked. Children waved as the bus swayed along the narrow street and finally came to a stop in front of the store.

Suitcases in hand, Masato led the way inside. A quick glance around the store told Nobuko that nothing had changed here, either. Just inside the door, a display table was piled high with linens, towels and bedding, another with American jeans and t-shirts, and yet another with school supplies and stationary. Along one wall were bins of fruits and vegetables. In the back were shelves of cooking utensils and dinnerware, and in one corner were tins of kerosene. In the middle of the store and surrounding the cast iron stove, shelves displayed everything from soap powder to cans of juice. Nobuko smiled as she inhaled the familiar smells.

Her mother-in-law stood behind the counter, one of many catalogues open in front of her. "So, you're back," she said.

Nobuko's smile wavered. "It is good to be home, Okaasan."

Mrs. Abi frowned. "I expected you yesterday."

Masato drew a breath and slowly let it out. "It was too late when we got to Sakayama, Mother. We were both tired."

"Tired? After you did nothing but laze about on a ship for nearly two weeks?"

Masato shook his head. Without further comment, he took their luggage through to their living quarters behind the store.

Mrs. Abi turned her harsh gaze on Nobuko. "I suppose your brother is married now." It wasn't a question.

"Yes. If you don't mind, I'm going to give Masato a hand."

"Don't take all day. I see Mrs. Tanaka coming along the street."

Nobuko escaped to their living quarters. Mrs. Tanaka, who had no doubt seen her and Masato get off the bus, would have a million questions.

Masato had already deposited their suitcases next to the large tonsu that contained their clothes and bedding. He stared out the window above the sink.

"How about a cup of tea and a neck rub," she said. "You first, and then me." Her mother-in-law could deal with mousy Mrs. Tanaka.

Over the next few days, Nobuko spotted John Sato's mother twice, but neither time did she come into the store. Nobuko had almost decided to approach the woman on the street when the bell above the door jingled and Mrs. Sato walked in.

Masato was out delivering mail. With Mr. and Mrs. Abi in their quarters and no other shoppers in the store, Nobuko was glad for the opportunity to speak undisturbed with John Sato's mother. "What can I help you with today, Sato-san?"

"I heard you went to America."

Nobuko's eyebrows went up at Mrs. Sato's straight-forward response. This might not be as hard as she'd imagined. "We did. I was hoping for an opportunity to tell you about it. Do you have time for a cup of tea?"

Mrs. Sato, whose gaze since entering the store had been everywhere but on Nobuko, gave an almost imperceptible nod.

"You'll need to excuse me a moment while I fix it." In the summer, the weather was too warm for a fire in the store's stove, where the rest of the year a water-filled cast iron teakettle always simmered. Nobuko needed to fetch hot water from the kitchen. "Have a seat in one of those chairs while you're waiting."

Mrs. Sato gave another of her brief nods.

Nobuko cast a glance over her shoulder before opening the door to their living quarters. The woman hadn't moved. Returning a few minutes later, Nobuko set a small clay teapot and two matching cups on top of the cold stove. "Won't you take a seat?" She again indicated the two western-style chairs in front of the stove.

Mrs. Sato hesitated, then sat.

Nobuko waited a moment for the older woman to settle before handing her a cup of tea. "I met your son, John, in Idaho, Sato-san. He asked to be remembered to you."

Mrs. Sato took a sip of tea. Her hands trembled, but she said nothing.

"He is the husband of my new sister-in-law's friend and was our host while we were in Idaho. With a partner, your son and his wife own a large farm."

Mrs. Sato's eyes widened. "My son owns a farm? How can that be? Japanese aren't allowed to own property in America."

"Those laws, which were only in a few states, are no longer enforced, and they didn't apply to those born in the United States, like your son," Nobuko said. To get around that law, many immigrant Japanese had once registered property in their American-born children's names.

Nobuko's father had planned to do the same when Mako turned eighteen and they could purchase the farm from the owner. Not that it would have mattered—even as property owners, her family would have been sent to that camp. Nobuko mentally shook herself. She needed to pay attention to Mrs. Sato.

"Is he okay, my son?"

"He is well. He said he'd written to you, but you didn't respond. He thought you had died."

Mrs. Sato's eyes widened again.

Nobuko studied her face. "Perhaps you didn't get his letters?"

Mrs. Sato frowned. She shook her head, but her shoulders eased, and she looked slightly more relaxed.

They talked for several minutes, mostly about John, his family, and the farm. Nobuko decided not to mention Mr. Sato, at least not now. Instead, Mrs. Sato surprised her by bringing him up. "My husband was sent to Siberia after the war."

"There were many Japanese captured at the end of the war that the Russians didn't repatriate," Nobuko said. "Instead they sent them to Siberia to work in mines or on a railroad. It was in the newspapers each time some were finally released. Not that long ago, the Russians said they'd released all the prisoners they'd taken."

Mrs. Sato's eyes fell to her clasped hands.

"If your husband is still there, why do you suppose he wasn't among those who were released?"

Mrs. Sato's answer was a near-whisper. "I don't know."

"How strange." Nobuko took a breath before asking her next question. "Has he contacted you?"

The older woman's eyes filled with tears. "No."

Nobuko felt dishonest for asking questions when she already knew the answers. She tried to make amends by patting Mrs. Sato's hand. "Perhaps he will contact you soon. In the meantime, at least you'll be able to write to your son. Let me get you his address."

Nobuko and Masato were overjoyed when their daughter, Sachiko, was born the following spring. The birthing was hard, but Nobuko delighted in holding her baby, feeding her, and brushing her wispy-fine hair.

If only those early days, when Sachiko was content to be in her arms, had lingered. Instead, she did everything early: sitting at four months, crawling at five months, walking at nine months. "I believe our daughter feels trapped in her infant's body," Nobuko told Masato with a sigh. Their daughter was now a year old, and while March winds howled outside, chaos reigned within. No longer willing to be confined in a pen, Sachiko thrilled in tottering through the store, squealing and pulling items from the shelves, often to the entertainment of those who had come to shop. Nobuko's mother-in-law did little to help, insisting her granddaughter needed the exercise.

"Let her be. She is doing no harm."

Nobuko didn't mind picking up after her daughter, but she didn't appreciate being countermanded when she told Sachiko to stay away from items that could break. The hot stove in the middle of the store was even more a concern until Masato erected a small fence around it. "I'm going to deliver this letter to Mrs. Sato," Masato said after the third time Nobuko replaced several cans of juice on a shelf. "Bundle her up, and I'll take her with me."

Nobuko smiled her thanks. "Another one from John?"

"No," said Masato, examining the envelope. "There's no return address, but it looks official and it was mailed from Tokyo."

Nobuko dressed Sachiko in padded pants and jacket, and, ignoring her protests, pulled a hat over her daughter's head, and tied the strings under her chubby chin. "She is ready." Two months later, when spring was in full bloom, the cherry blossoms showing their splendor, the leaves on the maple trees unfolding, Nobuko gathered pen and paper and sat down to write a painful letter to John Sato.

Mrs. Sato's was not the only death that spring. It seemed an entire generation was leaving them. Mr. Abi, who'd been ill for years, slipped out of their lives as quietly as he did everything else, by dying in his sleep one night. Mrs. Abi railed. Masato, so like his father, held his grief close.

Mrs. Mori also departed the world, moving into the afterlife without a struggle. She'd once told Nobuko she would be happy to join her husband and their grand-children. "He will be taking care of them, you know, Jiro and Myoko. And I will help him until the time comes that their parents arrive."

Although Nobuko didn't have Mrs. Mori's confidence in such a well-planned afterlife, she was saddened at the loss of her old friend and confidant, missing their gossipy chats and her funny sayings.

"Nishimi isn't the same with so many gone," she told Masato, who gave an absentminded nod in return.

Nobuko eyed him. Several times in the past year he'd complained of feeling tired. At the same time, he had no appetite. He looked rundown, and she encouraged him to make an appointment to see Chieko's brother, a doctor just as Chieko's father had been before he retired.

"I don't need to. I haven't slept well in the past few days, that's all."

"But you're not eating, either."

"Nobuko, stop fussing. I told you I'm fine.

Mrs. Abi chided him as well. "I made this soup for you, and you're not going to eat it? There is too much here for the rest of us. It will be wasted if you don't eat."

"Thank you, Mother, but I'm not hungry. Perhaps tomorrow."

When they'd first married, Masato had told Nobuko of his many bouts with malaria and dysentery when he was in the jungles of New Guinea, and the awful food they'd eaten, the insects that had attacked them. It was enough to make anyone sick. If only he'd see a doctor. "Men," she complain- ed to Chieko.

The bouts of fatigue and loss of appetite didn't last, and when they passed, he was the same Masato, chiding her about her needless worries, taking Sachiko on his mail delivery rounds, leading them on hikes into the woods to find fiddle-neck ferns for Nobuko's mother-in-law to cook.

Nobuko finished straightening a stack of towels when Chieko entered the store along with her young son. Akira looked longingly at the row of wrapped candies on a low bench near the door.

"Good afternoon, Chieko-san," Nobuko said. "I was expecting you earlier."

"I was helping my husband this morning," Chieko said, with a slight reddening of her cheeks. She turned to her son. "Very well, Akira-chan, you may choose one." Then, to Nobuko, "What do you have special for me today?"

Nobuko showed her friend the fish that had come in that morning from Sakayama, and the pork chops sent by Mr. Sanyo. Chieko chose fresh mackerel. "I'll have a block of tofu, as well."

Nobuko wrapped the tofu in paper, also the mackerel. "Do you need anything else?"

"I don't think so. Where is Sachiko?"

"She is with her papa. I'm not sure where they've gotten to."

A short time after Chieko and Akira, who'd finished his candy, left the store to begin the twenty-minute climb to their home, Masato and Sachiko returned, Masato dropped into one of the chairs next to the stove and leaned his head forward. Nobuko rushed to his side, concerned. "Are you okay?"

He waved her off. "I'm fine."

He did not look fine.

17
KEIKO

Oregon

Keiko stepped out of the cramped apartment she and Mako had lived in since their marriage. She wore her best suit and carried the fine leather briefcase that her father gave her when she graduated from law school. Today she would be appearing before a federal judge for the first time. Her hand trembled, but only slightly, as she pulled the door closed.

Her client was George Nakasoto, a veteran who'd been denied benefits under the GI Bill. George had been interned at Heart Mountain when the war started. He'd been an early member of the Fair Play Committee, which objected to Japanese-Americans being drafted from internment camps. Despite his misgivings on the constitutionality of the draft, George had registered and soon found himself in the Army.

He claimed not to mind it at first. He willingly followed orders, and he enjoyed the diversity of his fellow soldiers. "My doubts started when my cousin wrote to me about his experience at Fort Riley, Kansas," George told Keiko the first day he came to her office. "Jimmy enlisted in the Army a short time before Pearl Harbor. He was sent to Fort Riley for training, but when others in the unit went to Europe to fight, Jimmy and the rest of the Japanese-Americans—and there were quite a few in the unit—were ordered to remain behind. They were given menial assignments, like collecting all the garbage on the post."

George shifted in his chair. "Then President Roosevelt was schedule to tour Fort Riley. My cousin and the other Nisei, eager to meet their president, polished their brass and their boots until they gleamed, dressed in neatly laundered and ironed uniforms, then lined up where they were told to assemble." George's mouth twisted. "But instead of meeting President Roosevelt, they were marched to an empty building. At gunpoint, they were ordered inside. They stayed in that building under armed guard, until the President and his entourage left—first having toured the base and dined on a fine meal, of course." George nodded, as if to himself. "Only then were Jimmy and the others released and ordered to return to their barracks."

Keiko had heard of the incident. She waited for George to go on. After a moment or two, he did. "A couple of months later, my cousin was court-martialed and sentenced to fifteen years in prison at Fort Leavenworth for failing to obey a direct order. When I heard about it, I got so angry. My family was still locked up in a concentration camp, while I was treated with contempt by my government, the same government I'd grown up pledging allegiance to every day in school. I wondered why I should fight to defend something that treated me and other Nisei with such disrespect. If I'd been an animal, I would have been given more regard."

George said he started speaking out whenever he saw an injustice. He was fined and spent three months in the brig for hitting a corporal who called him a yellow-bellied Jap and a subversive. He eventually fought in France and Italy, but that earlier incident remained on his record. When the war was over, he received a less than honorable discharge, thus making him ineligible for all the benefits of the GI Bill, benefits like tuition assistance, a low-interest home loan and unemployment compensation.

Remembering her own impotent fury at being sent to Camp Minidoka and the treatment her family and over nine -thousand other Japanese immigrants and Japanese-Americans received there, she gladly agreed to represent George in trying to get his record cleared.

Mako was as indignant over George's treatment as Keiko. Several times they invited George to their apartment for dinner and the three of them discussed their experiences at Camp Minidoka, Heart Mountain and in the war.

Now the time had come to present George's case in court and Keiko was armed with both facts and the knowledge that right was on their side. She just hoped the judge would agree. Two weeks later, he did just that.

"Another win," Mako said, toasting her success the evening the judge announced his ruling. "You are making a name for yourself in the Japanese-American community."

"Good thing I can find work there, since none of Portland's law firms are about to hire me." It had turned out just as she and Virginia and discussed years before, when Keiko first brought up the idea of studying law. It had been impossible for her to find work with a traditional firm. Women weren't supposed to be attorneys, especially not Japanese-American women. Even within the Japanese-American community, it had taken Keiko months to get her first case.

Fortunately, Mako's landscaping business was doing well. With the help of a business loan guaranteed by the government, thanks to the GI Bill, he'd bought more property east of Portland to begin his nursery business. Another loan had allowed him to buy more equipment and hire workers for his lawn and yard maintenance business.

They decided, mostly Mako decided, that the time had come to buy a house.

After a year of searching for such a house proved fruitless, a determined Mako set his chopsticks on the edge of his dinner plate and leaned back in his chair. "There's a house for sale on SW 31st Drive I think we should look at. I saw the sign on the lawn when I was delivering some rose bushes a couple of days ago."

Keiko looked up from her bowl of noodles. "That area would be convenient, but what is the point? We've already had three offers turned down—people don't want Japanese-Americans in their neighborhood."~

"Maybe this one will be different. We can't quit trying."

"I suppose you're right. How big is it?"

"The house isn't so big, but it's located on a kind of dogleg and has a huge lot."

Keiko laughed. "Aha. I can see that you're already plotting. You'd have some fun with that."

Mako cocked his head and grinned. "Yes, I would."

"I'm not brimming with confidence it will come to anything, since nothing has changed," Keiko said with a shrug. "It won't hurt to look, though."

They looked, and both fell in love with the little two-bedroom house and its large backyard.

"With that full basement, I could set up a home office," Keiko said, already seeing it in her imagination.

"An office for each of us, and a workshop…and that yard…it's even bigger than I imagined."

Fortunately, the sellers, an older couple who owned the house outright, agreed to sell to them. "I'm sorry we can't guarantee the neighbors will be friendly," the man said. "My wife is German. She had a hard time here during the war."

Keiko's eyes shifted to the woman, who offered a weak smile.

"It's time to put the war in the past," Mako said. They all nodded.

With her father's and Tommy's help, they moved in as soon as the papers were signed.

Soon after, Keiko realized she and Mako were about to experience another milestone. She was pregnant. A baby would occupy the little house's second bedroom by the following spring.

"I just wish Mama could be with us," she told her father.

He smiled and patted her hand. "Oh, she's with us, Keiko-san. She will be with you when your baby is born, stroking your cheek, whispering in your ear to be brave. She will be there to see your baby's first steps, see his or her first tooth, share your joy when he or she begins school. She will be at your side at all those landmarks and more. Simply close your eyes and you'll know she is with you."

Tears gathered in Keiko's eyes. "You're right, Papa. She will always be with us. And I will be brave for her."

When the time drew near, however, Keiko didn't feel quite so confident in her bravery. She recalled her only previous experience with childbirth, the night Bella was born. What a frightening night that had been. At least she would be in a hospital. Her doctor had made the necessary arrangements with a maternity hospital in northwest Portland. Keiko thought of Bella's birth again. Virginia had intended to go to a hospital, too. Everything happened so fast, there hadn't been time for her brother to drive her the twenty miles to Twin Falls.

"Don't worry," Mako kept telling her. "I'll get you there in plenty of time." Keiko thought his assurances were as much to assuage his own worries as hers.

Her pains began early in the day. She called her doctor. He told her to wait until the contractions were five minutes apart, then to go to the hospital.

"They'll notify me when you get there and make you comfortable. Don't worry, Mrs. Abi. This is your first child. It will take a while."

Keiko thought once again of Virginia. Bella had been Virginia's first, too. She placed her packed bag beside the front door.

Mako had been working at home for the past week, designing and planting the yard. With watch in hand, he timed Keiko's pains and paced. "Okay, we need to go. Your pains are still ten minutes apart, but by the time we get to the hospital…"

Keiko was quick to agree with his unfinished judgment. "Yes."

Her doctor was right. At the hospital, they checked her contractions and made her comfortable. So comfortable, the pains stopped and didn't start again until late in the evening. "Don't worry," the nurse said. "Babies seem to prefer arriving at night."

The nurse was right. At 3:05 AM, Keiko held her daughter for the first time. For several minutes, she tried to comprehend what lay ahead for this tiny scrap. Then the nurse took her baby to the nursery, leaving Keiko with empty arms.

She recalled the look on Virginia's face when she'd held Bella the first time, and how her eyes kept traveling to her infant daughter, cleaned and lying on a folded blanket in an emptied drawer, before she finally fell asleep. Keiko wanted her baby at her side, too. She should be there, in the room with her.

They named her Amy. "She's American," Keiko said. "I want her to have an American name, not a Japanese one."

They were in the hospital for five days. Most of the time, Amy was in the nursery. Keiko held and fed her daughter every few hours, but Mako wasn't allowed in the room at that time and had yet to even touch their infant.

"I can hardly wait to get home," Keiko told him. "I want to have her all to ourselves. No more interfering nurses."

Of course, things didn't go altogether as Keiko planned. Why did her baby cry so much? Bella hadn't cried all the time. Bella had been an angel, content until Virginia picked her up and fed her. Not Amy. The doctor said it was colic. Colic. Such a simple word.

Then Mako broke his left leg jumping off the back of a truck. With him clumping around on crutches and baby clothes and equipment everywhere, their house, which had once seemed quite large, especially after their apartment, suddenly seemed very small.

Don't worry, Virginia wrote. *It's natural you're feeling stressed right now. After Neil was born, I thought I'd go crazy. John was no help—he just spoiled the baby rotten, picking him up the minute he let out so much as a squeak. Things will be easier with the next one, though. Mandy was just like Bella— remember what a good baby Bella was? I'm hoping this one will be like the two of them. If I have another Neil, they'll need to lock me up.*

Virginia was expecting later in the summer and swore it would be her last. Keiko could only imagine what it was like now the farm was so much bigger. And with Virginia in the last months of pregnancy, it would be especially chaotic.

John says he and Marc have everything under control. They plan to hire an assistant for Mrs. Perez—the daughter of a neighboring farmer. Bella is already a huge help, but her duties are in the barn and garden…shades of Suki, huh? I'm not sure she's as attached as Suki was to the cow, though. I remember when I was her age how much I hated farm life. I don't think Bella feels that way, but she is so self-contained, it's hard to know what she's thinking.

Keiko read Virginia's letter several times, smiling each time. It was nearly as good as talking to her friend. Suki's letters were just as reassuring, though she and Paul led a much different life. As he'd promised her, Paul had worked at the university only three years, then they'd moved into their home in Carmel Valley and he'd finished his book, a story about the war in the Pacific. It had been published to all the critical acclaim Suki had expected for it.

Suki had sent Keiko pictures of the house, which looked lovely, but was so different from homes in the

Northwest—long and low, with a vine covered porch in front and a pool and something called a loggia in the back. Suki said she was delighted to be near the ocean again. Without lectures to prepare and student papers to grade, Paul could devote all his time to writing a second book, this one about a Pacific island and its native people. It was also set during the war.

When Suki wasn't transcribing for Paul or taking care of their young son, Adam, she was doing her own writing. Whenever Keiko spotted Suki Franconi's name on the cover of a magazine, she bought it and eagerly read the story it contained. The stories were charming and there was always some bit of wisdom tucked within them, to think about and treasure. Plus, a happy ending—so Suki.

Perhaps, someday, she and Mako would take Amy and drive down to California for a visit. Keiko couldn't imagine the mild climate Suki claimed they enjoyed year-round.

Sudden crying came from the back of the house. Keiko put Virginia's letter down and went into the bedroom to retrieve her daughter; she was soaked up her entire back. Keiko sighed and went into the bathroom. She turned on the warm water.

Her daughter was four months old now, old enough for a babysitter. Keiko had two cases pending—it was time to return to work. Her clients had waited for her long enough.

18

VIRGINIA

Virginia held Opal in the curve of her arm while giving the large pot of oatmeal another stir. Mrs. Perez would take the oatmeal outside as soon as it finished cooking. The field hands ate at the two picnic tables set up in the shade of a large maple tree between the house and the garden, just as they'd done for years.

"I'll take Opal, Mama."

"Is everything on the table? The bowls and spoons? The cantaloupe?"

"Yep," Bella said. "C'mon. I'll take her."

Virginia slid Opal into Bella's arms just as Mandy ran screaming into the kitchen from the dining room, Neil in hot pursuit. "Mama, mama. Make him stop."

Virginia rolled her eyes heavenward. "Stop chasing your sister, Neil. And Mandy, you stop that screaming—it's the only reason he chases you."

Neil grinned and darted out of the kitchen. Mandy stuck her thumb into her mouth and clung to Virginia's leg.

"Let go, Mandy. I need to move this pot off the stove. I can't with you hanging onto me."

Mrs. Perez came in from outside and took the pot. "Mandy, you're too big to be clinging to your mama like that. Hold the door open for me instead."

Mandy didn't remove her thumb from her mouth, but she moved to the door and held it open for Mrs. Perez, following her out.

Virginia let out a slow breath. What she wouldn't give to be on a desert island, alone, no kids, no field hands, no… she was about to add no husband, but that wasn't true. She couldn't live without John, not even for a minute on a desert island. One with palm trees and native boys serving drinks in coconut shells. She sighed again and looked around the kitchen. Dirty dishes filled the sink and there would soon be more. The fan on the counter swung back and forth, moving the muggy, early morning air about.

Her mind moved from the clutter of the kitchen to the den where, along with a two-day stack of mail, there were several scraps of paper on the desk, each a note directing John or Marc to call someone. With fifteen-hundred acres under cultivation now, the den was the hub of a growing, thriving business. John and Marc handled operations, but Virginia, former hater of farm life, kept track of all the farm's administrative needs, placed orders for seed, put advertisements in the newspapers and magazines for help when they needed it, set up appointments with brokers, paid invoices, and ordered much-needed new equipment.

Since the war, a revolution in farm equipment had occurred. And the government was spending more money on farm research leading to better, hardier seeds and better ways of planting and harvesting. Every Monday morning, except during harvest, Virginia met with John and Marc to go over plans and forecasts. In full partnership with the men, she now thrived on all of it.

Thank God Mrs. Perez had come into their lives, she thought, filling the sink and plunging her hands into the hot, soapy water. Without Mrs. Perez, she would never have found her niche, her ability to keep a hundred balls in the air.

The first Friday in July, a small package for John arrived in the mail. Virginia stared at the return address, Nobuko Abi, General Delivery, Nishimi, Japan. What would Nobuko be sending John? She contemplated ringing the farm bell to call him but decided the package couldn't be that important. Probably just something Nobuko had found and thought John would be interested in. She set the package on the hall table next to the telephone and went about her work. But several times throughout the day she paused beside the hall table and ran her fingers around the package's sealed edges, trying to imagine the contents.

When John came in from the fields that evening, his face covered in so much dust that only his eyes and teeth gleamed, he was interested in two things, a bath and dinner. "I'll open it after we eat."

Virginia sighed and put the package next to his place on the dining room table. The children were already fed and had dispersed—Bella upstairs to her room with a book, Opal down for the night, Neil and Mandy outside, playing in the long twilight of an Idaho evening. Marc wouldn't be eating with them. According to John, he'd gone back to his own house to clean up and put one of Mrs. Perez's casseroles in the oven.

John ate with the gusto of a starving man, while Virginia, nearly overcome with curiosity, ate a few bites of string beans, then pushed the roast beef and potatoes around her plate. At last, after his second helping of everything,

John set down his knife and fork and leaned back in his chair. He picked up the package and frowned at the writing on the front. "I wonder what's in it."

Virginia's fingers itched to grab the package from John's hands and rip the paper away. "Open it. I've been dying to know what's inside ever since Mrs. Hancock delivered the mail this afternoon."

John, finally giving in to Virginia's curiosity, tore off the brown paper and unfolded the first letter the package contained. He stared at it for a moment and then began to read. *"Dear John-san, I am so sorry to convey the news of your mother's recent demise."*

Virginia caught her breath.

John closed his eyes a moment, then opened them and went on, his voice determined.

"As I told you some time ago, I spoke with your mother soon after Masato and I returned from our visit to America. Since that time, we've had little opportunity to talk with her about your father. Masato delivered your letters, but he said there was never one to you in response. I am sorry."

John's voice turned hoarse and he stumbled several times as he read on.

"In March, he delivered another letter to your mother, which I have enclosed here along with an older letter from your father and some pictures I thought you might like to keep. Also, a copy of the coroner's report of your mother's death. It is evident from your father's letter that he wasn't a spy, which I hope brings you comfort. Again, I am very sorry to be the bearer of this sad news. If there is anything Masato or I can do, please let us know. Sincerely, Nobuko Abi."

John dropped the letter on the table and gazed at it with dulled eyes. The expression on his face was one Virginia hadn't seen there before. Anguish.

Her heart ached for him. "John, I'm so sorry."

Without responding, he opened another of the envelopes Nobuko had included with her letter, this one with the Russian postmark. His fingers stiff and fumbling, he withdrew the letter. After a moment, he handed it to Virginia. "You read it." He shook his head. "I can't."

The letter was in Japanese script, but Nobuko had written the words in English beneath each line. There was no salutation, no Dear Wife, only the date, January 4, 1953. Virginia cleared her throat and began to read.

"I write this to inform you of our divorce. As you may know, I was taken from Japan to Manchuria and after the war, captured by Russians and brought here to Siberia. For seven years, I worked at a coal mine. An accident resulted in an injury to my right foot. Unable to continue working in the mine, I asked to be sent back to Japan, but instead was sent to work at a farm collective. The people here are hardworking. I met a young woman who has consented to be my wife. We have a son together. His name is Olaf. May you enjoy a happy life in Nishimi. The letter was signed, Yoshitada Sato.

Virginia put it down and looked at John. Her husband wasn't easy to read. What was he thinking? Like her, did he wonder how his father could be so heartless to his mother? And good lord, John had a half-brother, a Russian half-brother. To find out like this....

Whatever he was thinking, John made no comment. Instead, he picked up the pictures, each worn around the edges, and shuffled through them. One by one, he handed them to Virginia. "My brother and me. I must have been about fifteen and George would have been thirteen."

Two handsome teenagers.

He handed her a second. "My parents on their wedding day."

Virginia studied it. The solemn-faced couple stared into the camera lens as though it would tell them what their future held. "They look so young."

The next pictures were the ones John had sent his mother, the pictures of their family. The edges were bent and dirty.

"She may not have written back to you, John, but she obviously spent a great deal of time looking at these pictures."

John nodded and picked up another envelope. It looked official. Inside was a letter dated April 15, 1957. It came from someone in the government. Nobuko's neat printing translated the words that informed John's mother of her former husband's death. There was no indication of how that information came to the government's attention, just a brief two lines saying he was dead.

John straightened his sagging shoulders and reached for the final envelope. The coroner's report. Again, with Nobuko's neat printing below each line. Mariko Sato was dead by her own hand. The time of death was estimated to be on or around June 3, 1958.

He rocked back in his chair and rubbed his neck, sighing heavily. "I should have made more of an attempt to reach her."

Mandy's and Neil's piping voices drifted in through the open window.

John fingered the edge of the coroner's report. Virginia reached across the table for his hand. "What else could you have done? You wrote her—several times. She made no attempt to write back. If she'd wanted to, had given any indication, you know she would have been welcome to come and live with us."

John shook his head. Virginia resisted the urge to brush the hair off his forehead, the way she did Neil's when he was upset.

"I should have pressed harder," he said. "Now it's too late."

Thanksgiving and Christmas, despite the children's excitement and good spirits, did nothing to bring John out of his doldrums. In January, when snow covered the ground, Virginia decided he needed a change of scenery.

"Let's do something crazy," she said, sitting at her dressing table one evening and watching him in the mirror. "Let's take some money out of the bank and go somewhere warm. Just the two of us."

John said they couldn't afford it—like most farmers, they were rich in land and equipment, but had little ready cash. Virginia insisted, though, and a road trip to the warm beaches of southern California turned out to be perfect. On a blanket spread on a barren stretch of beach, John finally unburdened some of the feelings he'd kept locked inside for years.

"My father was a hard man, never giving an inch to George or me. He'd insisted on my brother coming to work with him at the lumber mill. I'd done the same, working summers, until I graduated from university, but George was never cut out for the rough work. When that load of logs fell on him, I think my father took his death especially hard because he'd insisted on George working there."

Virginia said nothing, not wanting to interrupt now that John was finally telling her things he'd kept buried.

After a moment, he resumed speaking. "My mother was a cold fish. She never argued with my father, but I never saw an ounce of affection pass between them. Nor did she show any affection for my brother or me. She apparently felt keeping us fed and in clean clothes was all that was required of her. When George died, if she shed a tear, I never saw it."

He glanced at Virginia and smiled. "I suppose I thought her behavior was normal, that she was a normal mother, until I saw you with Bella."

Virginia blinked back tears. "I'm so sorry, John. You must have had a very lonely childhood."

"Not really," John said. "I had plenty of friends at school and in the neighborhood."

"You told those government men that you and your father parted on bad terms. What was that about?"

"When they decided to return to Japan, my father demanded that I go with them. I refused. He wasn't used to being thwarted, especially by his son."

"But he must have understood that you were an American citizen, that this was the only country you knew."

"He didn't see it that way."

Gazing out over the ocean, Virginia followed the flight of a flock of gulls, wheeling and diving. Words couldn't express the sorrow she felt for the boy her husband had been. She'd had a cantankerous father, one who'd said and did hurtful things, but her mother had been as loving as her father had been ornery.

She picked up a handful of sand and let it run through her fingers. "What are you going to do about your half-brother? Olaf."

John shrugged. "What can I do? I just hope his mother can give him a decent life."

19

CHIEKO

Japan
While her son sprawled on the tatami-covered floor looking at a book about samurai, Chieko moved through the house. The quiet was interrupted only by Akira turning a page and the twittering of birds coming through the open windows. She paused to adjust the scroll hanging in the tokonoma, depicting the fall season, then stooped to inhale the spicy aroma of three yellow chrysanthemums arranged in the celadon vase Hirotaka had given her when they first married. The green vase was centered on a polished table beneath the scroll. The house might be small, so much smaller than her parent's house in Sakayama, but as she gazed around it, she felt both satisfaction and pride in its elegant simplicity.

A smile played across her lips, remembering how pitifully she'd behaved when Hirotaka first brought her to the house. She'd cried for hours, sure there was no way she could ever live in what she considered little more than a hovel. How foolish and naïve she'd been. Not only then, but later, when she realized she was pregnant with Akira and thought Hirotaka would be angry, sure he would say they couldn't afford to have a baby at that time.

Instead, her husband had been nearly as excited as her, vowing to be the best of fathers. "He will follow his own path, his own dream," he'd said soon after Akira was born. "Whatever his chosen path, I promise he will have my full support."

Chieko bit her lip in sympathy for her husband, whose own father had been unwilling to support his son's desire to be an artist. Many months after they married, having become more comfortable with one another, Hirotaka told her how badly he'd felt about never being able to please his father.

"He considered himself a modern man, although that never included the emancipation of women, certainly not my mother. Nor did it include letting his sons choose their own futures. He thought Japan should forsake the old ways of art and literature. 'Technology is the future,' he often told us. He forced my brothers and me to study in the fields he chose for us—business and engineering for Shunsuki and Kinya, economics for me. I never knew how she did it, but after two years at the University of Tokyo, my mother finally convinced him to relent and allow me to study art."

Chieko knew it was a son's duty to obey his father, or at least it used to be, but she couldn't imagine Hirotaka, the man she'd married so reluctantly seven years before, as anything but the fine artist he was.

Hirotaka. She blushed, thinking of her frequent desire for him, and laughed aloud remembering how she'd told her father that Hirotaka was so old, she'd be a widow by the time she was thirty. He wasn't old. He was perfect—a perfect husband, perfect lover and a perfect father.

The only damper on her good spirits was worry about her own father, who planned to retire in the spring. It seemed impossible to imagine her busy father with nothing to do and nowhere to go every day.

Hirotaka tried to allay her concerns. "Why don't you take Akira and go visit your parents for a few days. I can get along without the two of you for a while—just be sure there is plenty of rice on hand before you leave."

Chieko laughed and clapped her hands. "What a wonderful idea. Thank you, husband. I will write my mother and find out when will be convenient. You needn't worry you'll have only rice to eat, either. I will ask Tomiko or Ichiko to come and fix your meals while I'm away."

The next week, in a pelting rainstorm, Hirotaka escorted her and Akira to her parents' home. Her mother met them at the door. "Come in. Quickly, before you catch your deaths of a cold."

As a maid knelt and helped Chieko and Hirotaka remove their shoes, Akira kicked his into a corner.

Her mother pulled the boy to her and pinched his cheek "You are getting to be a fine big boy, aren't you my dumpling?"

Six-year-old Akira pulled back, frowning. "I'm not a baby, Grandmother."

"No, no. Of course, you're not."

Chieko watched, a slight smile on her lips. "How is my father? Is he at home?"

"No, he is at the clinic with your brother. He is still seeing patients every day."

After delivering Chieko's suitcase to her old room and Akira's to his uncle's former room, Hirotaka told Chieko he needed to leave. "My students will wonder if I am coming today. I will pick the two of you up on Friday." After donning his shoes once again, he lowered his head against the rain and darted out the door to the still waiting taxi.

Akira followed the maid. He would need to remain indoors, not something he normally relished, but Chieko knew he would find plenty of books in her brother's old room to keep him entertained.

A low table between them, she and her mother soon sat upon silken cushions and sipped tea from delicate china cups.

"Tell me about Father. Why is he choosing to retire when he is still young?"

"He is sixty-three—not all that young."

"But not that old, either."

Her mother put down her cup. "As you know your father came to my family as an orphan. His parents were distant relatives of my mother. Even though he was a teenager, it was understood that he would take the family name, become a doctor, and follow in my father's footsteps. After he finished medical school, he took over my father's clinic and went on to build the hospital—his only time away from his patients was when he served in the Navy during the war."

Chieko nodded. She'd been nine when he left them and nearly thirteen when he returned. Although she hadn't understood the danger he'd faced while serving on a Navy ship, it had disturbed her to see her mother frequently turn her head to hide her tears.

Her mother took another sip of tea. "Although he has been very successful, I don't believe his heart was ever fully engaged in the practice of medicine."

Chieko's brows knitted. "What career would he have preferred?" Just as she couldn't imagine her husband as anything but an artist, she couldn't imagine her father doing anything other than practice medicine.

"I don't know. He has always been interested in history. Maybe he would have preferred teaching."

Her father at the head of a classroom? "Really?"

Just then a knock sounded on the door and the maid entered and bowed to Chieko's mother. "Your husband is home."

Chieko was surprised the afternoon had flown so quickly.

Later, muted sounds came from the kitchen, where Chieko's mother was directing the preparation of the evening meal. Chieko, kneeling on a cushion opposite her father, poured tea. She was reminded of a similar evening when the two of them had discussed—rather, she had railed and her father had discussed—her proposed marriage to Hirotaka Katsuragawa.

She studied him as he picked up his tea and blew on it. He'd never seemed unhappy about his work, but maybe she'd been too involved in her own girlish problems to notice.

"How was your day, Father?"

Her father took a sip of tea before answering. "Your brother and I made rounds together. He will soon run the clinic and the hospital entirely on his own. He is well-suited—fortunately, he has always liked medicine and is a fine doctor."

"You are a fine doctor, too. Everyone says so. I wonder what you will do with yourself when you no longer have patients to see or administrative work to be done." He had always been so busy—growing up, Chieko often hadn't seen him for days at a time.

"Perhaps I will come and visit you and Hirotaka and my grandson."

Chieko blinked. Her father in their small house—how would they manage?

"You look shocked, daughter." He smiled. "Don't worry—I haven't always lived in such splendor as this. I grew up in a house very much like yours. At times I still miss it."

★

It was nearly eight months before Chieko's father kept his promise to come for a visit. Fully retired, he arrived in Nishimi in a shiny black car driven by a man in a dark green chauffeur's uniform. Chieko, who had hurried outside when she heard the car approach, watched with startled eyes as the man jumped from the car, ran around it, and, standing stiffly at attention, opened the door for her father.

"I don't know how to drive and I'm too old to learn," her father said after clambering out of the car's back seat. "I've hired someone to do the job for me." The chauffeur retrieved her father's small bag from the trunk and took it inside. "That's all," her father told the man when he returned to the car. "Pick me up in two days."

Chieko served her father a light luncheon of miso soup and rice balls stuffed with spicy baby shrimp and cucumber. "Would you like to look around outside, Father. The weather is perfect for a stroll."

Hirotaka had enlarged the garden, planting several rows of chrysanthemums and dahlias next to the rows of vegetables. She was pleased for her father to see their beauty.

"I'd like to explore what is left of the old estate."

The terrain was rough and often Chieko needed to lend her father a hand as they climbed over loose stone and clumps of weeds. They paused to look around when they came to a small cleared space. Chieko remembered her first visit to the site of what once had been the summer estate of the Katsuragawa family. Since that first visit, the shrubs and trees had grown even more out of control. Still, it was easy to see how beautiful the grounds must have been when Hirotaka was a boy.

Her father turned away from the gardens and studied what was left of the house's foundation. "It must have been quite large—and the roof was thatch, I understand."

"And dried out from the summer sun, which is no doubt why it caught fire so easily when lightning struck it."

Her father nodded. "I've seen enough. We can go back now."

That evening, Chieko's father and her husband put on jackets and went outside to sit on the bench Hirotaka had set near the edge of his flower garden. After dinner and after spending time with their son, sometimes helping him with his homework, it had become her husband's habit to sit on the bench for an hour or so each evening. Chieko never disturbed him, knowing how much he enjoyed his solitude. She was glad that he'd included her father, though—they needed the opportunity to get to know one another better.

It wasn't until her father had returned to Sakayama that Hirotaka confided what Chieko's father had proposed.

"He wants to rebuild my parents' house, turn it back into the grand estate it was before the fire, refill the koi ponds and bring in gardeners to refurbish the gardens and to prune and retrain the trees. I couldn't believe I was hearing correctly."

Chieko couldn't believe what she was hearing, either. She studied his face. "So that we could live in it, I suppose. Would you want such a thing to happen?"

"Of course not. I vowed to put all that behind me when I came back from New Guinea. I wanted only to be allowed to live here, in what was once the caretaker's house, in peace—I think we do that, don't we?" He gazed at her, a sudden look of doubt in his eyes.

Pleased with his answer, she leaned back on her heels. "Yes, we do. What did my father say when you declined his offer? Were you able to make him understand?"

Hirotaka shook his head. "I'm not sure. It is sometimes hard for me to know if he is following my logic or simply seeing and hearing what he wishes to see and hear."

Chieko nodded. She was not sure what her father was thinking either. He'd always been strong-willed, now he sometimes seemed like a child in his determination to get what he wanted. "Maybe he will forget the idea."

Chieko's father did not forget the idea. He hired an architect and sent him to view the estate and take measurements. Her husband found the man pacing off the crumbling foundations. Chieko watched Hirotaka send the architect on his way, making it clear he was not interested in rebuilding the estate. The architect departed, but only after casting a longing glance at the site.

Hirotaka then wrote her father, thanked him, and explained again that he didn't want the house rebuilt. Her father responded by sending gardeners, whom Hirotaka also sent away.

Chieko wrote and asked her mother to intervene. Her mother wrote back.

My dear daughter,

I do understand how your husband feels. Unfortunately, I can't seem to convince your father. He is determined that the Katsuragawa estate should be returned to its former splendor. I wonder if you and I might work out a compromise of sorts. What if we allowed your father to have at least the gardens restored? It might become a place the villagers could enjoy.

Chieko immediately grasped her mother's idea. She could imagine the villagers strolling along the paths Hirotaka's mother once walked, feeding the koi swimming in the green depths of the pond. They could create a place for picnics as well. She drew a shaky breath. A park was a splendid idea, but Hirotaka wanted nothing to do with revitalizing his family's estate. Could she convince him of the merits of such a plan?

20
YOKO

Japan

All spring and summer, dust and noise clogged the air. The street that ran through the middle of Nishimi was as busy as the streets in Sakayama. Yoko kept watch as the men and equipment came and went. First, they widened and smoothed out the track that led up the mountain to the Katsuragawa house. Next, they paved it, like was done to the street in front of the factory a year or two after the war ended. When that was completed, trucks filled with people and equipment streamed through the village and turned up the newly paved road.

The old Katsuragawa estate was being made into a park. There was to be a tea pavilion, too—as though people had nothing to do but stroll through a park, feed the koi, and drink tea. A vision of Hirotaka's father, frowning and fierce, appeared before Yoko's eyes. Ha! How quickly he would put an end to such foolishness.

From the doorway of the factory, she called to her son. "Kazuhiro, get away from the road. A truck might come and knock you down."

Her son looked like an urchin, his face, hands, and clothes covered in dirt and clay dust. When he was younger, she'd carried him in a sling on her back. Now, at seven, he was always into something, keeping Yoko on her toes. He threw a rock into the street just as a truck thundered past spitting up pebbles and dust.

"Kazuhiro! Did you hear what I said? Get away from there."

"Why? I'm not hurting anything."

Yoko sighed then turned to gaze toward the Abi store and beyond. Old Mori and Ishihara wouldn't recognize the village with all its city-style houses, dominated by large windows. Outside each were miniscule yards, where dogs were chained instead of being allowed to run free as they used to do. She had no idea why that was so. Behind her, next to the factory, was her own house. It, at least, remained unchanged. There was no need for more than three rooms, not when Takeda was so seldom in it.

The daughter-in-law of old Mr. and Mrs. Mori, both gone from this life, approached, a market basket over her arm. Like hers, the Mori house, the last house on the road through the village, was just as it always had been—though no longer the largest house in the village. Still, a dog was chained in the yard, just like the others. Yoko nodded a greeting to the woman, who said something to Kazuhiro before joining Yoko.

"He is getting to be a fine-looking boy, Yoko-san. You must be very proud of him."

"Yes."

"He will no doubt make a fine potter one day."

Yoko gave her son a fond smile. He threw another rock.

"The sensei's son, Akira, is also doing well. Sachiko Abi, too. She is getting to be a beauty. One day all the boys in the village will be fighting over her."

Yoko scowled at the thought of the gaijin's daughter becoming the center of attention, just like her mother.

"Kazuhiro, it is time for morning tea." She gave the foolish Mori woman a cool nod and retreated into the factory.

★

Takeda had taken himself off again. Yoko no longer bothered where he went or what he did when he boarded the bus and left Nishimi. He didn't trouble her in bed, so no doubt seeing a woman was part of the reason for his disappearances. It wouldn't be all, though. She continued to check the accounts book he kept locked in the drawer.

He wasn't using money from the factory, so he must have some other source of income. Yoko felt certain that he was back to black-marketeering. There were always things that people wanted. Takeda must have discovered a way to locate the goods and match them to those willing to pay his price. She didn't care what he was up to, so long as he took nothing from the factory except himself.

While he was gone, she used her wits to keep the factory from further decline. Ogawa spent more time trying to thwart her than he did working to improve his skills, but at least he wasn't tattling to Takeda all the time. She'd put a stop to that behavior when she discovered him sneaking off with several fired pots, planning to sell them and pocket the profits. She demanded to know how long he'd been stealing from the factory. At first, he tried to deny it.

Yoko was unmoved by his denial. "Perhaps I should call the police and let them settle this."

Ogawa hissed at her, glaring. Then one side of his upper lip drew up and he admitted he'd been stealing from the factory for a year. "But you, foolish woman, were too blind and stupid to see what was beneath your nose." He then slithered away like the snake he was.

Yoko didn't tell Takeda when he eventually returned to Nishimi. Instead, she held the information close, using it to check Ogawa's more egregious efforts to frustrate her.

One summer afternoon, she sat in the desk chair, her feet propped on an open drawer. Asai Sano sat on the packing platform. The factory's one-time master potter came the closest to being a friend that Yoko had ever had. After Takeda fired her, Asai began helping her forester husband with his business. When she came to Nishimi to shop, and she knew Takeda was away, she often stopped in the factory to visit.

Asai picked up a sake flagon waiting to be placed in a wooden box partitioned to hold it and two sake cups.

Yoko gave the flagon a dismissive glance. "Not so fine as you once produced—not with that graceless curve and the thickness of the lip. Is it a wonder we are losing business?"

Ogawa had a sixth sense where his predecessor was concerned. He slid open the door that led up from the production area and scowled at Asai. "What are you doing here?"

Asai ignored his rude question.

Yoko frowned. "What do you want?"

Ogawa sniffed, not answering, and retreated, sliding the door shut once again.

"The man is always skulking," Yoko said. "I wish I could get rid of him."

Asai stared at the closed door. "My son is sixteen now. He has an eye for form—I've long noted it."

"Kazuhiro will make a fine potter as well if he isn't first run over by a truck." Yoko said the words with cool detachment, but in reality, she felt great pride in her son's daring.

"Perhaps you need one of the village women to tend him—I'm sure you could find someone with a child near the same age who would be willing to take him for a little extra cash."

Yoko's brows drew down at the suggestion. She didn't want anyone else looking after her son. "This factory will be his one day. Even though he is not yet seven, he isn't too young to start learning the importance of work."

Asai nodded. "You're right. I need to go home and prepare my family's dinner." She rose from her seat on the edge of the packing platform. "I doubt you have much say in who your husband hires, but if you do, I hope you will keep in mind what I told you about my son. Takumi would make an excellent apprentice. Who knows, one day he could even take Ogawa's place."

After Asai left, Yoko smiled, enjoying the perfect irony of that thought—Asai's son replacing the man who had replaced Asai.

Several evenings later, an hour after the last bus to Nishimi had come and gone, Takeda arrived home. While Yoko prepared a meal, he absentmindedly played a game of quoits with Kazuhiro, who took his father's comings and goings without complaint. Mostly her husband stared into space.

The following day, her husband studied the accounts book. He then began taking a renewed interest in the running of the factory, an interest that went on for several months. He even spent a few hours each day working at the wheel.

Ogawa became grumpier the longer Takeda remained, perhaps thinking he was being eased out of his position as master potter. He would be eased out, but not by Yoko's husband. She and Asai had talked more about Asai's son, Takumi.

"It must not come from me or you," Yoko said. "Takeda would reject the boy on principle if he thought I favored him."

"Or if he knew he was my son."

"My husband has likely forgotten you, but I've no doubt Ogawa would remind him. I think your husband should be the one to propose him. One of the apprentices is leaving us—pottery-making has lost its appeal, or Nishimi has."

"He isn't from around Nishimi?"

"No. Takeda met him somewhere and sent him here. He was never suited—couldn't even learn how to wedge the clay."

Yoko had wondered about the boy, where he came from. City, not country. He'd seemed bright enough, but it was clear from the start he wasn't interested in making pottery for the rest of his life. She ignored the fact that, except for being several inches shorter, he bore a striking resemblance to her husband.

She nodded to Asai, a smile of anticipation on her lips. "The next time we fire the kiln, perhaps your husband can bring your son. Let Takeda think it is his own or your husband's idea to bring him on as an apprentice."

Yoko only needed to show Asai's son once how to wedge the clay. Just as his mother had predicted, he was a natural. His name, Takumi, meaning artisan, foretold it. He had a feel for the clay.

He also worked hard, making sure there was always clay wedged and ready for the potters. He carried the planks laden with just thrown soba bowls or plates, cups, or sake jars to the drying room, where he slid the planks onto racks. When it was time to fire the kiln, he worked tirelessly helping to load it and later, once the kiln was lit, feeding wood into the chambers at the precise angle.

Takeda was pleased with his selection. "I could tell just by looking at him that he had the making of a potter. I will teach him all he needs to know."

For weeks thereafter, Takeda had the boy throw nothing but cups. "It is the way we all learned." Day after day, cup after cup, until he finally allowed Takumi to move on to bowls. Yoko wanted to tell Asai of her son's progress, but so long as Takeda remained in Nishimi, Asai stayed away from the factory.

Yoko was surprised her husband remained—it had been years since he'd stayed in Nishimi so long, away from wherever it was he normally went. It was almost as if he feared going back.

She wondered briefly if it was overseeing Takumi's training that kept him in the village, then dismissed the idea. More likely some fix he'd gotten himself into. Or maybe he'd just mellowed with age—he seldom struck her anymore, and his insults were fewer. She'd long before given up her dreams of revenge.

Kazuhiro attached himself to the young man, tagging along after him, mimicking everything he did. Takumi would often cut off a chunk of clay for Kazuhiro to wedge or work. Later, when Takumi began working on the wheel, Kazuhiro would lean against a post, his eyes glued to the whirling wheel and Takumi's increasingly deft hands. At break time and lunch, when Kazuhiro and Takumi finished eating, Takumi frequently went outside with the boy to play catch. Yoko watched from the door, pleased to see Kazuhiro enjoying himself.

One day, Mrs. Abi and her granddaughter appeared at the same time Takumi and Kazuhiro were throwing a baseball. Mrs. Abi didn't need to encourage Sachiko to join them.

Mrs. Abi came to stand next to Yoko. "They are so close in age, less than a year apart, it is good for them to play together."

Yoko frowned. Her opinion of Nobuko Abi unchanged, she had no interest in a friendship forming between the gaijin's daughter and her son. Unfortunately, Kazuhiro had ideas of his own.

21

CHIEKO

Japan

Chieko followed her husband along the path that led from their house, around the garden and his bench, to the park. Eleven-year-old Akira, had gone ahead, calling over his shoulder, "I'll find us a good spot for our picnic." The park was well-used. Even in winter, a few hardy souls from the village would venture up the mountain to visit the beautifully bared garden, the limbs of its shrubs and trees limned with snow.

It was easier to convince Hirotaka of the wisdom of turning his family's former estate into a garden and park for Nishimi than Chieko had imagined. "I'm just ashamed I didn't think of it myself," he had told her. "I was being selfish. Of course, I could never afford what your father has done with it. I still wish there was a way to repay him for his generosity."

"Don't worry. My mother said he took great pleasure in overseeing everything. It was the perfect way to start his retirement."

The entire spring and summer the garden was being constructed, the big black car appeared on the track every few days with Chieko's father enthroned in the back seat, looking very pleased with himself. Chieko couldn't help be reminded of Akira with a new toy.

The park, completed three years ago, included a tea pavilion, stands of bamboo, hand-pruned rhododendrons and pine trees, maple trees and moss-covered rockeries. A graveled walkway wound throughout. On special nights, like Setsuban, the beginning of spring, and during Obon, when deceased ancestors were celebrated, the entire garden was lit with lanterns tucked into the rockeries and along the path.

"My mother says he has now taken such an interest in gardening that he spends all his afternoons in the garden he has created at their home." This was the closest Chieko could come to revealing the sadness that now flooded her heart whenever she thought of her father, the man she'd always looked up to, revered, even, now reduced to puttering in a garden. His skill as a doctor had once been sought after. She suspected he had known of his impending dementia, had recognized the signs, and that is what made him decide to retire at such a young age. How hard it was to see, and how hard it must be on her mother.

They reached the spot Akira chose for their picnic. Hirotaka spread a blanket and Chieko opened the picnic basket. Akira grabbed several pieces of fried chicken and a rice ball, then hurried off to feed the koi the breadcrumbs he carried in his pocket.

"My father used to get upset whenever he found us feeding the koi anything other than the special food he ordered for them. Even my mother would give them breadcrumbs from time to time, though."

"What do you suppose your father would make of this?" Chieko gestured around them, to the trails, the tea pavilion, the gardens.

"I'm not sure. At times, I've thought he'd hate it, but now…it was wasted before, as was this view, since my family only came for a couple of months in the summer. I think he might take pleasure in it. I'm sure my mother would." He sighed. "I wish you could have known her, Chieko. In many ways, your mother reminds me of her. My mother, also, was the family peacemaker."

Hirotaka had brought his sketch pad and pencils—he was rarely without them. While they chatted, he sketched her. She'd grown used to it. At first, she'd been embarrassed, especially when she was pregnant, and he'd insisted on posing her nude. Thank goodness, those sketches were never seen by anyone but the two of them. Several of her portraits, though, had been sold in the gallery in Sakayama.

Chieko hoped Hirotaka' reputation would continue to spread, hoped her father had been right when he said her husband would one day be recognized as a National Treasure. Unfortunately, Hirotaka didn't seem to share Chieko's ambition. He continued to consider himself nothing more than a humble artist.

Akira, always hungry, came back for more food. Sometimes Chieko worried that their son didn't make friends. He seemed to prefer reading or being off on his own, exploring. She often took him shopping with her, thinking he and Sachiko might spend time together. But Nobuko's daughter was generally somewhere else, most often with Kazuhiro Yoshida. Those two were inseparable.

Chieko could only imagine what Yoko made of that— did that woman never smile? She'd once asked Nobuko how she felt about her daughter's friendship with Yoko's son. Nobuko's answer surprised her. "I do not want to pass my prejudices to Sachiko. She must make up her own mind. Besides, despite his parents, Kazuhiro seems like a good boy." Sometimes she thought Nobuko almost too good—so serene, never complaining. Yet worries about Masato's health must plague her.

After they'd eaten, Akira and Hirotaka went off to see a bird's nest her son had discovered, while she packed away the remains of their meal. Then, with a linen napkin protecting her face from the sun, she stretched out on the blanket and dozed until her husband and son returned.

As always, the shiny blue car Chieko's father had bought her remained under its canvas tarp while she walked down the paved and tree-shaded track to Nishimi to do her daily shopping at the Abi store. When the bell above the door jingled to announce her arrival, a sight she didn't expect greeted her: Nobuko, her customary neat-as-a-pin hair hanging loose and wild, her forehead creased with worry.

"Chieko-san, I'm so glad you have come. Masato has grown worse. I have called a taxi to take us to the doctor's office. Can Sachiko stay with you when she comes home from school?"

"Of course. I will be happy to watch your daughter. Would you like me to mind the store until you get back? Hirotaka is in Sakayama today, so I am free to do so."

Nobuko's lips trembled. "Thank you, but I'm not sure how long I will be."

Chieko's lips trembled as well. "It doesn't matter. I'll be here—however long you need me."

The taxi came, and the driver helped Nobuko get Masato to the car, half-carrying him. Chieko brought a blanket and Nobuko draped it around Masato's shoulders. Masato didn't protest. His skin and the whites of his sunken eyes were a dark orange-yellow. He seemed only partially aware of his surroundings.

Chieko caught her lower lip between her teeth and her eyes stung from unshed tears as the taxi pulled away and sped off down the mountain. She'd talked to her brother, who'd taken over their father's medical practice, and from what he'd described, she understood Masato must be suffering from advanced liver failure. Poor Nobuko, what would she do—because Masato couldn't go on like this. Chieko's brother said that someday doctors would find a cure or a treatment, but that now, once the liver got to this stage, nothing could be done.

Oh, my dear, dear Nobuko. It is unfair that you have already suffered so much sorrow in your life. Now this. Chieko stopped trying to hold back her tears.

Masato was admitted to the hospital from the doctor's office. Nobuko called on the store's telephone, asking Chieko if Sachiko could stay with her. "My mother-in-law and I will take turns nursing Masato."

Chieko wondered if her friend realized how close they were to the end. She wanted to cheer her somehow, but didn't think there was anything she could do except take good care of Sachiko and be a support when the end came.

The end took less than a week to arrive.

Chieko continued to mind the store. Village women came daily to find out how Masato fared—Nobuko phoned every morning with an update. After closing the store in the afternoon, when Sachiko and Akira returned from school, Chieko would take them home, fix them a snack, and let them roam in the park. Often, she packed them a picnic dinner and they stayed outside until she called them in to do their homework and go to bed.

"This morning, on the telephone, Nobuko told me that Masato was able to speak with her," Chieko told Hirotaka on the third such evening. She worried about him. Masato was his best friend. "Perhaps my brother was wrong, and Masato will get better."

"I don't believe so." Hirotaka, his eyes cast down, fingered the edge of his soup bowl. "I went to the hospital after my class today. I saw death too many times in New Guinea not to recognize it. Masato knows the end is near—it was in his eyes." Without finishing his meal, he stood and went outside. Two hours later, he was still seated on his bench.

When night fell, he lay down beside her on their futon. Without words, he reached for her and held her close.

The following day Nobuko came home for a change of clothes. Chieko asked if she would like her to bring Sachiko to the hospital. "We can come on Saturday if you'd like."

Nobuko buried her face in her hands. "Oh Chieko-san, I'm not sure he'll last that long."

Chieko put her arms around Nobuko's quivering shoulders.

"I hate the idea of Sachiko seeing her beloved papa like he is now, but I'm afraid she'll never forgive me if she doesn't get the chance to say goodbye. Could you keep her out of school and bring her tomorrow?"

"Of course."

Chieko did her best to prepare the little girl for how ill her father was, what he might look like when she saw him. "He is very sick, Sachiko-chan, but he will love the strings of origami birds you've made for him," she said.

"I didn't have time to make enough. My teacher says there must be a thousand for him to get better."

Chieko smiled reassurance despite her jaw tightening at the thought of what Sachiko's teacher had implied. "He will like the ones you have made, and he will be happy to see you."

When they reached the hospital, Mrs. Abi led them to the room Masato shared with three other men. Sachiko hesitated at the door. Nobuko looked up and held out her arm. Sachiko rushed to her mother's side. Nobuko enfolded her.

Chieko felt as though all the joy in her heart had been sucked out. She backed from the room, swallowing repeatedly to force down the sobs swelling in her throat.

The rain that had started when their taxi was partway down the mountain had not subsided. With no umbrella, she ran two blocks before she came to a tea shop. Inside, she ordered a cup of tea. After an hour, she went back to the hospital to collect Sachiko.

"How is he?" she asked, staring at the thin body on the bed.

Nobuko's chin trembled. She shook her head.

Chieko bent over Sachiko, stroking her arm. "Did you give your papa a kiss goodbye, Sachiko-chan?"

"Yes." The little girl's voice was barely more than a whisper.

"Say goodbye to your mama, then."

Nobuko held Sachiko in her arms, her cheek pressed to her daughter's shiny black hair. Chieko could see in her face the effort it took to release the child. "Go with Chieko, daughter. I will be home soon."

Masato died that night.

22

NOBUKO

Someone arranged for a taxi. Nobuko helped her mother-in-law in then slid onto the seat next to her. "Do you want to come back to Nishimi with me, Okaasan?" Nobuko asked.

Mrs. Abi held a tissue to her mouth to muffle her sobs. She shook her head. "No. I…I will return to my friend's house." Mrs. Abi had moved to Sakayama the year before, claiming she should have done so when her husband died.

Nobuko gave the driver her mother-in-law's address then leaned back in the seat and stared out the cab's window at the dark and pendulous clouds pressing against the tops of the buildings. She shivered. Rain cascaded down, sliding off the taxi's windshield in sheets. The streetlights and the lights of approaching cars reflected off the wet pavement.

She felt disconnected. Empty. How could she go on without Masato beside her? From the first time they met there had been an intangible link between them. He was her counterpart. On her own, she wasn't sure she could function. She gulped back a sob. *Maybe Yoko Yoshida was right. Maybe I do bring bad luck—death follows me.*

The taxi driver pulled to a stop. "Madams, we have arrived."

Nobuko drew a shaky breath and turned to her mother-in-law. "I will escort you to the door, Okaasan."

The taxi driver came around the car holding a large green umbrella with prancing red horses printed on it. He held the umbrella over the women's heads while they walked the short distance. Without a word, Nobuko's mother-in-law went inside and slid the door closed. The driver continued to hold the umbrella above Nobuko's head, the rain pinging against it, while they retraced their steps to his vehicle.

Once underway again, Nobuko leaned against the seat once more, this time closing her eyes. How was she to tell her daughter, who so loved her papa, that he was gone from them forever?

Her heart pounded, and she feared she would be sick. She rolled the window down a few inches and let the wind and rain blow against her face. Her mind emptied and after a few minutes, she rolled the window up.

Chieko waited for Nobuko at the store. "I've put Sachiko to bed. Would you like some tea?" Tears stood in her eyes.

Nobuko shook her head wearily. "I couldn't. I can't talk tonight, Chieko-san. I just need to lie down and close my eyes for a while. I'm very tired. The taxi driver is waiting for you—he will take you home."

Chieko nodded, grasped Nobuko's hands one more time and left.

Her footsteps echoing on the store's wood-planked floor, Nobuko walked between the display tables and shelves of canned goods to the living quarters behind. A few of Masato's things were still about, though Chieko had tidied and put most away. Sachiko lay curled on her futon. Nobuko got into her night clothes and slid in beside her. She pressed her lips together to keep the sobs inside. If she let them escape, she didn't think they'd ever stop.

"I love you, Mama," Sachiko whispered.

The whole of Nishimi attended Masato's funeral, approaching the familiar Buddhist Temple in a slow procession, accompanied by the solemn, steady banging of drums. Like heartbeats. Masato's flower-draped casket, carried by six of his friends, including Hirotaka Katsuragawa, was placed at the front of a large room smelling of age and incense. Sunlight filtered through narrow windows but failed to provide Nobuko with warmth. Dressed in funereal white and seated on a cushion next to her daughter, she shivered. Mrs. Abi, also in white, was on her right. In front of Masato's casket stood a low table where incense burned in an iron urn.

A priest entered the room and began to chant.

Hirotaka, clad in formal attire, his family crest embroidered on the back of his black kimono, his family sword swinging at his side, helped Nobuko to her feet. Ready to offer his arm, he walked with her the short distance to the low table. Nobuko lowered herself onto a cushion and stared at the casket that would soon carry her beloved husband, whose body she had washed and prepared the previous night, into a great maw of fire. She bit back a low moan.

A rope of beads looped around her clasped hands, she brought them to her forehead and bowed three time. She then added a pinch of incense to the urn. While the priest droned words that meant nothing to her, she rose on shaky legs. With Hirotaka once more at her side, she returned to the cushion next to her daughter.

Mrs. Abi, her friend and Hirotaka supporting her, made it to the low table next. She groaned and collapsed onto the cushion Nobuko had vacated. She continued to moan and cry throughout the ritual.

When Mrs. Abi was back in her seat next to Nobuko, Hirotaka sat on the cushion in front of Masato's casket. Then Chieko. Finally, the rest of the villagers paid their final respects. Even Yoko Yoshida.

Through it all, Nobuko sat, numb and slightly groggy from the sedative Chieko had insisted she take that morning.

Sachiko's small, cold hand slipped into hers. Nobuko squeezed it. Poor child. She is too young to understand what the loss of her father will mean.

She had tried to talk with her daughter, prepare her for what the future would be like. But even though Sachiko had witnessed death in the form of animals and insects, how could she grasp the total absence of someone who'd been so present during the first ten years of her life?

In the days that followed Masato's funeral, Nobuko felt she was disappearing into a deep, black hole. She had to fight her way out—for Sachiko, for herself, for Masato. When her brother, Mako, arrived from America, she collapsed against him and wept.

His voice rumbled against her ear. "I'm sorry I couldn't be here in time for Masato's funeral."

Nobuko nodded, unable to speak.

Mako patted her shoulder. "Keiko sends her love. She wanted to come, but she has a court case she couldn't postpone—a case that has drawn out for months. Also, Amy is in school and has already missed several days because of the flu."

Nobuko straightened and backed away. She wiped her eyes on a tissue. Mako was making small talk. Everything was small talk now. Nothing mattered. No, that wasn't true. She swallowed and took a deep breath. "It is good of you to come." She took another breath. "How was your flight?"

"Long, but not bad. The train ride from Tokyo to Hiroshima was interesting. The other passengers did nothing but eat—everyone had baskets of food, plus food vendors boarded the train at every stop, pushing carts down the aisle and selling passengers the specialties of their towns. I was struck by the colorful displays."

Nobuko dabbed at her eyes again and nodded. "Speaking of food, can I get you something? She gestured to the store shelves. "As you can see, we're not lacking."

"No thanks. I had lunch at the station in Sakayama, before getting a taxi to bring me up the mountain. I can't get over how small the fields are in Japan."

"Masato couldn't get over how big they are in America." Nobuko's voice cracked. She closed her eyes and drew several more breaths before she could speak again. "Let me show you where to put your things."

When Sachiko came home from school, Nobuko felt less awkward. Sachiko and her uncle had no trouble communicating. Sachiko had learned English at the same time she learned Japanese. Nobuko and Masato had often laughed when their daughter started a sentence in one language and finish it in the other. She closed her eyes at the memory. There were so many memories. They tumbled one after another.

She lifted her chin. "Sachiko, perhaps Uncle Mako would like to go for a walk. You could show him the Buddhist Temple and the garden next to it." The temple priests had designed the garden to be a replica of Buddha's universe: a raised hillock to represent Mount Sumeru, white gravel to symbolize Lake Muncisunochi, and several rocks in the gravel 'lake' to represent the nine islands and eight seas of the Buddhist creation myth. Masato had once explained it to Nobuko.

"I'll get Kazuhiro," Sachiko said. "He can come with us."

After they left, Nobuko put the 'closed' sign on the door and lowered the blinds. She didn't expect any more shoppers. Most bought what they needed early in the day. She fixed tea and poured herself a cup. She was glad to see her brother, but would have preferred he'd waited and come later, when she was more prepared to enjoy their time together—if she could ever enjoy anything again. Tears threatened once more to overwhelm her. She shook her head and bit down hard on her lower lip. *No. Do not go to that place. It is self-defeating.*

Shoulders stiffening in resolve, she took a sip of tea and thought of Sachiko. Sachiko would be her purpose in life. She must now be both father and mother to her daughter.

By the time her daughter and Mako returned, Nobuko had regained her composure. She felt more prepared to spend time with her brother. After her daughter went to bed that evening, they talked of the past, and about the future.

"Keiko and I think you and Sachiko should come to Portland for an extended visit. Would you like to do that? Amy wants to meet her aunt and cousin, too. We have plenty of room. Even though you've lived in Japan for twenty years, you still have U.S. citizenship. You might like Portland so well, you'll want to stay."

And yet, Nobuko thought, despite that citizenship, following the war she'd initially been denied the right of return. When she and Masato had traveled to America for Mako's wedding, she'd managed to put aside her long-buried anger at the country of her birth. Even so, the thought of living there was so foreign to her now, she found herself grasping for something to say. "The store, who would run it?"

"Masato's mother? She actually might contest your ownership of the store."

Nobuko shook her head. "Masato had her sign a document before she left Nishimi. Even if she did, I couldn't leave. This is our home."

Mako nodded, understanding in his eyes. "Well, I'm glad she signed something. Keiko was worried. It is too bad Masato's mother couldn't appreciate you as her daughter-in-law, when it was obvious Masato loved you. If she had, you could support each other now."

Tears spurted to Nobuko's eyes, but she managed to smile through them.

"Always remember. If anything changes, you and Sachiko have a home with us."

On Sunday, Nobuko and Sachiko took Mako to the park, where they met Chieko and her family. The two children went off to explore. They were closer now, no doubt due to the time they'd recently shared. Chieko took Mako to see the koi pond. Nobuko's friend had learned English in school and, after some initial embarrassment, was growing more confident using it.

After they left, Hirotaka cleared his throat. "We haven't spoken much since Masato left us, Nobuko-san. I hope you know that I will be here for you, whatever you need."

Nobuko fought to keep control of her voice. "I know, Hirotaka-san. Your friendship with my husband was forged in the caldron of war. Nothing can break that bond, not even death. I know you will be a good friend to me, also."

They sat on in shared solitude, waiting for the others to return.

Mako stayed until the end of the week. Nobuko was sorry to see him go, but she also felt relieved that she no longer needed to assure him she was okay. Okay was something she felt sure she never would be again. She was, however, gaining the strength she needed to face each new day. Her daughter needed her, needed her to be strong—for both of them.

23

KEIKO

Portland, USA

The fifties gave way to the sixties and Keiko's law practice continued to grow. She sometimes found she was too busy to eat the lunch Mako prepared for her.

"I don't mind," he'd said when she had at first protested that it was her job to fix their meals, including lunches. She stopped protesting when she realized his lunches were far superior to the ones her efforts produced.

She was reading her case notes one day, when her receptionist stepped into her office and said Rose Ochi was on the phone for her. Keiko quickly took the call.

"You are making quite a name for yourself up there in Oregon," Rose Ochi said. Although Keiko hadn't met the woman, a fellow attorney, she'd long admired her. "Even down here in L.A., we're hearing good things about you."

Keiko's cheeks flushed with the compliment. Rose Ochi had already graduated from university when Pearl Harbor was attacked. After the war and after being released from Manzanar, she went back to school and earned her law degree. She, too, had needed to work in the Japanese-American community before gaining a reputation as an astute civil rights attorney and activist.

Keiko picked up a pencil and bounced the eraser end on the desk blotter. "Thank you. That's very flattering to hear. What can I do for you?"

"A group of us here in California are trying to gather support for getting Manzanar designated as a historic site," Rose said. "We hope to get people from all the internment camps involved. Every camp should be recognized."

Keiko put down the pencil, intrigued.

"Would you be interested in working with a group from Minidoka?"

Keiko grinned. "Absolutely."

At home that night, she told Mako about the call. "She knew who to contact," he said. A gleam of pride shone in his eyes, quickly replaced by a look of concern. "But how are you going to find the time? You're already working ten to twelve hours a day. Amy barely sees you."

Keiko pressed her lips together. She didn't like being reminded, but Mako was right. Most mornings she was out the door while her daughter was still asleep, and many evenings, when she came home, it was to find Amy's nanny had already fed her dinner and put her to bed.

Mako worked long hours, too. He'd recently opened a nursery with an adjacent store selling pots, yard tools, and a variety of seeds and indoor plants. The new store and his landscaping business required most of his attention. Keiko was proud of his accomplishments.

"Our daughter is growing up without us," Mako said.

"We need a bigger house," Keiko said.

Mako frowned. "What would a bigger house accomplish? We'd be too busy to enjoy it anyway."

"If we had a larger living room, I could have the committee meetings at home."

Outside Keiko's office window, the November skies were blue, but thunderheads billowed on the horizon. Rain was in the forecast. She'd just hung up the phone when her secretary flung open the office door. Keiko's thoughts still on her what she and Rose Ochi had just discussed, she frowned at the interruption. "What is it?"

"It's the President," she said. "He's just been shot!"

Keiko sprang to her feet. "What?"

"A friend called me and I turned on the radio. It's true. President Kennedy was shot—in Dallas, Texas."

That evening and over the weekend, Keiko and Mako sat on their living room sofa and watched the continuous coverage on television of the nation saying its final goodbye to John Fitzgerald Kennedy. Keiko's eyes filled with tears as a horse-drawn caisson slowly carried the body down Pennsylvania Avenue to the Capital building where it would lie in state under the rotunda. She nearly choked at the sight of young John Kennedy saluting his father's flag-draped casket, sure the image would be etched in her mind forever.

Her thoughts turned to Amy, playing quietly in her room. Mako had been right, their daughter was growing up without them. Perhaps she did need to spend more time at home. If they were to get that house on Council Crest they'd looked at, there would be room for her secretary to have a small office and she could even see clients there.

Keiko and Mako were once again on the living room sofa. They had been transfixed for days, watching yet another replay of the shooting of Lee Harvey Oswald, the man accused of assassinating President Kennedy.

"Why would he do it?" Keiko said, not sure if she referred to Oswald, or Jack Ruby, the man who'd somehow managed to kill Oswald while he was in police custody. Her mind was awhirl, unable to grasp the convoluted details of assassination followed by assassination.

"I can't imagine what the world is thinking of us right now," Mako said, shaking his head. "We must seem like a nation of mad and lawless gunmen."

Keiko leaned her head on her husband's shoulder. "Why are the good men taken from us so early? Men like Kennedy. And Masato Abi. I feel so sorry for your sister, losing him. He was so young. Poor Sachiko, too. She will miss her papa dreadfully." She sighed. "Sometimes, Mako, I don't like this world very much."

24

VIRGINIA

Idaho

Bella's letter lay open on the kitchen table. Virginia absently thumbed its edge. Her daughter wanted to bring Grace, Virginia's six-year-old granddaughter, back to Idaho.

She needs proper schooling, Mom. We could send her to a boarding school, but Bill and I both think she would be happier on the farm with you, going to the same schools I did, helping you and Mrs. Perez when she gets a bit older. What do you think? Are we asking too much?

Were they asking too much? Opal was seventeen already. Like Neil and Mandy, she too would soon be off to college. On the other hand, maybe the timing was perfect; there'd be another young person in the house. Mrs. Perez was semi-retired from her role as housekeeper and cook, but she still lived with them. She might like having another child to take in hand.

Virginia picked up Bella's letter and reread it.

A rust-colored sky had already darkened into night, and moths flitted around the security lamp outside. "What do you think?" she asked John as they enjoyed their after-dinner coffee on the screened-in porch. A welcome breeze brought the scent of new-mown hay.

"Honey, it's entirely up to you—you're the one who'll be the most involved. Did you ask Mrs. Perez? What does she say?"

"You know Mrs. Perez could never deny Bella anything—this would be no different." Virginia took a sip of coffee. "I think we should do it. It will be good for us, keep us young. Mrs. Perez, too. If it's truly okay with you, I'll write Bella tomorrow and tell her we'd be delighted to have Grace."

Bella arrived with Virginia's granddaughter two weeks before the beginning of the school year. Bella planned to stay for a month, giving Grace time to adjust and settle in. Grace, however, seemed far from pleased with the idea of staying in Idaho without her mother.

"This was your mama's old bedroom," Virginia said, easily understanding how overwhelmed the child must feel. "Did she tell you that she was born right here in this house?"

Grace, wearing pigtails and a frown above a hand-smocked yellow dress with puffed sleeves, looked around the room without commenting on its blue flowered wallpaper, dotted-Swiss curtains and matching bedspread, the white painted desk and chair next to the bed, or the new rug. Virginia and Mrs. Perez had earlier agreed that any little girl would love such a room.

Bella tried to engage her daughter. "This is so pretty. Look, Gracie, there's a cupboard for all your books." She moved to the window. "I think that's Papa John, way off in the distance, driving the tractor. Do you see him?"

Grace turned in the direction of the window and gazed out. Her frown didn't soften.

Bella's shoulders sagged.

"She'll be fine," Virginia mouthed to her daughter, hoping it would be true.

The second day of school, dressed in a starched yellow blouse and matching skirt, Grace stuck out her lower lip and declared she wouldn't go. "It's stupid. My teacher is stupid. Why can't I be with you and Daddy?"

"You know why, Gracie. I've explained a hundred times." Finally, after much cajoling and Grace's feet dragging every inch of the way, Bella managed to get her daughter to the end of the lane where they waited for the school bus.

Virginia watched their progress from the kitchen window. Her concern they all might be making a mistake deepened when the bus pulled to a stop and Bella put a wildly resisting Grace on it.

Eight years before, Bill McKnight had swept Bella off her feet, carrying her away to exotic places. Virginia had hated seeing her daughter go, but Bella was so happy, and when Grace was born two years later, that happiness only increased. Bill's engineering job took him all over the world, though, and they never stayed in one place for long. Not exactly ideal for raising a child.

Bella returned to the house shaking her head. "I don't know how this is going to work out, Mom. She's such a stubborn thing. But Bill and I can't school her ourselves. He's nearly finished with this Egypt project, but then we're scheduled for the Congo." She sighed. "At least we'll be back here for a couple of weeks at Christmas."

"She should be settled in by then," Virginia said, trying to reassure her daughter.

"I hope you're right." Bella looked away, but not before Virginia saw the look of doubt on her face. Her daughter turned to face her once again, a determined smile on her lips. "So, what do you hear from Neil these days?"

Virginia laughed at the question. "Nothing." Her son was a junior at the University of Idaho.

Bella chuckled as well. "You probably won't either unless he needs money. But he'll be home for Christmas, right?"

"Yes, Mandy, too."

Mandy attended college in Oregon. A music and voice major at Portland State, she lived with the Itos. Keiko's and Mako's daughter was a couple of years younger than Mandy, but despite the age difference, the two girls had become good friends—likely from their mutual interest in music.

"Amy wants to spend the summer here—if her mother will allow her to miss her piano lessons for such an extended period. The girls are counting on it, but I think it doubtful Keiko will let her stay so long."

"Isn't Amy old enough to make her own decisions about such things?"

"You know your Auntie Keiko. She has plans for Amy—wants her to become a world-famous pianist. Reliving her own dreams, I suspect." Virginia doubted Keiko had even asked Amy what she wanted.

"That hardly seems fair."

Virginia watched Bella's face register disapproval and then doubt. Might she be reconsidering her and Bill's decision to force Grace to go to school in Idaho? But what other option did they have?

They spoke for a few more minutes, then Bella excused herself to go straighten Grace's room and her own. "And I need to write to Bill and let him know my flight information."

Left alone, Virginia's mind drifted ahead to Christmas, when all the family would be back home. It would be hectic, of course, but well-worth whatever effort it took.

When Bella left, Grace became so distraught, Virginia thought she might make herself ill. But after a week of tears alternating with fits of fury, she finally settled down and they established a routine. Virginia walked her down the lane to catch the bus every morning and met her there every afternoon. Despite Virginia's questions, Grace rarely offered anything other than to say her day was 'okay.'

"She's so different from the way Bella was at her age," Virginia told John. "Bella used to jump off the bus, hopping and skipping all the way down the lane, full of all that had transpired at school. You remember what she was like. Joyful, but pliant."

Throughout the fall, Virginia detected little change in her granddaughter. She hoped the anticipation of Christmas would spark her interest. She and Opal put up the tree and brought the ornaments down from the attic.

She told Grace stories about the ornaments, the ones from Sweden, where Virginia's grandmother was born. Grace looked at one, a small nativity scene, but made no comment. "Your mother made this," Virginia said with a smile. Bella's plaster handprint from kindergarten caused whichever branch it hung on to sag. Grace placed her hand over her mother's imprint but found her hand much larger and put it aside. The rest of the ornaments collected over the years made little impression on her granddaughter. While she and Opal decorated the tree, Grace wandered off.

Nor did her granddaughter want to be involved in making the traditional Christmas dishes. Even when

Virginia invited her to help decorate gingerbread cookies, she shook her head and left the kitchen.

Then her parents arrived, and like a dam burst, Grace started talking, telling them all about school, about her teacher, about how she could read like a third-grader. Virginia was encouraged. Maybe Grace was adapting better than she had thought.

Grace wouldn't let her parents out of her sight, though, and when they returned to Africa the week after the Christmas break ended, the parting was even harder for Grace than when Bella had left in the fall. She wouldn't speak to anyone for days, at home or, apparently, at school. Her teacher called, full of concerns.

With Bella and Bill gone and Neil and Mandy returned to their respective schools, only Opal remained at home. But Opal was busy being a junior in high school—in drama and debate, playing volleyball in the fall, basketball in the winter and planning to run track in the spring. She was seldom home in time for dinner. On the weekends, she breezed in and out with her friends. Mandy and Neil had been the same.

Mrs. Perez tried to help, playing games with Grace, attempted to teach her to cook, as she'd taught Grace's mother and aunts. She even tried to teach her Spanish. Nothing seemed to help. Sometimes Grace would go through the motions, mostly she didn't even try. It nearly broke Virginia's heart to see how dreadfully she missed her parents.

She was writing to Bella and Bill, explaining her concerns and telling them they needed to reassess—*it's simply not working out, I'm afraid*—when a car approached, driving slowly down the lane and pulling to a stop in front of the house.

Virginia, looking out the window, was reminded of the day the government men drove down the lane to bring John news of his father. This time, a man wearing a tight-fitting white collar and a black suit stepped out of the passenger side of the car. The driver was from Bill's firm.

Bella was dead. Bill, too. Swerving to avoid a head-on collision with a runaway truck, their car went off the road and into a river at the bottom of a deep ravine. It took two days to retrieve their bodies, which were being sent home for burial.

When Virginia finally took in the words, she began to scream.

★

Virginia sat motionless in a chair by the window, her cheeks wet, staring mindlessly at the fields, the sky and the few clouds moving through it. There seemed no end to the tears a body could produce.

Marc pulled a chair next to hers. "I remember the night Bella was born. I was so scared. Poor Keiko, she was just as scared as me, but she was a trooper and I was a coward."

Virginia gave no sign of hearing her brother's words, but somewhere inside her they registered. How could she forget that night, her fear, and then her pride when Keiko placed Bella in her arms.

"She was like sunlight, Virginia. You did a wonderful job bringing her up. You and John."

John, she thought. "Where is he?"

"He's out on the porch. You've got to come out of this, Virginia. You've been like this for weeks, not talking to anyone, eating hardly anything. It isn't John's fault. It isn't anyone's fault."

"I shouldn't have let her go. I should have kept her with me. Safe."

Marc cleared his throat. "You couldn't. She was crazy about Bill from the get-go. You thought he was taking advantage of her, her being so much younger than him, but John could see Bill was just as crazy about Bella as she was about him. I could, too."

"He said I had to let her go."

"He was right. And she was happy as a clam in the going. You know she was, Virginia. And she's left you something special. Grace is a lost little soul right now. You've got to come out of this and start taking care of her. You owe it to Bella to take care of her daughter."

Virginia finally tore her gaze away from the window and looked at her brother, fresh tears welling in her eyes. "I'm not sure I can. I'm afraid all the mothering in me died with Bella."

Marc grabbed her hand and squeezed it. "That's crazy talk and you know it. You've got Opal right here in the house. She's been tip-toeing around you, but she still needs you—she just lost her big sister, for God's sake. You're not the only one devastated by this, Virginia. Neil and Mandy are, too. They'll be home again in a couple of months. Bella was not your only child. You have responsibilities to all of them. John, too. Me as well. This farm. Everyone relies on you. And poor Mrs. Perez is inconsolable—you know how she doted on Bella."

Virginia closed her eyes. A moan escaped before she could hold it back. "You're asking too much."

"No. I'm not asking too much. You're the strongest woman I know. You've just got to come back to us and get on with things. No one knows better than a farmer that life goes on."

"I'm not a farmer."

"Yeah, you are. You're as much a farmer as John and me."

Virginia's shoulders rose and fell. She moved back in her chair a fraction.

"Grace needs you. She's not even seven, and she's lost both of her parents. You've got to help her get through this."

Virginia gave a slight nod.

"And you've got to quit blaming John."

"I don't blame him."

"He thinks you do."

Marc stood and left Virginia sitting alone in the living room. A few minutes later, his voice and John's sounded from the porch.

Marc was right. She needed to pull herself together. She wasn't even sure what month it was. April, maybe. She looked out the window again and saw a few green buds on the cottonwood tree. Yes, probably April. Two months since…. She closed her eyes again, took a deep breath, and stood.

Summer arrived with little fanfare. Virginia stood at the kitchen counter, cutting up cantaloupes. Summer had always been Bella's favorite time of year. As a young girl, she'd loved it when the laborers were at the farm. All her children had.

Things were so different now with all of them grown, or nearly so. Mandy had brought Amy with her from Portland. Amy had flown over for the funeral in February with her parents, but this was the first time she'd come on her own with a plan to stay for the summer. Virginia didn't ask how she'd convinced Keiko.

Neil, out in the fields with John and Marc, would be graduating the following spring. Thank God the war in Vietnam had ended and her son wouldn't be drafted. She couldn't bear to lose another child.

Her thoughts went to the evening before. She'd looked around the dinner table at her family, knowing she should be happy to see everyone gathered, but for some reason, even though Bella had married and left home years before, the presence of the rest of the family seemed to make her oldest daughter's absence more pronounced. Down the table and sitting next to Opal, who was talking across the little girl's blond and pig-tailed head to Mandy, Grace had fiddled with her food.

Virginia glanced out the open kitchen window. From far-off came the sound of a tractor—John or Marc. She reached for another melon to cut. It seemed like she'd become a shadow hovering on the perimeter of life. Like Grace, she was just going through the motions. She thought a gaping hole had replaced her heart, a hole that might never be filled. She swallowed the bitter taste that rose in her throat as she reached for yet another melon.

The weather turned hot as the summer moved on. Every afternoon, a layer of yellow heat haze was thick enough to cut. Flies banged against the window screens. Virginia kept busy—if not busy, she dwelt too much on Bella, reliving the day her daughter married and left home and the day that she left home forever. Time and again, she recalled herself to the present, knowing that thinking about Bella wouldn't bring her back. Still, melancholy kept her in its grip.

One sultry evening toward the end of summer, Neil and the girls gathered in the living room, as they frequently did after dinner. Amy pounded out *People Get Ready* on the upright piano and all four sang the words with gusto. From that, they rolled into *Take Me Home, Country Roads,* exaggerating West Virginia whenever they came to it. Even clowning, Mandy's voice soared. Such a gift.

The window in Virginia's office was open, and warm air laden with the scent of ripening corn drifted inside. John had already gone upstairs to bed. She'd join him as soon as she finished entering some new figures in the ledger. To relax, she'd read another of Suki's stories. Her sister-in-law had sent a brief note along with the book, the third collection of her short stories, saying she and Paul were going on tour in the fall. Virginia had a hard time imagining shy little Suki on tour, maneuvering her way and Paul's through strange cities and hotels. But each time they came to the farm, Virginia's admiration for her sister-in-law grew. How well she handled Paul, his blindness, his buried anger. At least the anger had eased a bit.

From thinking about her younger brother, Virginia's thoughts moved to their sister, Irene, and the long-ago week she and Bella had spent in Portland with Irene, who worked in the shipyard while her husband was off fighting in Europe.

Despite the war and Roosevelt's death the month before, Portland had been beautiful in the spring of 1945. Irene, who'd taken a few days off work, had toured them around, to the zoo, Chinatown, and Portland's huge department stores. Not even Boise had anything to compare with those department stores.

The morning before she and Bella were to return home, the city erupted with the sounds of church bells and sirens. Hitler was dead, Germany had conceded defeat. She and Irene had jumped up and down like school children when they'd turned on the radio and heard the news. Bella, a toddler, had looked at them as if they were crazy. Instead of the picnic they'd planned, the three of them went downtown, into a crush of jubilant people, laughing, hugging, and throwing streamers and confetti. Strangers embracing strangers. Never, before or since, had Virginia seen so many people so deliriously happy.

That night, though, when they returned to Irene's tiny apartment, Irene confessed to having an affair with a co-worker. The last time Virginia heard from her sister, she was in Austin, Texas, with husband number four. *Where are you now, Irene, and when are you going to settle down? Dad's gone, so it's safe to come home.* But it hadn't been safe for Leo. There'd been too many memories for him here, she thought.

She entered one more set of figures before closing the ledger with a snap.

Neil, Mandy, Opal, and Amy had moved on to *Joy to the World.* Virginia smiled, thinking how smitten Neil seemed to be with Amy. At first, she kept time to the music by bobbing her head, until the chorus began…Joy to the world, all the boys and girls…and once again, melancholy washed over her. How could she feel joy in a world without Bella? Children aren't meant to die before their parents, she wanted to rail. But she had long since learned that the more she railed, the worse she felt.

An image of her daughter holding out her hands came to her, as though Bella was trying to defy the eternity that now separated them, pleading with her. Virginia's hands reached out but found only empty air, and she dropped them in her lap. She hung her head. "I'll try harder to reach her," she whispered, nearly strangling on the words. "I promise." After a few more minutes, she straightened, wiped her eyes on a tissue, switched off the light and stepped out of the office, softly closing the door behind her.

Grace sat at the bottom of the stairs, her head leaned against the bannister.

Virginia froze. She closed her eyes and once again saw her daughter's imploring face. She moved closer to Grace and reached out to smooth her granddaughter's blond hair—so like Bella's.

"Wouldn't you like to go in and sing with them, Gracie?"

At Virginia's words, Grace jumped to her feet and disappeared into the kitchen. A moment later, the outside door banged shut.

BOOK TWO

2000 - 2010

Hayoto and Helena

A Love Story

1
SACHIKO

Japan

Just as she'd promised her father, Sachiko left Nishimi to attend the University of Tokyo. But instead of returning home after she graduated, she'd found a job in Sakayama. She needed to earn and save money for when she and Kazuhiro Yoshida married—the wedding kimono alone would cost thousands of yen. Plus, they would need to provide food and gifts for their guests, and money for their honeymoon.

All those glorious plans had come to nothing, though, and now, over two decades later, she lay on her futon and thought of her son's future—a future that was firmly tied to a past rooted in pain and violence, beginning with his conception.

For years she'd tried to forget that day. Sometimes she managed to bury it for a while, but it was always there, ready to spring to the surface, always at times she wasn't prepared. Now it came bubbling up again. She sighed with resignation and let the memory play out.

It had been a beautiful day when she'd boarded the Nishimi-bound bus that Friday after work. The dogwood blossoms looked like lace against the sweeping boughs of tall cedar, the cherry trees were budding out. All contrasting against an iris-blue sky.

She hadn't been home in weeks and couldn't wait to see Kazuhiro. Maybe he'd think the time was finally right to announce their engagement. She hoped her mother would be pleased for her. She and Kazuhiro had been soul mates since they were children. They'd done everything together— explored the woods, hunted fiddle-necked ferns for their mothers to cook, climbed trees, flown kites in the fall, and in winter played in the snow. Her favorite memory was sliding down the track from the Katsuragawa's house to Nishimi, then turning around and climbing back up the mountain for another exhilarating ride, yelling and laughing all the way.

They'd only separated when Sachiko went away to university and Kazuhiro stayed in Nishimi to learn how to manage what would one day be his, the pottery factory. As the bus rumbled its way up the mountain, she'd wrapped her arms around her stomach in anticipation of the future, hers and Kazuhiro's.

When the bus stopped in front of her mother's store, Sachiko was surprised he wasn't waiting for her. He knew she would be home that weekend. She'd written and told him. She carried her small bag into the store and called out to Nobuko. "Mother, I'm home."

Kazuhiro didn't appear that evening, nor the next morning. Sachiko's nerves grew raw with waiting. She wanted to go to the factory but felt it might be unseemly to interrupt his work. What would his mother think? Sachiko was half-afraid of Yoko Yoshida, known for her sharp tongue, and didn't want to do anything that would invite her future mother-in-law's displeasure.

To keep busy, she helped in the store. She straightened rows of canned goods and waited on her mother's customers, all of whom wanted to know how she liked working and living in Sakayama. Sachiko answered their questions as briefly as possible, wishing they would finish their shopping and leave.

Finally, the bell above the door jangled and this time it was Kazuhiro. "I'm sorry I can't stay, Sachiko-san, but we have a large order from a new customer, and we want to impress them with a fast turn-around. My father insists that I oversee it from start to finish. Maybe I can spare some time later to see you."

"I understand." Although Sachiko spoke in her usual soft voice, her insides trembled like a block of fresh tofu. She looked down, not wanting him to see the tears pooling in her eyes. "Work must come first." Just as it had for the past four years. She looked up in time to see Kazuhiro hurry out the door, the bell jingling in his wake.

What has happened since we last saw each other, she wondered. *Has he changed his mind about us getting married, has he found someone else? Or was it as he said, work?* She refolded a stack of tea towels, but her eyes constantly flicked toward the window. A sliver of blue sky was visible below the short metal awning shading the window.

I will go for a walk, she thought. *A walk in the woods will clear my head and chase my doubts away. Who can be sad on such a fine spring day?*

Sachiko sat up on her futon, her heart suddenly pounding. Such a simple decision that had been. A walk in the woods. How could she have known it would end in a nightmare? That Kazuhiro's father, Takeda Yoshida, would follow her into the woods and brutally rape her?

She'd stopped to watch a wren perched on a branch, its head cocked, when she heard footsteps. She'd grinned, thinking it was Kazuhiro, that he'd changed his mind. How often, along with the other village children, they'd chased one another through these woods, playing samurai or hide and seek. With a chuckle, she ran ahead down the pine-needle strewn path, jumping over tree roots, but soon came to a skidding halt. Takeda Yoshida stood in the center of the path, blocking her way. His mouth was twisted in a sneer. Filled with instant fear, she'd scrambled back the way she'd come, getting only a few steps before Takeda's long arms reached out, grabbed her from behind and threw her to the ground.

Kensai Hara had found her on the path near the school, disheveled and confused. She told him she'd fallen. His face flushed with purpose, he'd escorted her up the mountain to Nishimi, leaving her at the door to her mother's store.

The memory of that day had her heart pounding. She felt clammy all over. And dirty—even though she knew the shame had been his and not hers. He'd been an evil man. The whole village knew it. She'd been glad when he'd disappeared.

She rose unsteadily to her feet and went to get a drink of water. The window over the sink showed the night still inky black. She returned to her futon and closed her eyes, willing herself to go to sleep. Her mind, however, couldn't let go of the past.

When Sachiko realized she was pregnant, she returned to Nishimi. This time she went directly to the pottery factory and demanded that Kazuhiro accompany her. He followed her into the woods, taking the path she'd taken that dreadful day. With blunt words she told him what his father had done. "He raped me. Now I'm pregnant."

Kazuhiro collapsed onto a fallen log.

"If we marry right away, we can say the child is yours," she said.

Kazuhiro jumped to his feet. "I can't marry you. I would never touch my father's leavings. You are used goods. Besides, how do I know the baby is his? You could have been with someone in Sakayama."

Two weeks later, two weeks after Kazuhiro's heartless rejection, Sachiko inwardly trembled as her mother gaped at her. "Kensai Hara? But, daughter, I thought you would marry Kazuhiro. What possessed you to accept Kensai's proposal? You aren't cut out to be a farmer's wife. You will go crazy living on that farm, miles away from everyone. His father is mad. Besides, Kensai is much older than you."

Sachiko steeled herself to keep from howling. "He asked. I accepted. It is settled."

After their brief wedding ceremony, Kensai walked beside her down the track, past her old school, where the sing-song voices of children came through an open window, into a narrow valley and up the side of another mountain, making their way toward what would be Sachiko's new home.

Her fingers clenched and unclenched as she thought of a future without love. She swallowed hard and renewed her determination to make this marriage work. "I will be a good wife to you, Kensai-san. I promise."

He nodded.

She swallowed again. She hadn't lied. Theirs might not be the love-match marriage she had always dreamed of, but she would make every attempt to make it a successful one.

When they finally reached the farm, she took in the large rooms, the high ceilings and thought how nice the place would be, especially compared to the cramped quarters behind the store where she'd grown up with her grandparents and parents all crowded together.

Then she met Toshio Hara, Kensai's father. To say the man was mad, was an understatement. For some reason, he held a special hatred for Sachiko's mother, calling Nobuko a soul-sucking witch. Eyes wide, Sachiko gawped at him, unable to comprehend even half of his rant.

In the days and weeks that followed, she often needed to wipe tears from her eyes and cheeks as she went about cleaning the farmhouse, which had not seen a woman's touch in twenty years. None of what she did was to her father-in-law's satisfaction. The old man continually complained. His food was cold or tasteless or there wasn't enough of it; the dog barked too much, a sure sign he wasn't being fed; at night, his futon wasn't arranged the way he liked. Kensai, though he didn't say cruel things as his father did, didn't support or defend her, either.

She missed her mother. Her stomach ached with the need to see and talk to Nobuko. Beg her forgiveness for being such a disappointment. Nobuko had warned her that she wasn't suited to the loneliness of farm life. She'd been right. Even though Sachiko had done little more than make sure advertising sales agreements were signed correctly before filing them, she'd loved her job. Just as she'd loved Sakayama. Tokyo had been fun, but it was too big and impersonal. Sakayama was just right. There were plenty of shops and plenty of things to do. A late coffee after a movie, picnics and hikes with friends. She'd had so many friends. She missed them. She missed everything.

If only she could unwind time and go back to that moment when she'd decided to take a walk in the woods. What a different decision she would make. But she couldn't go back in time. She couldn't go home to Nishimi, either, not pregnant—her mother, who'd had enough sadness in her life, must never know her daughter's shame. Her mind shied away from any thought of Kazuhiro Yoshida and his abandonment of her. He'd said it was her fault, that she should never have gone into the woods on her own— something she'd done since childhood. How had she so deluded herself about his character?

Kensai had to know he wasn't the baby's biological father, but he never said the words. During her pregnancy, she worried she wouldn't be able to bear touching it when it finally came, that it would remind her too much of the degradation Takeda Yoshida had inflicted upon her.

Instead, from the first moment she held her infant son in her arms, she was overwhelmed by the emotions that swelled her chest, made her throat thickened and tears spring to her eyes as she gazed at him. Her cheeks flushed with the fierceness of her need to protect him. He was so small though, and for days he suckled only half-heartedly.

Snow lay deep on the ground. Kensai had gone to the barn to feed the sow he'd bought from Sanyo, and the ox, which was no doubt enjoying its winter respite. Sachiko's father-in-law sidled up to her. His mouth pursed with distaste when he looked at the baby in her arms. "He is so puny, he is sure to die before the end of the week. Your witch mother has probably put a curse on him."

Sachiko cried out. "Don't say such things. My son will live."

For two months, she feared Toshio might be right. Day and night, her every thought and nearly every action was for her son. After the first week, Kensai did nothing to help and the old man harangued her even more. But Sachiko persevered. Over time, her son grew stronger and then began to thrive.

Her son was nearly six months old before Sachiko climbed the mountain track leading to Nishimi. The glorious early summer weather did nothing to lessen her apprehension. Kensai traveled with them as far as Sanyo's farm, where he said he had business. "When you're at your mother's store, get my father some tobacco. It's been a long winter and he is out."

The closer Sachiko came to Nishimi, the tenser she became. Hayoto was still small for his age, small enough she could pass him off for younger. Her mother was very astute, however.

Nobuko's mouth dropped open when Sachiko entered the store carrying her son in a sling on her back. "What is this?"

"His name is Hayoto, Mother. He is your grandson."

At some point during the night, Sachiko fell asleep. She woke in the morning to find tears on her cheeks. She thought about her sixteen years on the Hara farm, watching Hayoto grow from baby to teenager, the long hours of work in the fields, taking care of the house and her increasingly difficult father-in-law.

Following old Toshio's death, her husband had become more secretive and odd by the day. He'd always rambled, often about things she didn't understand, but with her father-in-law's death and then the failure of their rice crop, he became even more strange.

One night, he'd come after Sachiko with a hoe, ranting that, like her mother, she was a witch, that she'd killed his seed and ruined his life. Hayoto had tried to stop him, but Kensai was out of control. When he turned on the dog chained in the yard, hacking the poor beast to death, Sachiko and Hayoto escaped and fled to Nishimi, arriving at dawn on her mother's doorstep, blue-lipped and shivering.

The sun splintered the remains of the night, pouring onto the tatami mat next to her futon. Sachiko shook her head, as though to forcibly rid it of the past. She dressed and went into the store to light the fire in the stove. A moment later, her mother appeared, shrugging into a light jacket.

"Would you like to join me on my morning walk?" Nobuko asked, her voice now reedy with age.

"Yes. I think the fresh air will do me good."

"I heard you cry out in the night. Bad dreams?"

Sachiko nodded. "I was thinking of Kensai." She lowered her voice. "And Takeda Yoshida."

Nobuko squeezed her arm. "Then let us go quickly."

In silence, they passed the Shinto shrine, the Buddhist temple and the grove holding the meditation garden. Sachiko felt a chill when she glanced at the grove, where Kazuhiro's body had been discovered three years before, his severed head placed on a large rock at the edge of the garden. His death had nearly destroyed the village. Yoko, had been convinced the Japanese mafia had murdered her son because he'd borrowed money from them and couldn't repay it. The yakuza hadn't done it, though. The murderer had been much closer to home.

"I need to tell Hayoto about his father," Sachiko finally said. "He's eighteen now. Grown up. He needs to know the truth."

Nobuko peered up at her. "Do you think he heard Kensai that day, ranting about not being his father?"

The day Kensai had gone completely mad. Even now, Sachiko felt her heart nearly stop as she remembered walking into the store with her mother to find Kensai there, holding a knife to her son's throat.

"Bring me Kazuhiro Yoshida's mother," Kensai had demanded of Sachiko's mother.

When Nobuko had returned from the pottery factory with a spitting mad Yoko Yoshida, along with Hirotaka Katsuragawa, the sensei, Kensai started ranting about Hayoto not being his but the spawn of Yoko's devil son.

Then he further shocked everyone. "I killed Kazuhiro Yoshida," he announced. "His father destroyed the bridge in New Guinea before everyone could safely cross. It was Takeda Yoshida's fault my father was taken prisoner by the

Australians. The greatest shame for a soldier is capture by the enemy, and that shame haunted him for the rest of his life. It was the reason for his illnesses and for the many failures of our crops."

"You? You did that terrible thing to my son?" Yoko, her fingers extended like claws, had lunged at Kensai. The sensei had barely been able to restrain her.

Kensai ranted on, claiming it was fitting that he had killed Kazuhiro with the sensei's family sword and fitting that the sensei's son had been charged with the murder. "Because you did nothing to keep Takeda from blowing down the bridge. You were the lieutenant. You were in charge."

Terrified for her son, Kensai's accusations made no sense to Sachiko. New Guinea and the war had happened before she was even born—it was ancient history. She'd tried to reason with her husband, but he ignored her. Just as she thought he was about to kill Hayoto, he'd pushed the boy aside and plunged the knife into his own belly.

Later, after the coroner had taken Kensai's body away and the doctor had given Hayoto an injection, saying he would sleep the rest of the day, Yoko had claimed that Kensai had been right when he'd said Hayoto was Kazuhiro's son.

"There is no way Kensai Hara, with his jug ears and gaping teeth, produced that boy," she said. "He has Kazuhiro all over him—his good looks, his height, those broad shoulders. He has the making of a potter—the clay is in his blood."

When Sachiko denied that Kazuhiro was Hayoto's father, Yoko slammed out of the store. After she left, Nobuko cleared her throat. "I hate to add to your woes this day, daughter. But Yoko is right. My grandson does have the look of Kazuhiro.

The red in Sachiko's face receded. "Hayoto is not Kazuhiro's son, Mother. He is Kazuhiro's brother. Sixteen years ago, Takeda Yoshida raped me."

Nobuko had cried out. "Sachiko, my dear child, why didn't you tell me?".

Sachiko dropped her gaze to her tightly clasped fingers. "I was too ashamed," she whispered.

Three years had passed since the day Kensai killed himself. Her son was no longer a fifteen-year-old child. It was time he knew the truth. But how was she to tell him?

"He rarely says anything about the past," Sachiko said to her mother. "And he's never spoken of that day. I don't know if he was aware of what anyone said, or if he was too frightened to take it in."

As it always did when thinking how close she'd come to losing her son, her throat tightened. "He needs to know the truth, though. He also needs to know he has options. We have the farm; someday he'll have the store; he can go to university, as both his grandfather and I did; or, if he wishes, he can become a potter, like Takeda and Kazuhiro."

"You are right about the factory," Nobuko said. "Neither Kazuhiro's widow, nor his two sons appear to have any interest in it. Yoko runs it now, but, like me, she is an old woman. What will happen when she dies?"

Sachiko gave a determined nod. "I will talk to him. I've put it off too long."

They reached the park, tarrying for a while near the koi pond before they returned to the store. After the morning rush of customers, Sachiko asked her mother to mind the store for a couple of hours.

She led Hayoto along the path she'd taken the day Takeda Yoshida followed her into the woods and again the day Kazuhiro had rejected her. She glanced over her shoulder at her son, who towered above her and most everyone, men included. As usual, he walked with his shoulders hunched and his head thrust down, as though he was ashamed of his superior height.

When they reached the clearing, as gently as she could, she told her son what had happened all those years ago, when Takeda Yoshida stole her innocence. During her recital, her gaze focused on a spot on the ground. When she looked up, it was to see Hayoto's eyes filled with tears.

"I thought you would never tell me," he said.

"You knew?" Stunned, Sachiko stared.

"I heard what Kensai said that day, but even before, I'd begun to suspect something. I was so much taller than Kensai, and I looked too much like Kazuhiro. Everyone said Kazuhiro was the image of his father."

"Why did you not say anything?"

"Even though no one from the village has seen or heard from Takeda Yoshida since he disappeared, he and his evil behavior are legend. I knew you'd been hurt, either by him or by Kazuhiro. I didn't want to hurt you more."

It took Sachiko several moments to find her voice. "Well, now that we have spoken of it, you have a decision to make. You need to decide what you want to do with your life."

"I already know, Mother."

Sachiko looked at him, her head tilted to one side, trying to read his thoughts.

"I want to be a potter," he said.

She would have preferred him to say he wanted to go to university, but for some reason she wasn't surprised. Although Yoko was wrong in thinking Hayoto was Kazuhiro's son, she was right when she'd claimed that the clay was in his blood.

"You're sure?" she asked.

"Yes."

Resigned, Sachiko rose from her seat on the same fallen log Kazuhiro once sat upon. "Very well. I will see Yoko and make the arrangements."

"One thing, Mother. I cannot keep the name Hara, and I will not take the name Yoshida. I would like to be known as Hayoto Abi."

Sachiko nodded. "And the farm? What shall we do with it?"

"It is yours. You should keep it—lease the paddies and fields to another farmer."

The fields had lain fallow for the last three years. Sachiko had wanted to sell the farm, but had waited until Hayoto was of an age to participate in the decision. Now she nodded once again. "That is a good idea. We can use the farmhouse as a retreat. Your grandmother says it was once a peaceful place. Perhaps we can make it so again."

That evening, Sachiko waited for Yoko to leave the factory. The older woman was almost to her house when Sachiko approached.

Yoko glanced at her, then opened the door and gestured for Sachiko to enter. "I suppose you're here to talk about my grandson."

"I'm here to talk about Hayoto, yes, but he is not your grandson, Yoko-san. He is your husband's son. He is Kazuhiro's half-brother."

Yoko blanched. Her eyes narrowed, but she said nothing.

"Takeda Yoshida raped me," Sachiko said.

Yoko flinched and briefly closed her eyes before finally speaking. "What do you propose?"

"My son would like to become a potter."

"Not to mention that as a Yoshida, he would also like to inherit the factory."

"As you suggest, it is his heritage." Sachiko's chin lifted. "I believe I earned it for him. Hayoto doesn't wish to take the Yoshida name, however. He will be known as Hayoto Abi."

"Yet you expect me to take him under my wing and teach him what he needs to know about pottery and managing the factory—why should I?"

"Partly to make right what Takeda did to Kazuhiro and me—I did love your son. We planned to marry until Takeda ruined it." At the mention of Kazuhiro, Yoko's lips tightened. Sachiko went on. "Also, because there is no one else. Kazuhiro's sons have no interest in the factory." She didn't refer to Yoko's age. Yoko would know better than anyone that if the factory was to continue after her death, she needed to pass it on to someone.

"You're sure he won't reconsider about the name? Until Takeda spoiled it, Yoshida was an honorable one."

Sachiko hoped Yoko wouldn't refuse Hayoto's wish based on his refusal to be known as Hayoto Yoshida. She was glad he didn't want the name—it would be a constant reminder to her. "He is sure."

Yoko gave an almost imperceptible nod. "I'll give him a month. If it turns out he has talent, I'll keep him on. If not, he goes."

2
HAYOTO

Japan

Hayoto was glad that Nobuko lived to see him finish his apprenticeship at Nishimi Pottery. His grandmother had been suspicious of Yoko fulfilling her promise.

"I'm not sure she can be trusted." Nobuko's spirit was still strong, but her voice had grown weak with age and he had to bend to hear it. "You are my grandson and she has always blamed me for the death of her daughters. She claims I brought the earthquake that killed them."

Hayoto straightened. "I think she would do anything she considers in the best interest of the factory, Grandmother, including training me."

That training had been merciless and took nearly two years. Each morning, Takumi Sano had worked to teach Hayoto everything about making pottery, starting with wedging the clay, then throwing cups—thousands of cups. After the cups, it was bowls, then plates. He could throw them in his sleep.

Two afternoons a week were like high school chemistry class, only harder, because each of the chemical used in the glazes reacted differently, needed different combinations to create different colors, and different temperatures to stabilize those colors.

The other afternoons, Yoko took over. "You didn't grow up around this place as Kazuhiro did. You need to learn everything about running the factory from scratch."

She started with some of the factory's history, telling him about two old men, Mori and Ishihara, who'd helped her run the factory while Takeda was off fighting in the wars. "He was gone over a decade. I doubt I would have managed so well without those two, even though they were a couple of old gossips, always putting their noses where they didn't belong." A corner of her mouth lifted in a wry smile. "Ishihara knew everything there was to know about clay, though, just as Mori knew everything about firing the kiln. Mori died first. Ishihara soon followed him to the afterlife." She sighed. "I suppose he couldn't bear to be parted from his old friend."

Hayoto met the vendors and learned about the factory's regular customers—restaurants in Sakayama and even as far as Hiroshima, plus several department stores.

Yoko showed him the accounting system she used, going over the books back to the war years. They were dusty and covered with fingerprints, but he could see from them much of how the factory had operated over the decades. "I see there are no expenditures for chemicals in 1944 and 1945," he said. "Why is that?"

"Because there were no chemicals to buy. It all went to the war effort. Instead, Mori showed the potters how to make tactile decorations with paddles and incising. Burnishing, too."

"Why don't we do that now?"

"We could, but as Takeda once impressed upon me, this is a production factory. Chemicals are faster."

Hayoto nodded, but tucked the information away, planning to find out more about both techniques. He went on studying the accounts. Although he said nothing, he noted the loss of profit during the years Takeda Yoshida managed the factory.

When his finger hesitated over several of those columns, Yoko cleared her throat and spoke. "Unfortunately, your sire didn't take much interest in the factory. His attentions were elsewhere."

"Where?"

"Besides women, I'm not sure. For the year following the war, it was black-marketeering. I suspect it was more of the same later. He continued to leave Nishimi once or twice a month, never saying when or where he was going. Maybe he was yakuza."

Hayoto's eyes widened and he gave an involuntary shudder. The yakuza were gangsters. Could his biological father be even worse than he'd imagined? A sudden heaviness grew inside him, as if a large stone had settled in his stomach.

Eventually, Hayoto knew everything Yoko Yoshida and Takumi Sano could teach him. Still, he wanted more. What held his interest were large, ornamental pots—he wanted to make them. But to continue to employ the villagers, the factory needed to keep going in the way it had done for the past two-hundred years. For the present, at least.

Before she died, Hayoto's grandmother called him to her. "I won't be here much longer, Hayoto. There is something I need to tell you before I go."

Hayoto sat on a cushion next to Nobuko's futon, where she'd been confined for several weeks. He leaned close to catch her whispered words. "What is it Grandmother?"

"It is about Takeda Yoshida," Nobuko said.

Hayoto's lips grew firm. "What about him?"

"I believe Kazuhiro killed him. I suspect his body is somewhere in the woods." She gave a vague wave.

"Because of what he did to my mother?"

"Yes."

Hayoto's lips tightened further. "He deserved it."

She indicated he was to lean closer. "I never told your mother what I suspect happened to Takeda. She had enough sorrow to deal with. But I wanted you to know."

Another ugly thing to add to his less than illustrious lineage. Once again, Hayoto was forced to swallow his shame. "I understand, Grandmother."

Nobuko died soon after their talk, with Hayoto and Sachiko kneeling beside her.

"I will wash her and prepare her for cremation," Sachiko said after the coroner left.

That night, they sat up with the body. His grandmother's iron-gray hair was spread out on the futon. The scar on her face, the one she got in the earthquake that killed so many of Nishimi's children, was barely discernable.

"I need to write to my Uncle Mako and tell him," Sachiko said.

Hayoto nodded. "Someday I would like to travel to America and meet these relatives I've only heard of."

"Uncle Mako came to visit after my father died. He and my mother were a great deal alike—both reserved, but also strong. Later, Uncle Mako, my Aunt Keiko and their daughter, came and stayed for two weeks. Aunt Keiko is even stronger than my mother and Uncle Mako put together. She was a lawyer and then a judge before she finally retired." She chuckled. "My cousin was afraid of her mother. I didn't blame her. Aunt Keiko scared me, too."

They talked on through the night, telling each other stories of his grandmother, stories they both knew well, especially of how badly Nobuko had been treated during the years of the war.

"It is hard to imagine such ignorance as thinking someone brings bad luck," Sachiko said. "As a girl, I hated the gossip about her, and I hated how Yoko and even my own grandmother disrespected the woman I held most dear. My father tried to explain, but I wanted no part of an explanation. Seeing her treated that way crushed me."

Hayoto thought of how he'd feel if his mother had been shunned—which she no doubt would have been had she not married Kensai.

"My mother was modest and traditional," Sachiko said. "But she dared a great deal. Like coming to this country, a place she'd never been, intending to stay three years with people she didn't know. That alone must have taken much courage."

"Or going swimming in her underwear in the irrigation ditch near her home in California—with girls and boys alike."

Sachiko chuckled. "Oh, yes. She told me that story when I was growing up, as an illustration of how not to behave."

"She said your grandfather beat her brother for not protecting her modesty, while she spent the rest of the summer in the fields or in her room."

Sachiko gazed at her mother's calm features. Without looking up she said, "I wish you could have known your grandfather, Hayoto. He was a wonderful man, and so wise. The love he and Mama had for one another was so strong, even as a child I could see it in the way they looked at each other, respected each other. I hope one day you will have a marriage like that."

"I'm sorry that you didn't, Mother."

"No. Kensai tried. And he tried to be a good father to you. Until the madness took him." She sighed. "Papa used to take me on his mail rounds from the time I was a toddler. When I was older, he taught me to fly kites. In the springtime, we'd hike up the mountain to hunt fiddleneck ferns for Mama or Grandmother to cook."

"And now you sell them in your store."

"They don't taste the same as the ones we found in the wild."

The next day, Nobuko's body was conveyed to the Buddhist temple atop the shoulders of six village men and accompanied by solemn music. Hayoto and his mother followed, walking together up the graveled walkway, beneath the ancient gingko trees, to the steps leading up to the temple. The temple's broad, gold-painted eaves swept up at the corners. In front of the temple, a row of white flags fluttered in the breeze.

The room where his grandmother's body lay was crowded with villagers who'd come to pay their respects.

The Katsuragawa family was seated in front. Despite his age, the sensei still came to the factory once a week to paint in sumi-e style insects, birds and flowers on large platters and bowls. Ten years before, the government had designated him a Living National Treasure, a preserver of important cultural heritage. Hayoto aspired to the same honor someday.

Behind the Katsuragawa family sat young Mrs. Mori, who was no longer so young, her husband, his crutches resting on the floor next to him, and two of their grown children. Some of the many mourners were longtime friends and neighbors. Others were relatively new to the village. All were customers of the Abi store.

"I never expected to see so many people here," Sachiko whispered.

Hayoto nodded in reply. He, too, was surprised. His grandmother had always been unassuming. He'd had no idea she was beloved by so many.

Once the priest began the sutra, one by one people went forward, knelt on a cushion, and honored his grandmother with incense and prayers. Sachiko suddenly gasped and grabbed Hayoto's hand. He followed his mother's gaze and took a sharp breath. Yoko Yoshida walked slowly down the aisle toward his grandmother's coffin.

No doubt like his mother, Hayoto feared Yoko was about to do something to disrespect Nobuko, her supposed enemy. He started to stand but resettled when Yoko did nothing but follow the same process of kneeling and offering a prayer before getting to her feet and walking back up the aisle. Neither Hayoto nor Sachiko took their gaze from Yoko's retreating back until she was safely reseated in the rear of the room.

"Amazing," his mother muttered, turning to face the front of the room once more.

Yoko surprised Hayoto a few weeks after his grandmother's funeral by telling him she planned to retire.

"Before I do, however, there is something I need to show you."

She then escorted Hayoto to her house and took out a drawer in a tonsu. She pulled the back of the drawer out to reveal a considerable space filled with large denomination yen notes.

Hayoto's eyes widened at the sight.

"It is from when I managed the factory during the war. After all my work, I wasn't about to turn everything over to Takeda. He told me what a foolish woman I was not to have reaped more profit in ten years, but he never knew about this secret cache. After Kazuhiro was murdered, I gave some of the money to my daughter-in-law to pay off the yakuza—of all the foolish things, Kazuhiro had borrowed money from them to enlarge the factory; they were making threats. Until Kensai Hara confessed, I thought it had been the yakuza that killed my son."

Hayoto was always surprised Yoko seemed to bare him no animosity since he'd been raised by the man who had killed her son. Not to mention that he was her husband's illegitimate offspring. Yoko was a strange woman, though. There was no accounting what she was capable of—that she loved the pottery factory, however, he had no doubt.

"This money is to be used only for the factory. When I'm gone, you will know it is here for that purpose alone. This house will be yours as well. A lawyer has seen to everything."

Hayoto bowed his head. "Thank you, Yoko-san."

"You know, I used to dream of killing Takeda. I'm glad I didn't. If I had, there would have been no Kazuhiro. There also would have been no you." She stared at him a moment. "How strange that you, Hayoto, the grandson of my enemy, the woman I once hated, have answered my prayers."

Her faith in him filled Hayoto with humility. He was about to say so when Yoko went on.

"I have no doubt that even at this moment, the rats in the attic are howling with glee at my feeble attempts to shape the future. But so be it. It is done." With that final word, she dismissed him.

As easily as she dismissed Hayoto that day, Yoko seemed to dismiss life. She died five weeks later. Cancer, the doctor said.

Each month after Hayoto took over, the factory's orders increased to now include restaurants and department stores as far away as Kyoto and Osaka. The Japanese economy seemed robust once again.

Yoko had been right, too, in realizing that young and upcoming adults would pay handsomely for pottery fired in an earthen kiln—getting back to the fundamentals of living, they called it. Except for her strange belief that his grandmother brought bad luck, her belief that anyone could single-handedly cause an earthquake to happen, Yoko had been an astute woman and an enterprising businesswoman. He sometimes imagined he heard her sharp tongue in his ear, giving him advice, urging him to take on more and more work. He hired another apprentice.

When he had time, Hayoto experimented with the large pots he'd once only dreamed of making. Some were so large, he had to rearrange a wheel and lie on his side on the ground so that he could turn the wheel with his bare feet. These pots were also fired in the old earthen kiln in the rear of the factory, each taking up an entire chamber. The regular production work, directed by Sano, was done in the gas-fired kiln installed when Kazuhiro had enlarged the factory.

Just as Kazuhiro had long ago envisioned, visitors often came to the factory, especially during the spring to view the cherry blossoms, and in the fall to see the colorful foliage. They arrived by the busload and, just as Kazuhiro had foretold, they were served tea and cakes on the patio. The waterfall was not quite so splendid as Kazuhiro had planned, but its soothing sound accompanied a woman who knelt beside it and played the koto. When the visitors left, they carried away platters and bowls and vases in bags with Nishimi Pottery printed on the side. They also admired Hayoto's large pots. His reputation grew.

Nishimi thrived along with the factory. Hayoto's good friend, Kotada Katsuragawa, the sensei's grandson, had graduated from university with his degree in architecture—a subject he'd often talked about when they were at school together. Hayoto remembered the many sketches of buildings, from traditional to modern, that his friend had surreptitiously worked on instead of listening to their teachers.

"I think Nishimi needs an inn," Kotada said.

"Oh? And I suppose you plan to design and build it?"

"Of course. Will you support me?"

"Why not? I know a banker…"

Kotada laughed. "As it happens, I'm well acquainted with one, too. He is talking of retiring soon and taking my mother to Hiroshima to live. I'd better hit him up for a loan before he does."

Before the inn got underway, however, Hayoto was approached by the owner of the Sakayama gallery that showed his work. "I've been asked to see if you would be interested in traveling to America, where you would give lectures at various schools and galleries."

Hayoto didn't hesitate to say yes.

3

HAYOTO

Idaho

The moment he stepped out of Idaho's crushing heat on the tarmac and into the blessed relief of the air-conditioned terminal, Hayoto spotted the two young women waiting for him. The shorter one, whose black hair was bobbed just below her ears, approached him, a wide smile on her face.

"I'm Nori Sato, granddaughter of your great-aunt and uncle, Mako and Keiko Ito."

Hayoto bobbed his head while accepting the proffered hand. "Good afternoon."

Nori stretched her arm to the other woman, hanging back a few feet. "Hurry up, Helena." She turned back to him. "This is my cousin, Helena Franconi."

Helena was tall and slim, with almond-shaped hazel eyes and cream-colored skin. Her last name told Hayoto she must be related to his prospective hostess, Virginia Sato née Franconi, the near life-long friend of his great-aunt.

He bowed then straightened and smiled at her. "How do you do, Miss Helena Franconi? It is a pleasure to meet you." He turned back to Nori. "And you as well, cousin."

"We're all cousins around here," Nori said. "In spirit if not in blood. You'll meet another at the house. Lily's an artist, too."

Hayoto's eyebrows went up. He was always interested in meeting fellow artists. "Oh? What medium?"

"You and Helena go claim your bags," Nori said. "I'll get the car and bring it around front. You and Lily can talk all about art when we get to the house." She took off without waiting for either Hayoto or Helena to reply.

"The baggage claim is this way," Helena said in flawless Japanese.

He walked a step or two behind, admiring the way her long, mahogany-colored hair swung around her narrow shoulders.

The Sato home, nestled in the bend of the rippling Snake River, spread in two wings from a grand foyer. Hayoto had seen many such houses on his recent travels, including the home of his great-aunt and uncle, where he'd stayed while lecturing in Oregon. He couldn't fail to compare them to homes in Nishimi, any of which were a tenth of the size with a thousand times less grandeur.

"Put your bag there," Nori said, indicating a spot next to the door. "Someone will take it up to your room." She and Helena led him past the stairway leading to the second floor, down a wide, Oriental-carpeted hall. His eyes traveled across the photographs of farm scenes, people and animals that lined the walls. The women gave him no time to stop and study the photos, as he would have wished, but hurried him down the hall and through a large, raftered room, complete with what looked to be a five-foot fireplace at one end, to a wide, covered patio beyond.

Hayoto paused in the doorway to take in the space, crowded with people and noise. A broad expanse of lawn ran out from the patio to the river, and the sheer face of rock on the river's opposite side. The setting sun gave the rock and the sky above it a warm rose, lavender, and yellow glow. He took a step forward, eager to explore.

Nori touched his arm, recalling him to where he was. He reluctantly pulled his gaze away from the river and the rock. She introduced her parents, Neil and Amy Sato. Neil was tall and broad-shouldered and his burnished cheeks revealed the many hours he spent in the sun. Amy was of medium height and plump. Neil pumped Hayoto's hand and Amy welcomed him.

Nori then introduced her father's sisters and several more cousins. The number of people claiming some sort of ancestry or relationship nearly overwhelmed Hayoto. "There's Lily," Nori said. "I'll introduce you later. First I want you to meet my grandmother." She led him to a tall slim woman standing next to an even taller man and a small Japanese woman.

Hayoto was immediately struck by Virginia Sato's direct and un-faded, navy-blue eyes, which belied her ninety years. "Welcome to Idaho," she said.

He bowed. "Thank you for allowing me to share in your birthday celebrations."

"I'm delighted to have you. Many years ago, your grandparents were welcomed visitors to our home. Your grandmother's story intrigued me from the first time Keiko told me about Mako's missing sister. She was a remarkable woman."

Hayoto briefly closed his eyes. "Yes, she was."

Virginia introduced her brother, Paul Franconi, and his wife, Suki. It was easy to see that Helena Franconi had gotten her height from her grandfather. Her bird-like grandmother, who was more than a foot shorter, didn't appear in the least intimidated by her tall husband.

"Keiko and I met at Camp Minidoka, where we washed dishes every morning in the dining hall." She grimaced. "We met Virginia when we went to work in the fields of her family's farm during the summer."

"That must have been hard work. Were you from Portland, too?" Coming from Portland's mild climate would have made working in Idaho's summer heat even more difficult.

Suki shook her head. "Seattle. You probably know they'll be here in a couple of days. Keiko and Mako, I mean. We use Virginia's birthday as an excuse for our annual get-togethers. No one will want to miss her ninetieth."

While the four of them stood talking and sipping wine, Hayoto's eye followed Helena Franconi.

That night, after all the other guests had left, including Nori, Helena, and Lily, who had the same Navy-blue eyes as Virginia, Nori's mother led him up the stairs to the bedroom she'd allotted him.

"My mother sends her regards," he said.

Amy Sato nodded. "We had great fun when my parents and I visited Nishimi."

"That's what she told me. Since you and my mother are cousins, does that make us second cousins or cousins once removed?"

Amy chuckled. "I have no idea. Those connections always baffle me."

"Your daughter says we're all cousins here, in spirit if not in blood. I like that."

"Me, too." Her round face lit with pleasure, she smiled at him over her shoulder. "Here's your room." She opened the door and ushered Hayoto inside. "The bathroom is through that door. The bedroom on the other side is empty, so you don't need to worry about disturbing anyone."

The room faced the river. When the door clicked closed behind his hostess, he opened the window wide and breathed in air redolent of grass and earth. A breeze licked his skin. The river murmured. From a distance, an owl called. He drew in another lungful of the cool night air, glad that he'd made time to come and see this place and these people he'd heard spoken of for years.

He removed his shoes and shirt and padded into the bathroom. While brushing his teeth, he thought of Helena Franconi. He'd learned on the drive from the airport that she was from Palo Alto, a town not far from San Francisco, where he needed to be in ten days. He would pick her brain as to what he should see while in that city.

She was an interesting young woman. Incredibly intelligent eyes. A writer, like both of her grandparents. She'd given him the titles of some of her grandfather's books. Hayoto recognized two of them, both about the war in the Pacific. Well worth re-reading. Maybe he could find a copy at the airport.

He slipped between crisp sheets and turned off the bedside lamp. Moonlight shone through the open window.

He'd also look for a copy of Helena's book, though she'd assured him that he probably wouldn't be able to find one. "It's long been out of print," she'd said. "But if you're truly interested, I'm sure there's a copy somewhere in this house. I'll ask Virginia or Amy when things are less chaotic."

Hayoto liked Helena's naturalness and her lack of self-importance. He also liked the warmth of her smile and the quiet way she laughed.

Over the next few days, Hayoto was shown around the area by Helena. Their first stop was Camp Minidoka, the place where his grandparents and his great-uncle and aunt were interned during the war.

When they arrived in the graveled parking lot, Hayoto's gaze wandered to a barbed-wire fence. The water in the canal beyond the fence was dark and silent as it rushed between its earthen banks.

"It's part of the Northside canal system. Two internees drowned in it, so the other internees dug out a big swimming hole—it's over there." Helena nodded to where a large sign was posted. "Well, the site of it. It's blocked off, so empty now."

Except for a hawk circling above them, its outstretched wings seeming not to move, they had the place to themselves. The quiet solemnity felt temple-like. The only sounds were their footsteps on the graveled path and the rumble of a far-off tractor. And the wind.

The sign Helena had pointed to was of a large photograph showing a crowd of people, adults and children alike, scattered throughout the swimming hole and lining its banks. Prior to seeing it, he'd had a difficult time imagining the quiet, rural landscape filled with nearly ten-thousand people.

"Keiko says they took photographs of kids playing basketball, women doing needlework, that garden at the front entrance for publicity—propaganda, to assure the American public that internees were being treated well and liked where they'd been put. I suspect she's right."

Hayoto nodded.Didn't all governments use propaganda when it suited them, his own included?

"It's thanks to Keiko," Helena continued, "who, with others, made numerous trips to Washington DC to lobby for it, that all the internment camps have been recognized as national historic sites."

It was a piece of history with which Hayoto was largely unfamiliar. "I should know more about this time and place since it includes my family's past, too. Thank you for bringing me here."

Helena's eyes lit, obviously pleased. "Part of the reason I left California and moved up here is to research and tell the story of Camp Minidoka. I tried for many years without success to get my grandmother to talk about her experiences during the war. Keiko and Mako, too, although Mako left two years before they did—to join the 442nd in Europe. Those who were interned here have seemed almost ashamed of what they endured during the war. Until now. Suddenly, they're talking—Grandma Suki, too."

"Why would they have felt shame?"

"I don't know—they shouldn't have. They weren't the enemy. They were victims of prejudice and fear."

Hayoto admired Helena's passion, the way her face glowed and her eyes widened as she spoke.

"There were lots of Japanese-Americans who acquiesced to being rounded up and put behind barbed-wire, with guard towers and rifles aimed at them. They got along and followed the rules without protest."

"Typical of what everyone assumes is the Japanese character, right? Follow orders, do what you're told?"

Helena stood on one foot, prying a pebble from the sole of her shoe. She glanced up at him, her eyes narrowing a bit. "The 442nd was made up almost entirely of Japanese-American volunteers and draftees. It became one of the most highly decorated units in the war." She straightened and threw the pebble onto the gravel path. "But others were fiercely opposed to what the country did to them—Keiko, for instance. And John Sato, Virginia's husband. Many young men refused the draft—No-No boys they were called."

Hayoto frowned, curious. "No-No boys?"

"They said they couldn't legally be drafted from the camps. They claimed the government should release them, let them go home, and then they'd join the army. The government countered that if they didn't answer the draft, they'd go to jail. Some did."

Hayoto looked at the barbed-wire, pictured the guard towers, the tarpaper-covered barracks, the people crowded into them. Hadn't that been jail enough?

"Was Virginia's husband a No-No boy?" he asked.

Helena shook her head, her mahogany hair swaying. "Though Grandma Suki said Virginia feared he might become one. He ended up in the 442nd, too. He was injured twice."

Hayoto suddenly felt torn, divided between two countries. His own, Japan, and America, which was part of his heritage. And if he felt torn, how must his Grandmother Nobuko have felt? "When will your book be published? I want to read it."

Helena smiled. "Next summer," she said, and then asked if he was hungry. "Have you had a hamburger since you came to America? You know they are a staple in this country—one of our basic food groups."

"Of course," he said, feeling a bit lighter. "I've had plenty of hamburgers in Japan, too. You may not know it, but we have McDonalds there."

"Really?"

"Absolutely."

Helena laughed. "Well, I'll take you to a place that makes much better hamburgers than McDonalds."

They drove to a diner in the nearby town of Jerome. When their hamburgers and French fries were set before them, Hayoto's eyes widened. "Do they really expect one person to eat all this?"

"Well, they have doggy bags if you can't manage it." Helena's laugh was low and throaty. Intimate sounding. He studied her, not attempting to hide his attraction. She stared back, her eyebrows raised. He smiled. After a pause, they attacked their hamburgers.

Hayoto was first to concede defeat. He watched Helena try to keep hers from breaking into pieces while juice ran over her fingers. He handed her some extra napkins.

"How did you come to speak Japanese so well?" he asked.

Helena, too, gave up and put what remained of her hamburger on her plate, took a proffered napkin and wiped her mouth and hands. "I wanted to learn all I could about the culture of Grandma Suki and my mother."

"Your mother?"

"She and my father aren't here. They own several tech companies in Palo Alto—Silicon Valley. I'm sure you've heard of it. They're always in the middle of a merger or a buy-out. They never have time for anything else. I'm surprised they found time to have me."

Hayoto's eyebrows drew together. "That doesn't sound like a very happy childhood."

"Oh, don't worry. I had a great childhood. Suki and Paul made sure of that. I spent most of my summers with them. Lots of weekends during the school year, too. And when not in Carmel Valley, I was with my mother's aunt and uncle in Salinas—that's in California, too. Or I was up here in Idaho carrying on with Lily and Nori."

"I get the impression Nori is not interested in men, romantically."

"Funny you should sense that after such a short time. You're right, though. She came out to us when she was a teenager, but she's been terrified of telling her grandmother. You've met Keiko—well, of course, she's your great-aunt—but I doubt you know how intense she can be."

"When my mother was a girl, Mako, Keiko and Amy visited Nishimi. She told me that even then, she recognized that Keiko was a force to be reckoned with, that she and Amy were both half-frightened of her."

Helena chuckled. "I can imagine. There was a time I thought Amy was still frightened of her mother, but later I realized that she always listened politely to whatever Keiko had to say and then did exactly what she wanted. It took a while for Nori to realize her grandmother has a very soft heart buried beneath the bluster."

She stopped speaking to take a sip of her milkshake, her eyes smiling at Hayoto over the rim. He wondered how she remained so slim.

"Just recently, Nori finally got up the nerve to tell her grandmother she's lesbian—by introducing Keiko to her girlfriend. You'll meet her—Susan. She's a veterinarian and was working last night."

"How did Keiko take the news?"

"She said, 'You could have told me sooner. I wouldn't have wasted my time introducing you to all those men.'"

Hayoto laughed. "You still haven't told me how you learned Japanese so well."

"Well, I took classes, of course. I also had my grandmother and my aunt and uncle to practice on. My question is how do you speak English so well?"

"That's easy—my grandmother and my mother—they always spoke English to each other. And to me, though not until I was older."

"I'd love to meet them some day. I've heard Nobuko came here years ago for Keiko's and Mako's wedding."

"I'm afraid you won't have the chance to meet Nobuko. My grandmother died four years ago." Hayoto's throat tightened as he said the words. He didn't think he'd ever get used to her being gone.

Hayoto was impressed by Lily's work. She tried to dismiss her talent, but she blushed with pleasure when he told her how much he liked the paintings she showed him as they toured her studio. The studio, obviously old, had been remodeled—she told him it used to be called a prove-up, a house a family had to live in for a year before they could claim unsettled land from the government. It was located next to a big farmhouse that Lily, Nori, and Helena shared.

"I especially like these," he said, pointing to two paintings leaning against the wall. "They look as though the colors of Africa influenced you."

"Well, they did," she said, smiling. "I'm glad you saw that."

"I like the painting above the mantle at Keiko's and Mako's house in Oregon, too." The painting was of an African woman carrying a child in a sling on her back. He'd studied it several times, admiring the way the artist had captured the woman's calmness. "And its mate at Virginia's." It was only as they strolled through Lily's studio that he realized she was the artist of both. "Have you lived in Africa?"

They walked on to another of Lily's Africa pieces, this one more abstract than the others.

Lily shook her head at his question. "Africa has always fascinated me, though. My grandparents lived there. My grandfather worked as an engineer and built bridges. You've met my mother, Crazy Grace. She was born in Kenya. When she was six or seven, my grandmother brought her back to Idaho to live with Virginia and John and to go to school here. They were killed soon after in a car accident."

Hayoto started to express sorrow for her loss, but Lily waved it aside. "It's hard to miss someone you've never known." She paused and looked up at him. "You may have gathered, or someone might have told you, that Grace is an addict? I hated her for years—wouldn't have anything to do with her. She used to blackmail Virginia to support her drug habit, using the threat of taking me back—she had me when she was fourteen, and left me with Virginia and John to raise. Now, I'm trying to help her." She shrugged. "I'm not even sure what changed. Maybe I just grew up."

As a teenager, Hayoto had shuffled his feet when he walked, his shoulders slumped, looking at the floor or the ground, trying not to remind people of his height. Because of Takeda Yoshida, because he was Takeda Yoshida's son. Although he no longer tried to disguise his height, the shame he'd felt then was sometimes still close to the surface. "I guess we have no choice sometimes. It's either grow up or stay in a not very happy place."

"You'll only be here another week—why don't you come stay at the farmhouse with us? We could paint together."

"I would like that, Lily. Thank you. But is there enough room for me here?"

"Well, Grace went into rehab—you're the first one to know besides Nori and Helena. You can stay in her room."

Hayoto stretched out on the bed that night and thought of the three young women on the floor above him. Lily was sweet and generous—if he believed in such things, he'd think she was a yōsei, a fairy or spirit. Nori was outgoing and quick. He felt sure she'd make a success of her new law practice—assuming people didn't shun her because of her lifestyle. Attitudes about homosexuals were changing in Japan, at least with young people. He hoped the same thing was happening in America as well.

The woman who interested him the most was Helena. He suspected she'd been hurt by a man—maybe not that long ago. Much as she'd made light of it, he suspected her parents' indifference to her had inflicted more pain that she let on, too. Maybe more than she even realized. He hoped to know her better, know what made her happy, and what she was thinking about when she looked so solemn. She had an understated sensuality—it was in the way she moved, in her throaty laugh. When she spoke, Hayoto felt like they were the only two people in the room. He wondered what she would be like in bed, if she would lose her quiet reserve.

The day of Virginia's birthday started bright and clear, just as every morning had begun since Hayoto had been in Idaho. It was early, but when he went into the kitchen, Nori was already there.

"I like getting up early," she said. "Especially today. Virginia's birthdays are always on a grander than normal scale."

"I would be happy to help."

"I'll take you up on that. First let's have some coffee. We can take it out to the porch and watch the corn grow. I do that every morning. It gives me a chance to get centered."

"My grandmother used to walk in the woods every morning. Now my mother does."

"Rituals are comforting," she said. They settled into wicker chairs, coffee cups in hand.

Hayoto gazed at the fields of wheat and corn that spread almost as far as he could see. The corn was nearly five feet high. The wheat looked ready to harvest. Insects buzzed. Machinery of some sort rumbled in the distance. Mountains filled the horizon.

"Keiko and Suki used to work here, you know. When they were at Camp Minidoka—the government let the internees out to work in the fields, since most of the men were off fighting. That's how they met Virginia. I guess internees saved the day for the farmers around here."

"I didn't realize they'd made such an impact, nor that this was the old Franconi farm."

"Virginia and John raised Lily; she deeded the house over when Lily turned twenty-one. The fields still belong to Franconi & Sato Farm, of course."

Hayoto nodded, thinking of his mother's farmhouse, separated now from the fields that were worked by a neighboring farmer.

"There were five Franconi kids—Virginia and Paul you've met, Marc and Leo—they're both dead now. And a sister. Irene. She's gone, too. Married I don't know how many times, she'd go for years without contacting anyone. Driven by something, I guess."

Hayoto was surprised at the casual way Nori spoke of these people—ancestors should be honored—but he didn't comment.

She continued. "They had a miserable father. Paul told us yesterday about something that happened when he was still a boy." She scowled and took a sip of her coffee.

Hayoto had sensed something was wrong yesterday, when Helena had returned from Virginia's, but she hadn't said what was troubling her. That night, all three women had been unusually quiet. He gave Nori a quizzical look.

Nori set down her coffee cup. "Their father took part in the murder of an entire family."

Hayoto stared at her. "Murder?"

Nori nodded. "They were Asian, Paul said. It happened several years before the war, but even then, there was a lot of animosity directed at Asians—Orientals as they were called then."

"Helena told me how our great-grandmother Ito lost her citizenship for several years because she married an immigrant."

Nori nodded. "That law was changed in the early thirties, but there were lots of other laws like it—they were the reason my grandmother says she became an attorney, in fact. She wanted to help get those laws changed."

"Oh?" He would like to have known more, but before he could ask, Nori went on.

"Anyway, some men, including Paul's father, took the family—mother and father, a little boy, and a toddler—to a place called Lizard Butte. It's a big lava outcropping in the desert, not far from here. They killed them. Brutally. Even the children." Nori's face twisted. "Poor Paul—he tried, but he was only fourteen and too young to stop them."

Hayoto's lips thinned and his thoughts once again flashed to Takeda Yoshida. As he thought of his father and his father's depraved doings, he was overcome with empathy for the tall, thin blind man who was Helena's grandfather.

"He never told anyone else in the family about it. Only Suki, before they married—he said she needed to know that about him. I guess guilt has been eating him alive for all these years."

Nori wiped a tear from her eye, while Hayoto watched a fly climbing the screen. In silence, they finished their coffee, each lost in thoughts of the past.

After some time, the door behind them opened and Helena came out on the porch with her own coffee. She was dressed in shorts and a t-shirt. Gladly putting thoughts of his father aside, Hayoto rose to greet her. At the same time, he noted her fine long legs.

"Big day," she said, taking a third chair. It appeared she was making the effort to put Paul's revelations aside, at least for the time being.

"Is Lily up?" Nori asked. "I stuck my head in earlier, but you know Lily. She'll sleep until noon if we don't get her moving. Then blame us."

"She's up," Helena said, smiling into her coffee cup.

Nori laughed. "What did you do—pour water on her?"

"You didn't hear the scream?"

Hayoto laughed with them. This must be what it would be like to have brothers or sisters.

After breakfast, Lily told Hayoto, Helena, and Nori to go over to Virginia's to help set up for her birthday. "I need to finish Virginia's gift. Just a couple of extra touches. Then go see Grace."

Nori smiled and touched Lily's shoulder, Helena gave Lily a hug. "Tell her hello for us."

When they reached the big house, which is what Helena, Nori, and Lily called the house on the river, Keiko greeted them. "Mako is already down on the river, fishing." She looked at Nori. "Where is Susan?"

Hayoto had noticed when he was staying with them in Oregon that Keiko never wasted time on niceties, but always came directly to the point. In a strange way, she reminded him of Yoko Yoshida. He smiled at the idea of the two crossing swords.

"Susan is checking on a Bassett Hound whose puppies she delivered by cesarean section yesterday afternoon," Nori said. "I'm going to see if Grandfather has had any luck."

"I'll come with you," Hayoto said.

Helena went to help Nori's mother in the kitchen.

Hayoto wished his mother could be with him, see this place, but especially, he wished she could spend time with her uncle. Mako looked so much like Nobuko. It was his calm manner, though, and the seriousness in his eyes that most reminded Hayoto of his grandmother.

After greeting his great-uncle and spending a few minutes talking about fishing, he left the two and strolled along the river. Green water rippled and gurgled over mossy rocks, splashing up against larger ones. The canyon wall across from him was a soft rosy-gold in the morning sun. He thought about what chemicals would create that color. His fingers itched to be in clay.

When he returned to where he'd left Nori and her grandfather, a swarm of people had arrived and were setting up for what almost looked to be a carnival, with food wagons and games. Helena greeted him and took him on a guided tour.

"What are they doing?" Hayoto asked, pointing to a tree and two men with a ladder.

"Putting up that piñata," Helena said, nodding to a large, colorful, crepe-paper covered figure of a donkey. "It's filled with candy and toys. The children, blindfolded, will take turns trying to hit it with a stick until the piñata breaks, then everyone will dive for the goodies that will be scattered over the ground."

"I've seen pictures, but I've never seen it done. Shall we help?"

That was the beginning of what seemed to Hayoto a whirlwind of events. Virginia Sato's birthday party was attended by her large family, farm workers, their wives and children, the children racing across the grass from game to game, neighbors, local politicians, and even the governor. The evening culminated in a twenty-minute display of fireworks.

The next afternoon, following a lazy morning of recuperating. Hayoto happily joined Lily in the quiet of her studio.

"I can't get over the panels you painted for Virginia, Keiko and Suki."

One women's portrait dominated each of the large panels. Virginia's showed her gazing down at an infant, cradled in her arms. Surrounding her were vignettes: a baby, with a man, John Sato, kneeling beside her on the lawn; laborers in the field; four children sitting on the front steps of the farmhouse; a young woman and man holding hands; a bridge in Africa; Grace; and Lily.

The portrait of Keiko showed her as a young woman standing in the sugar beet field, leaning on a hoe, a slight smile on her face, gazing at the distant mountains. Surrounding her was the Portland skyline, including its many bridges; Mako in front of his first garden shop; a courthouse; sailboats on the lake; Amy as a toddler and at the piano and again with Neil, together holding their baby daughter; Nori in cap and gown.

Suki's panel showed her in the garden at the farmhouse, with Paul sitting nearby in a chair under a sunshade; a house with a swimming pool behind, where Helena said she, Nori, and Lily swam and played as kids, splashing water onto the surrounding garden and lawn; Paul's award-winning books; a bit of Stanford University; Helena's parents; Helena in front of a computer and Helena napping by a waterfall.

Prominent, but not dominating each of Suki's and Keiko's panels were a watchtower and strands of barbed wire—reminders of Camp Minidoka. In one corner of both Virginia's and Suki's panels was the place called Lizard Butte.

"Helena tried to explain to me what the pictures depicted," Hayoto told Lily. "But I think it would take years to understand what everything meant."

"I tried to paint their lives," Lily said. "The good with the bad."

While they talked, she showed him how to mix colors.

"Working with glazes is entirely different," he told her. "Because the chemicals change color when the clay is fired."

"That would drive me crazy."

Hayoto was amazed when Lily said she heard a car in the drive. "Helena or Nori. It must be getting close to dinner time."

He'd been so engrossed he hadn't realized so much time had passed. "You are a good teacher, Lily. If I didn't need to go to San Francisco, I would stay on so that you could continue to instruct me."

"That would be lovely." She gave him a grin. "I think Helena would like that, too. Why don't you come back after you've done whatever it is you need to do in California?"

That evening, Lily, Nori, and Susan conveniently or diplomatically had something to do elsewhere. Hayoto and Helena sat in the wicker chairs on the porch, drinking wine and enjoying the long sunset.

"Will you come to San Francisco with me?" He'd been thinking of it for days. "I only need to be there to give an artist talk at a gallery that's showing my work, but we could stay on a few days and you could show me around the city."

The hazel in Helena's eyes reflected the color of the setting sun. "I would like that, Hayoto." Her voice was soft. She smiled.

4

HELENA

California

Helena stared out the cab's window as it sped along the freeway toward San Francisco's iconic skyline. At the recommendation of the owner of the gallery where Hayoto's work was being shown, Hayoto had made reservations for them at a small boutique hotel near the center of the city. She didn't know if he'd booked one room or two and was too nervous to ask.

One.

They shared the elevator with an older couple and a young woman talking about their visit to the Legion of Fine Arts. Unsure where else to look, Helena stared at the floor numbers flashing above the elevator doors—two, three, four…. What is the matter with me? It isn't like I've never been with a man before.

The elevator dinged and came to a stop on six. Hayoto took Helena's elbow. "This is our floor."

Her entire body was stiff with tension. Could he feel it?

Their suitcases were already in the room with the bellboy. Hayoto paid the young man, who studiously avoided looking at the size of his tip before slipping the bill into his pocket and leaving them.

Hayoto asked her if she'd like to go out for a late dinner. "There's supposed to be a good restaurant in the next block."

Helena was quite sure she wouldn't be able to swallow a bite. "I'm not really hungry." He was behaving so casually—he must do this sort of thing often. She kept her eyes averted from the bed.

"Let's go for a walk then. This city must be beautiful at night."

After nearly an hour of walking, legs and feet tired, they finished off with a nightcap at the Top of the Mark. From seats by a window, they viewed the panorama of the city. As he told her more about his home and his work, Helena relaxed.

"Shall we go back to our hotel now?" Hayoto asked, when she finished the last of her drink.

She nodded.

Helena stretched languorously and rolled onto her side, facing Hayoto. A wave of bliss washed through her, bringing a warm flush to her smooth skin. She felt beautiful and special.

"You are the most giving woman I've ever met," he said.

"I don't know why I was so nervous." Helena fingered his long hair, spread out on the pillow. During the day, he wore it pulled back in a ponytail. It was nearly as long as hers, but straight and black. "You could be a Native American."

"Perhaps, millions of years ago, some of my ancestors were among those who crossed on the fabled land bridge to North America." He stroked her cheek.

Helena captured his hand and studied it, running her fingertips over his. They were all callused.

"From the clay," he said.

They talked on, sharing stories of lonely childhoods an ocean apart, until the traffic noise below their window began to fade. Helena drifted into sleep, Hayoto's hand cupping her breast.

It was past ten when she awoke to the sound of light knocking. Hayoto, already showered and dressed, crossed to the door. "Breakfast has arrived," he said.

Helena pulled the blankets higher. A young man in the hotel's livery wheeled a cart filled with covered plates into the room. She relaxed when he'd gone and Hayoto removed the covers from two plates.

"I didn't know what you'd like, so I ordered a bit of everything."

Even though it rained off and on, to Helena the day was perfect. It started with a cable car ride down California Street to Market Street and the Embarcadero, the cable car's bell clanging at every intersection. She sat on an outside bench with Hayoto on the step facing her. He held on to a metal post. The wind chilled her cheeks and blew her hair about.

"You're beautiful," Hayoto said.

"So are you."

He threw back his head and laughed.

Helena glowed, inside and out.

The sun broke through the clouds. Hands joined, they strolled among the other tourists to the waterfront, where Hayoto bought them t-shirts with the Golden Gate Bridge printed on the front and San Francisco printed on the back. From Pier 39 they watched the large seals, stretched out with their harems on specially built rafts, barking furiously at smaller seals trying to slither aboard.

"You need to see Chinatown. It's not far from our hotel."

Hayoto looked down at her, his eyes twinkling and leering at the same time. "I'd rather have lunch and go back to our room. We can save Chinatown for tomorrow."

Helena gurgled. She couldn't remember a time when she'd felt so carefree.

Late in the afternoon, they visited the gallery where Hayoto would give his talk the next evening. While Hayoto spoke with the owner, a short and energetic man whose hands never seemed to stop moving, Helena strolled through the gallery, studying Hayoto's work.

There were vessels as tall as a man with colors varying between bright and subtle, the sides of the vessels undulating. Other works were smaller, their color more evocative of the earth they came from.

"I can't wait to hear your talk," Helena said, over their dinner of Dungeness crab, sourdough bread and salad.

"You could be disappointed—you may be the only one there."

She smiled and raised her wine glass in a toast. "You'll be wonderful, no matter how many people turn up."

After dinner, they walked back to their hotel. "These steep hills remind me of Nishimi—nothing is flat there, either. We don't have all these buildings or the view of the Bay or the ocean, but it is filled with unexpected beauty. I hope you will come and see it for yourself."

Helena was too overcome to speak. Hayoto didn't appear to expect her to say anything. That night their lovemaking was even more wonderful than the night before.

After Hayoto had fallen asleep, Helena thought of her former lover, Bill Sheppard. Although she'd known him slightly when she was a graduate student, they didn't connect until later, after she'd become an adjunct professor, teaching three classes a week. Fortunately for her finances, her first book did relatively well, at least for what most would consider an obscure subject matter—Anti-Asian laws in early 20th century California. Her grandfather claimed he had nothing to do with the book's moderate success, but Helena was sure the name Franconi had added some cachet—both for book sales and for Bill Shepard.

Bill claimed his wife didn't understand him. He was going to leave her as soon as their daughter was a little older. "Next year," he'd promised. But the next year came and went, as did the one after. *How could I have fallen for such an obvious line?* It had been a sordid affair that in the end, brought only shame.

Helena had told Nori the sex with Bill hadn't been that good, but she'd lied. It had been good, just nothing like what she experienced with Hayoto. With Hayoto, she soared.

The following evening, Helena sipped wine and listened to rhapsodic praises being heaped on Hayoto's talent. He needn't have worried no one would attend his talk—nearly seventy-five people were crowded into the gallery to hear him.

Earlier, the gallery's owner had pointed out a local art critic to Helena. When the man stopped at a large grey vessel with the figure of what looked like a prehistoric bison on its rounded side, she edged her way toward him.

The animal was drawn in dark lines, and looked about to charge. Within the lines were blotches of subtle shades of rose and lavender, blue and yellow, ochre and rust, over-lapping and bleeding together. Helena fought the urge to stroke the beast's sides, to gentle it.

"It almost breathes, does it not?" the critic said. He looked to be in his early fifties, with a grizzled goatee, neatly combed hair and piercing brown eyes.

Helena nodded.

"I saw you come in with Mr. Abi. Are you Mrs. Abi?"

Helena shook her head. "Just a friend."

"I wonder if you might tell me something about him."

"I'm sure he'd be happy to speak to you himself. Would you like me to introduce you? I'm Helena Franconi." She offered her hand.

"Mark Maffei," he said, grasping her hand in a firm shake. "Any relation to Paul Franconi?"

Helena nodded, accustomed to the question—most knew her grandfather had a Japanese-American wife. Her parents, too, were well known in the Bay area. "My grandfather," she said.

The gallery owner interrupted further talk when he tapped the side of a podium set up on one side of the crowded room. He introduced Hayoto and the crowd clapped politely. Helena felt a warm glow of pride when Hayoto, dressed in black jeans and a plum-colored shirt, open at the collar, stepped up to the podium. A well-cut tweed jacket emphasized his broad shoulders and tall, lean frame.

He gave the crowd a warm smile. "I was raised on a farm in the mountains near Hiroshima. I'm not sure when I knew I wanted to be a potter, but I knew from an early age that I didn't want to be a farmer." Laugher rippled across the gathering. "There was an old man in our village who'd once taught tea ceremony to important geisha. He came to Nishimi during World War Two and stayed. He taught my grandmother the art of tea ceremony, and she in turn, taught me."

He held up a lovely but rather primitive looking small bowl, held it in the palm of one hand and slowly rotated it with the other.

"Part of tea ceremony is appreciating the simple beauty of the bowl in which the tea is served—turning it to examine each side. The process teaches one to take the time to really see."

He set the bowl down, pausing a moment before he went on.

"The heart of Nishimi is the pottery factory at its center . It has been part of the village for over two-hundred years, after an enterprising villager traveled to Korea to learn the art. It is now run by a friend and former teacher."

Helena observed how carefully Hayoto avoided saying the factory belonged to him. She wondered if he was that modest, or if there was another reason.

"My studio is next door to the factory." He spread his arms to include the works on display. "As you can see, I like to play with the historical boundaries of clay and push the limits as far as possible with color, shape and texture."

After concluding his talk and then answering several questions, Hayoto bowed. "Thank you all for coming." The applause that followed was more than simply polite. Hayoto bowed several times. When the applause finally concluded, several people—mostly women Helena noted—surrounded Hayoto, asking more questions.

She made her way through the crowd with Mark Maffei. She introduced the two men, who arranged to meet the following morning for coffee. After that, Helena stepped back and allowed Hayoto to continue taking questions from his many admirers.

Mark Maffei remained at her side and together they watched Hayoto deftly field questions. "You'd better get used to it," he said. "He's going to be famous, you know."

"I know."

At some point, Hayoto must have thought about the prospect of becoming famous. Would he want that—people recognizing him and stopping him on the street to ask questions? Helena's grandfather had that kind of notoriety—his first book had been put up for a Pulitzer, his second book had won. He and her grandmother lived such quiet lives in Carmel Valley, though, Helena didn't think he was often bothered by 'groupies.' Such might not be the case with Hayoto. He was so incredibly good looking and virile, he could never escape notice of either fans or the press.

She pondered the question and asked Hayoto later, over a glass of wine in the small restaurant near their hotel.

He shook his head as soon as the words were out of her mouth. "I want my art to be recognized and appreciated. I want people to look at one of my pieces, no matter how small, and say, 'oh yes, that's by that artist—what is his name?' If people would say that, I'd be happy."

Helena nodded. Exactly so.

"A man from our village, an artist and a nobleman by birth, has been designated a Living National Treasure. That's what I want someday, to be a *Ningen Kokuhō.*"

He flushed, and looked slightly uncomfortable. Helena understood that he was embarrassed to have confessed such a desire. It made her like him more. She reached across the table and squeezed his hand.

He gave her a sheepish smile. "To have that title stamped next to my name on all my work—what an honor."

"What an honor that would be for Nishimi—two Living National Treasures from one small village." Helena laughed. "People would say there is something in the water."

After two more days in San Francisco, it was time for Helena to return to Idaho and Hayoto to Japan. A taxi took them to the airport.

"You have promised you will come to Japan when your book about Camp Minidoka is finished." They stood next to the security line that would take Hayoto to the international departure section. He stroked her cheek, making it tingle. "I will hold you to that promise."

"I will be there," she said.

Helena spent the next several hours in the airport lounge before her flight was called, her mind a jumble of memories and feelings and thoughts of the future. Lily picked her up at the airport in Twin Falls.

"I was hoping Hayoto would be with you. I told him he was welcome to stay here as long as he wanted."

Helena rested her head on the back of the truck's seat, pleasantly exhausted, but full of purpose. "I'm sure he appreciated your offer, but he needed to get back. He'd already been away nearly six weeks."

"So? How was it? Tell me everything."

"I will not tell you everything, but I will tell you it was wonderful. I'm in love, Lily."

"I can see it. I don't think you've touched ground yet."

"He wants me to come to Nishimi."

"Will you go?"

"As soon as the Camp Minidoka book is in my editor's hands."

"Suki and Paul will be heading home at the end of the week. Keiko and Mako, too."

"Then I'll need to go over to the big house and get whatever more from them I can. Did anyone notice I was gone?"

Lily laughed. "Of course. They've talked of little else. Keiko is totally convinced she is responsible, because she arranged for him to come here."

"Ha! She probably sent him for Nori—a last ditch effort."

"Well, she isn't acknowledging that was her motive."

"Speaking of Nori, what are she and Susan up to? Are there plans for Susan to move in yet?"

"Oh yeah. Love is in the air everywhere."

Helena reached across the seat and put her hand on Lily's shoulder. "It will be your turn soon. Someone special is on the horizon, waiting for you."

"Well, right now I'm concentrating on my painting and on Grace."

"How is she doing?"

"Pretty miserable still, but finally through withdrawal and ready to start therapy."

"You realize with her history this likely won't be the last time—she's been an addict forever."

Helena ached for Lily, who didn't deserve the pain Grace had put her through over the years. Put Virginia through as well.

"I know," Lily said. "One day at a time."

"I love you, you know."

Lily smiled. "I love you, too."

5

SACHIKO

Japan

Sachiko knelt on a cushion, content to see her son home and relishing his meal. "The food wasn't as good in America?"

Hayoto put down his chopsticks. "It was delicious and plentiful. And different. Someday I'll tell you what they do with buta."

"Pig?"

"Yes. I enjoyed myself, Mother. America is many things—the landscape alone varies so much. I enjoyed my time in Portland with Mako and Keiko—they are very wealthy, you know. Their house has this magnificent glass piece hanging from the ceiling. It's by an artist named Dale Chihuly. It is so intricate—tubes of glass, each a different intense color, coil around each other like a nest of disturbed asps."

Sachiko's eyebrows shot up and her mouth pulled down at the corners. "That doesn't sound nice at all."

"Oh, but it is. If I weren't a potter, I'd be a glass-blower like that Chihuly fellow."

She nodded. Even though she couldn't imagine beauty in what her son had described, the passion on his face, in his eyes, told her that he saw it.

"When Uncle Mako came to visit us, after my papa died, I found him to be very nice, and interested in everything. When he later brought his wife and daughter over, I suspected they must be wealthy, to afford such a trip. But wasn't he a simple gardener?"

"No, nothing like that. He was a landscaper and designed parks for cities all around the country. I saw a spectacular one in Seattle. He also owns plant stores, nurseries they call them, throughout the states of Oregon and Washington. Keiko was a Federal judge when she retired. I met their granddaughter in Idaho. She is also an attorney."

Sachiko studied her son, hoping his head hadn't been turned by this trip.

"I met someone else in Idaho, Mother. Her name is Helena. I've invited her to come to Nishimi."

Sachiko sat upright, no longer relaxed. "You are interested in a gaijin? A foreigner?"

"Yes. I hope to marry her."

"Hunh…and how does she feel, this Helena." She pronounced the name Herena.

"Helena, Mother. I believe she feels the same as me." Her son drew a deep breath. "I've never felt such an immediate connection to anyone before—it's like we've always known one another, like we are two parts of a whole. I don't know how else to explain it."

After Hayoto left for the house he'd inherited from Yoko, now updated and slightly enlarged, Sachiko washed up and readied herself for bed. Herena. She was prepared to welcome the girl—after all, her own mother had been a gaijin, but that was what worried her. Nobuko's life in Japan often had been difficult. If Hayoto and this young woman were to marry, how would she manage the possible suspicion and animosity of the villagers?

She switched off the light and slipped under the blanket on her futon.

Nishimi had changed since Nobuko's time, though. It was no longer isolated. Many now traveled the country— traveled the world, even. Just last year, Mr. and Mrs. Ishi had taken a cruise in South America, coming home to rave about a Brazilian dance they'd learned called the samba.

Yes, things had changed since her mother's time. But that still didn't mean an outsider, an American, would be welcome in Nishimi.

A thought niggled at Sachiko's conscience—was she resisting because she was jealous, because she'd never had a love-match marriage like her parents had enjoyed, and like Hayoto wanted? No. She would not allow herself to be so small.

Her mind went to Kazuhiro Yoshida. She'd loved him as a girl, as a teenager and as a young woman. But as she grew older, she realized he was a weak and self-centered man. She doubted that a marriage between them would have been happy.

She sighed. Her life now might be simple and uneventful, even lonely at times, but it suited her. She rolled onto her side and went to sleep.

She rose early the next morning. Fall was in the air and mornings were growing cooler. She donned a light jacket before stepping outside for her customary walk. Instead of the woods, she turned up the road toward the Katsuragawa house, past the Shinto Shrine and the Buddhist Temple.

Eventually, she turned onto the path that led to the park, created years before from the overgrown gardens of the Katsuragawa summer estate. The park was just steps from the caretaker's house, where Hirotaka and Chieko Katsuragawa lived, and had lived for decades. Funny how everyone still referred to it as the caretaker's house. Even those like herself, not born until long after the war and the fire that had destroyed so much of the estate, including the main house.

At the top of the steps, she followed the path leading to the koi pond. She'd brought some breadcrumbs to feed the fish. When she came to the arched bridge spanning the pond, she discovered Chieko already on it. "Good morning," she called.

Chieko, who'd been gazing into the water's green depths, lifted her head and spotted Sachiko. "You're up early."

"I would say the same about you." Sachiko joined her mother's old friend at the rail. She took the breadcrumbs from her pocket and dropped them into the water. Orange and black fish swirled and the breadcrumbs disappeared.

"I used to imagine Hirotaka's mother doing that, resplendent in silken kimono and artfully coifed hair. It was an image I envied, fearing I could never live up to it." Chieko's voice was soft with nostalgia.

"Where is the sensei this morning?"

"He is sitting on his bench in his garden, enjoying his morning tea."

The sensei had looked well the last time Sachiko had seen him, but he was getting old. "He isn't ailing is he, Chieko-san?"

"No, no. He's fine. Don't worry, I won't be a widow for a while. I'm dreading that time, though. The loneliness…well, I don't have to tell you. You know how it is to miss a husband."

Sachiko didn't know. Since she'd never loved Kensai Hara it was hard to miss him. He'd tried to be a good husband and father. Unfortunately, with Toshio Hara as his role model, he didn't know how to do that.

Toshio Hara, Takeda Yoshida—two men who'd fought in New Guinea during the war and returned to their homeland forever changed. Her father and the sensei also managed to come back, but they were fundamentally the same, or so everyone claimed. Was surviving war whole and decent a fifty-fifty chance? Or were Toshio and Takeda flawed vessels before they were thrown into the crucible of war? Were they like those pots and bowls piled up behind the pottery factory, an air bubble or a thinning in their walls that made them unable to survive the heat of the fire? Sachiko supposed she'd never know.

Chieko straightened. "I must go and prepare breakfast for Kotada. He is leaving for Sakayama this morning and will remain with his parents for several days."

"Ah, you will miss him."

"He's going to his father's bank to see about getting a loan. You know he wants to build an inn in Nishimi."

"I'd heard that from Hayoto, but I thought he might be joking."

"He is very serious."

"Well, I wish him luck in his endeavor. An inn." Sachiko gave a thoughtful nod. "Yes, perhaps Nishimi does need such a thing. The village has changed so much from when I was a girl."

"Even more since I came here as a bride, fifty years and more ago."

"My mother used to speak of how it was then, before newcomers came and brought with them modern houses replacing the unpainted shacks lining the only street through the village. No more outside toilets and smelly ditches."

"Thank goodness for that. And with electricity to every house, no more need to go outside and build a fire beneath the ofuro."

Sachiko laughed. "Oh yes! I remember as a girl when it rained, holding an umbrella over Grandmother Abi's head while she heated the water for my grandfather's bath."

They talked for a few minutes more, then the older woman left, her footsteps sounding hallow on the bridge and then making a crunching sound on the gravel path. Sachiko remained, looking down at the water and thought more about the many changes in Nishimi, including the park she was now enjoying. Even more changes were apparently to come. An inn, for instance. What might be next? A theater? More shops? After several minutes of contemplating the future, Sachiko retraced her steps and headed down the mountain toward Nishimi and the store.

Later that morning, while Sachiko arranged a new line of cosmetics on a front shelf, the well-traveled Mrs. Ishi entered. Sachiko looked up when the bell jingle. "Good morning, Ishi-san."

"My son and his wife are coming for dinner tonight. What do you have that is special?"

Sachiko showed Mrs. Ishi the fresh eel that had arrived on the morning bus from Sakayama. Mrs. Ishi selected two, along with a chicken breast, fresh daikon, and ginger. She also bought a new lipstick and face powder before taking her leave.

The Abi store's longtime customers, like Mrs. Ishi, came every day to shop, just as they'd always done, and the constant flow of newcomers to Nishimi found the store's convenience hard to ignore. It wasn't the future Sachiko had envisioned when she went to work for NHK television nearly thirty years before, but she enjoyed the continual challenge the store presented.

The fall leaves brought the usual busloads of tourists to Nishimi, and once again Sachiko thought of Chieko's grandson, Kotada, and how right he'd been about the village needing an inn. The building had already begun. She was sure that when it was complete, there would be many guests. They would need to be fed. Sachiko jotted a reminder to herself in the notebook she kept on the counter next to the cash register to talk to Kotada about supplying whatever his cook would require.

It seemed no time before snow blanketed the landscape in white. Takumi Sano sent someone from the factory to shovel the snow in front of the store. "I believe we're in for a difficult winter," the young man said when Sachiko offered him a cup of tea after he'd finished. "I don't remember this much snow this early in the year. It is still October."

He was right in his prediction—the winter was harsh, but not only for reasons of weather. As it went on, Sachiko became more aware of the importance of the American woman to her son. Although Hayoto diligently visited his mother several times a week—sometime for a meal or a cup of tea, sometimes just for a brief visit and to pick up something he needed—he spent most of his time working on a series of vessels and wall plaques titled 'Rivers and Buttes.'

"I plan to dedicate the series to Helena," he told Sachiko. "She showed me much of the country near her home—it is so big and primitive, Mother. A person would never tire of discovering some new view, some new aspect of all that vastness."

Perhaps Hayoto would decide to move to America, to be near this Herena—he seemed to be that serious. Maybe it made Sachiko a selfish old woman, but she didn't like the idea of a future without her son nearby. Not that he needed to stay in Nishimi. He could move to Sakayama or even Hiroshima. But to go as far away as America…that thought she didn't like.

Through the long, cold winter, while Sachiko waited on customers, visited with them, restocked shelves and went about the myriad things she normally did, she worried about the possible bleakness of the years ahead. She had not missed Kensai after he was gone, but she would miss Hayoto. Dreadfully.

Spring finally arrived and again Nishimi was inundated with tourists. Sachiko became so busy, she almost forgot her concerns about Hayoto and his possible desertion. Her son brought her brief serenity to an end.

"I'm going to Hiroshima tomorrow, Mother. Helena is arriving from America."

6

HELENA

Japan

Helena flew into Osaka, and an hour later caught the shinkanzen, the so-called bullet train, to Hiroshima. The train left the Osaka station and minutes later was out of the city and picking up speed. Before long, blasting along at two -hundred miles per hour, the countryside beyond the window became a blur. Helena leaned back in her seat and closed her eyes, forcing herself to relax.

Hayoto had been an interested and attentive guest in Idaho—it had been fun showing him around. They'd shared a marvelous five days in San Francisco. Helena had never felt like he made her feel—she'd walked on air for weeks. And since his return to Japan, his emails had been filled with funny and loving reminders.

Before leaving Idaho, she'd been eager to come to Japan. Now she wavered, unsure she'd done the right thing. Waffling was unlike her. She was a planner. She liked goals, liked to know where she was going. Looking at the landscape rushing past…it seemed she was hurtling toward an unknown destiny.

An hour and thirty minutes after leaving the Osaka station, a soft female voice on the car's loudspeaker announced they'd arrived in Hiroshima. People stood and gathered their things. Helena did as well. She stooped to peer out the window. No Hayoto.

Suitcase in hand, she stepped off the train. Still no Hayoto. Judging by the determined looks on the faces of her fellow travelers, most were eager to be home or checked into their hotels. She found herself swept on a human wave up the steps and over several sets of tracks, before descending once again and entering the terminal.

She scanned the crowded space, her nervousness mounting. Why isn't he here? Maybe he'd missed his connection from Sakayama. Maybe he'd changed his mind, decided he didn't want her in Nishimi after all.

Just as she was about to surrender to panic, Hayoto appeared. Relief poured over her. Her smile spread wide, she would have fallen into his arms had he opened them to her. Instead, he bowed. Uncertain, she bowed her head in return.

He seemed like a different person in Japan. Gone were the jokes, the twinkling eye, the teasing suggestions and innuendos. Instead, he was all business, taking her bag and hustling her to another track for their trip to Sakayama.

Once the Sakayama-bound train was underway, they spoke of impersonal things, like how the economies of both their nations were showing improvement after near collapse, how Helena had left everyone in Idaho in good health, the weather. When they'd exhausted their supply of small talk, a silence fell between them.

Helena's lips trembled. Tears pricked at her eyes. She stared out the window and tried to blink them away. *To have come all this way…I was a fool to expect so much from our short time together. We were carried away. Coming here was a mistake.*

"Helena…"

"Yes?"

"Helena, I'm sorry."

Helena took a breath and straightened her shoulders before turning from the window to face him. "There's no need to be sorry for anything, Hayoto. You don't need to make it a big deal if you've changed your mind about having me here."

"Changed my mind? I haven't changed my mind."

"You haven't?" She brightened, but then frowned. "Then why are you sorry?"

"Well, after San Francisco, I thought you might expect something similar. The thing is, Nishimi is a small town, with small-town minds. We won't be able to be together, at night I mean. I should have explained to you before you came over. That's what I'm sorry about, not that you're here."

"I understand." She didn't, but at least he still wanted her. "Where am I to stay?"

"With my mother. Although a friend is building an inn, it isn't as yet complete."

"Oh."

"Don't worry," he said. "My mother is very kind. She's looking forward to meeting you."

He took her hand. At his touch, an electrical charge went up her arm, and she caught her breath.

Helena gazed at what appeared to be nearly an acre of bicycles parked in front of the train station in Sakayama.

"Everyone rides bikes in Japan," Hayoto said. He gave her a questioning look then grinned. "Don't worry. I'm not going to make you pedal up the mountain to Nishimi. My truck is parked in a lot around the corner."

"What is it about artists and trucks—Lily drives one, too, you know."

"Well, they are useful when transporting work to and from galleries."

"That's what Lily says." Helena smiled, thinking of her cousin.

It wasn't long before they were out of the city and traveling up the mountain. "Speaking of Lily—how she would love to see this. She'd probably set up her easel right here on the side of the road to capture that view. My goodness, how lovely. That isn't a rice paddy, is it? We grow rice in California, but it doesn't look like that."

"Lotus. But you'll see plenty of rice paddies, too." He pointed. "Over there is millet." A man and a woman, wearing loose-fitting clothing and cone-shaped straw hats, followed a cart pulled by an ox.

The road steepened. They left the fields and paddies and wound through stands of cedar trees waving their fragrant boughs, past granite escarpments. After rounding a sharp bend, a picturesque village came into view.

Helena caught her breath. "Is that Nishimi?"

"It is," Hayoto said, a note of pride in his voice.

The main street was narrower than Helena had expected. The side streets more so—she was sure no car was small enough to drive up one. Most of the houses were white stucco. "You told me that the countryside around

Nishimi was beautiful, but I didn't realize the village would be so interesting and quaint. The blue tile roofs remind me of Greece. How many people live here?"

"It's grown in the last few years to nearly seven hundred."

Helena laughed. "Only slightly bigger than Eden, Idaho. Do you remember Eden?"

Hayoto nodded and smiled. "How could I forget? It was in Eden that I decided to ask you to accompany me to San Francisco."

He pointed to a building with a wooden porch across its windowed front. Baskets containing fruit and vegetables stood near the door. "My mother's store." Helena's gaze lingered as they drove past. "The gas station was built when I was a kid. The post office, too—it used to be in the store. That's the pottery factory," he said, and nodded to a sprawling building with a large covered area to one side and a patio set with tables and chairs and with what looked like a miniature waterfall at one end. A graveled parking lot was in front. "My studio is just beyond."

"What about your house, where is it?"

"Behind the studio." He pulled the truck into the lot. "I'll show you around tomorrow." They climbed out of the truck and Hayoto reached into its bed for Helena's suitcase. "Let's go see my mother."

When they neared the store, Helena studied its wooden siding where a row of black umbrellas hung. "What are all those umbrellas for?"

"They've been a custom in Nishimi for as long as I can remember."

Helena's head tipped to one side as she considered the umbrellas. "But why? What are they for?"

"The bus from Sakayama stops in front of the store. If the weather has turned inclement, there is an umbrella for anyone in need, to borrow until the following day."

Helena smiled her pleasure. "What a wonderful idea. I bet they're always returned, too." She had heard about the honesty of most Japanese.

"Of course." Hayoto opened the door and called out. "Mother, we're here."

A woman who looked to be in her mid-fifties came through a door at the back of the store, wiping her hands on a dishtowel. "I am very glad you are home, son. A policeman, a detective has been here. You just missed him."

Helena's eyebrows went up while Hayoto frowned. "What did he want? Wait, before you tell me, I want to introduce Helena Franconi. Helena, my mother, Sachiko Hara."

Helena bowed while Sachiko reached out a hand. They both laughed, then Sachiko bobbed her head as Helena shook her hand.

"After such a long trip, you will wish to freshen yourself," Hayoto's mother said. She led Helena and Hayoto to her living quarters behind the store and showed Helena to the WC. "Hayoto will put your suitcase in your room." She gestured to a sliding door.

A few minutes later, they were seated on cushions around a low table set with tea things. "Now Mother, tell me what the detective wanted," Hayoto said.

Sachiko finished pouring tea into Helena's cup. She set the clay pot down and gazed at Hayoto a moment before speaking. "He wished to inform you that the remains of Takeda Yoshida have been found."

Hayoto looked stunned at his mother's words, but Sachiko's face was impossible for Helena to read.

"How? Where?" Hayoto said.

"A hiker from Sakayama found him. He had been buried in a shallow grave not more than five kilometers from here. The rains this spring washed the dirt away. He was stabbed. The murder weapon was also in the grave."

Hayoto's eyes narrowed."How do they know it is him?"

"His billfold remained intact."

"Twenty-seven years and he's been here all the time." Hayoto shook his head.

Helena frowned, her gaze going from one to the other. "Who was Takeda Yoshida? Someone from Nishimi? A relative?"

Sachiko said nothing, but looked at her son. Hayoto breathed deeply. "Takeda Yoshida was my father."

Helena's eyes widened. Neither Sachiko nor Hayoto showed any sign of grief or remorse.

Hayoto stood and bowed. "Excuse me. I must go. I will return."

Helena stood as well. "Shall I come with you?"

Failing to look at her, he shook his head. "I won't be long."

After Hayoto left, Sachiko busied herself with dinner preparations. When Helena offered to help, Sachiko insisted the kitchen was too small for more than one person. Instead, she suggested Helena might want to rest before they ate. "You've had a long flight and train ride."

Helena took the hint and retired to the little room where the rolled-out futon took up most of the space. She had a leaden feeling in her stomach. Hayoto had shut her out. So, too, had Sachiko. Well and why shouldn't they… she was a stranger, an outsider…a gaijin.

But the feeling she'd sensed between them was equally strange. The man had been gone for twenty-seven years. Hayoto would have been no more than an infant, so it was perhaps understandable he felt no grief. It was more than a lack of grief, however. There was some underlying feeling she couldn't understand. Maybe it was just shock that the man who was his father had been murdered. That must be it.

Despite his assurances not to be gone long, Hayoto didn't return in time for the evening meal his mother prepared. Helena kept looking toward the door leading to the store, expecting to see him enter.

Sachiko didn't appear disturbed by his absence. "You must have more rice than that little bit." Using chopsticks, she served Helena breaded chicken breast and tempura vegetables. "Tempura is Hayoto's favorite."

"Will he be here soon, do you think?"

Sachiko shrugged. "He sometimes goes off when he needs to think."

While they ate and talked of the differences between Japan and America, Helena wondered how this romance, or whatever it was, would work if there were walls and secrets between them? Since Sachiko made no mention of the dead man, Helena refrained from asking about him.

7

HAYATO

Japan

Hayoto's emotions kept changing, going from relief to satisfaction to curiosity—relief that he would never need to meet Takeda Yoshida, satisfaction that Takeda had gotten what he deserved, and curiosity over who had done it.

Those weren't his only emotions. He was running away. He'd been unwilling to look at Helena and see the shock and dismay he knew would be on her face, and that made him a coward. The thought sickened him.

Still, he jogged on, leaving Nishimi behind, taking the track that led past Sanyo's farm and the schools he'd once attended, toward the farm where he'd spent his first fifteen years of life. It was past eight when he arrived at the path leading up to the farmhouse, past the rice paddy where he and his mother had hidden when Kensai went on his wild rampage. The moon's glow washed the thatched roof of the farmhouse and lit his way to the front door.

Sachiko had taken Hayoto's suggestion and leased the fields to another farmer, but kept the use of the farmhouse for them—mostly Hayoto. Inside, things were much the way they'd been when he was a boy. The kitchen was tidy, everything washed and put away. So, too, was the room where Kensai Hara, Sachiko and Hayoto had slept until Kensai's father—old, mad Toshio Hara—had died.

Hayoto had found Toshio that day, slumped over in the only western-style chair in the house, his mouth hanging open, his eyes wide and staring. He'd felt no remorse at Toshio's death, either. Did that make him abnormal, he wondered.

But he'd felt sorrow when Kensai Hara had died. Kensai had tried to be a good father. Hayoto had grown up thinking Kensai was his father. He'd loved Kensai as a father. Then, to have the man turn on his mother and him…he'd tried to hate the man, but he couldn't. Even as young as he'd been at the time, he'd realized Kensai was as much a victim of Takeda Yoshida as anyone. Toshio Hara as well, Hayoto supposed—all victims of Takeda and a war that must have seemed like it would never end.

Exhausted, he rolled out a futon and without taking off his clothes, collapsed on it and pulled a light blanket over his long frame. Sleep, however, was beyond his reach. He stared into the rafters above his head. Who had done it? Kazuhiro? Hayoto's grandmother had once claimed so. She'd been right when she told him Takeda was dead. Could she have been part of it?

Hayoto immediately dismissed that idea. If anyone had justification for killing Takeda Yoshida, it was Hayoto's mother, not his grandmother. That thought made his stomach churn, but logic soon calmed it; his mother would never have done such a thing. It must have been Kazuhiro. Or Yoko. She'd certainly had every reason for wanting to see her husband dead. She'd even told Hayoto she'd planned to kill him once. He sighed. The truth might never be known.

He awoke with the morning sun on his face. His first thought was of Helena. She must think him a fool, rushing off without a word of explanation. Would she forgive him? She must.

An hour later, he paused in the doorway of his mother's store, relieved to see Helena still there, helping Sachiko dust and rearrange shelves. A chore he'd done in the past.

"Your breakfast is in the kitchen," his mother said. "Helena will get it for you."

Helena appeared nervous, as though she didn't know what to do with the dust-rag in her hand. Well, Hayoto was nervous, too. He gestured for her to precede him to his mother's living quarters.

Opposite him, Helena seated herself on a cushion. A tray on the table between them held Hayoto's breakfast. Ignoring it, he took a breath and began. "Helena, I hope you will forgive me for leaving you so abruptly last night. It was inexcusable, but if you will listen, I will try to explain."

"Of course, I will listen Hayoto."

"I never met Takeda Yoshida. Nonetheless, he was a big part of my life." Hayoto shifted on the cushion and cleared his throat. "He had the reputation of a brutal man— everyone in the village was afraid of him, including, I'm told, his wife, Yoko, and his son, Kazuhiro."

Hayoto paused a moment, searching for the right words to explain to her, make her understand.

"Although I had suspicions earlier, I didn't know until I was eighteen that Takeda Yoshida was my father, that he had raped my mother."

Helena gasped. Her hand, resting on the table, clasped, but she said nothing.

"I was sickened to know my mother had been so brutally attacked. And I was sickened to know that I was the result, that a man like Takeda Yoshida was my father. I couldn't hold my head up. I hated myself, my height, my looks—I was very much like his other son, Kazuhiro, whom everyone said had been the image of his father."

Helena studied his face, her eyes questioning. "You speak of Kazuhiro in the past. Did something happen to him, too?"

Hayoto closed his eyes, wishing he needn't go on, knowing he must. He opened his eyes and gazed at her. "That is what makes this story even more difficult. The man who raised me, Kensai Hara, my mother's husband, went mad and killed him, blaming the ills of a lifetime on Kazuhiro and his father."

Hayoto willed her to understand all that he'd said and even that which he'd left unsaid. "So, you see, Helena, there is a good deal of shame in this family, in my family. It is why I must be so careful of my mother's reputation and my own."

Helena took his hand in both of hers. "You have no reason for shame, Hayoto. None of this is your fault. As you learned in Idaho, my family also has some unpleasant history. We will speak no more of it unless you wish to." She released his hand. "Now, you must eat the breakfast your mother prepared, though I'm afraid your egg is cold."

Hayoto took one more deep breath and exhaled. The tension coiled at the base of his neck dissolved, his demons retreated. "Thank you."

After he'd eaten—with gusto since he'd eaten nothing the night before—Hayoto took Helena on a tour of the pottery factory, introducing her to Takumi Sano and the rest of the workers. She picked up a piece of clay and worked it between her fingers while Hayoto explained the process of making and firing pottery. He was showing her the kiln when a bus loaded with chattering tourists arrived.

"This was Kazuhiro's vision, having tourists see the factory, enjoy tea and pastries on the patio, then buy our products. It has worked very well, but it will be impossible for us to hear ourselves think with them about."

"They don't disrupt what the workers are doing?"

"The workers have grown accustomed to it." Hayoto didn't add that the workers also had to deal with a certain amount of breakage from clumsy fingers picking up and dropping a vase or a bowl. What the tourists bought, however, easily offset whatever damage they caused. "And it is good business. Come along and I'll show you my own studio."

Helena was full of praise for Hayoto's *Rivers and Buttes* series. "You told me what you were doing, but I had no idea how well you would capture Idaho in clay. The colors are perfect—that rosy yellow of the cliffs in the afternoon sun. And I think I've been to that very bend in the river."

She eyed his easel. "You've been painting on canvas as well. Wait until Lily hears. She'll want photos. She'll probably have something to say about your technique, too."

Hayoto frowned. "What's wrong with my technique?"

Helena's throaty chuckle sent a pleasurable jolt to his loins.

"Nothing, silly," she said. "Lily will claim she taught you well. So, do the tourists come in here also—do we need to brace ourselves for an onslaught?"

"Occasionally Takumi will send someone over, someone who specifically asks to see my work or shows a knowledge beyond the others. Some of my things are in the factory showroom, some smaller pieces. The rest are in various galleries, like that one in San Francisco."

Hayoto couldn't keep his chest from swelling a bit as he said the words. He was proud of his work and what he'd accomplished—even before reaching thirty, which was the age he'd set for himself to succeed as an artist. If he hadn't made it, he'd had the factory to fall back on, but recognition and success were so much better.

He smiled at Helena. "Let's go see the rest of Nishimi."

He pointed out an open gate set into an earthen wall. Beyond it was a long white building with a partially thatched roof. A worker stood on bamboo scaffolding arranging bundles of straw thrown up by another worker. "My friend's inn," he said. Once passed the inn, they turned up a narrow road, passing the Shinto Shrine and the Buddhist Temple. "Behind the Temple is a rock garden tended by the Temple priests."

He didn't add that Kazuhiro Yoshida's decapitated body had been found in the rock garden. Helena had enough unpleasant news about his family to assimilate. Besides, Hayoto was done with the past, with Takeda, and with Kazuhiro, too. He wanted only to think of the future and hoped that Helena wished to be part of it.

"Can we see it?" she asked. "The garden?"

He hesitated only a moment, then led the way to a path winding through the tall green grass. With the heat of summer fast approaching the grass would soon turn yellow and smell of sunshine.

Helena silently surveyed the two rugged boulders positioned among the white rocks of the garden. The white rocks were raked in swirls around the boulders, like the sea. "I've seen pictures, but this is the first time I've actually been to such a garden. It is very restful, isn't it?"

"And contemplative."

After a few quiet minutes, they returned to the track and continued up the mountain. Hayoto wanted Helena's reaction to the view from the park, something he never tired of seeing. When they arrived, he wasn't disappointed.

"It's stunning, Hayoto. No wonder you love Nishimi so. The blossoms of the cherry trees scattered here and there look like puffs of cotton among the dark green of the cedar and the other trees. Maple and oak?"

"Yes. And mountain ash. The leaves are beautiful in the fall."

"I can only imagine."

"I hope you will stay and see it for yourself."

Her eyes flashed from the view to him. "You must know I can't impose on your mother that long."

Hayoto looked down at her lovely face, caressing it with his eyes. "Perhaps there is another solution."

Helena stared back at him. "Hayoto, please don't joke about this."

"I'm not joking."

"Then what are you saying?"

"I'm saying that I'm in love with you and I hope one day you will feel the same and we will marry." He couldn't say it any plainer. He held his breath. He'd handed her something he could never reclaim, his heart. He hoped she would treat it with tenderness and care.

She stepped forward and looped her arms around his neck. "I'm afraid I'm dreaming, but before I wake up, I will say I already do love you." She laughed her throaty laugh. "And I will marry you whenever you get around to asking me."

His arms flew around her and he pressed her close. "I'm asking you now."

"Then my answer is yes. I will marry you."

Hayoto's breath exploded in a shout of victory. He pulled her even closer and rained kisses on her forehead, her eyes, her cheeks and finally, her lips. He vowed he would worship her forever. Treasure her. "You'll never have cause for regret. I swear it."

Eventually, they calmed down enough to talk about such things as where they would live.

"Nishimi, of course," Helena insisted. "You have your studio, the factory. I can write anywhere. And it's lovely here—paradise."

"We'll spend time in Idaho, too."

Helena sighed. "You will need to meet my parents. I'm sorry, but it can't be avoided. You will love my Aunt Millicent and Uncle Henry, though. They live in Salinas and are really my great-aunt and uncle."

"When?"

"When what? When should we get married?"

"Yes. I say, let's get married right away and then I can meet your parents."

"That might not be fair to you. After you meet them, you might want to back out."

"Helena, they can't be that bad."

"No? Well, you'll see for yourself soon enough."

8

HAYATO

California

Hayoto and Helena once again landed at the San Francisco airport. This time, instead of taking a cab into the city, they rented a car and Helena drove them to Palo Alto, where they checked into the Stanford Park hotel.

Hayoto glanced around their room. "When are your parents expecting us?"

"They're not."

"You mean you didn't tell them when we were getting in?"

"I mean I haven't told them anything."

He looked intently at her. "Not even that we're married?"

"Nope."

Hayoto frowned, unable to understand the relationship Helena had with her parents. She was such a loving and understanding woman, but there was no give in her when it came to her parents. How badly they must have hurt her.

"They can keep until we've seen your aunt and uncle and your grandparents," he said. "Let's get something to eat, then I have a plan for that bed, which looks large enough to land a helicopter on." He raised his eyebrows, wiggling them suggestively.

Helena giggled and cast a flirtatious look in response.

"On second thought," Hayoto said. "We can eat later."

After breakfast the next morning, Helena drove them toward the coast. She'd told him the state's reservoirs were at historical lows and that California was in a drought. Even when they were so near the Pacific Ocean, the signs were evident. The rolling hills were the color of dried millet. Even the leaves on the scattered oaks seemed to crackle with the lack of rain.

"Everyone is fearful of fires this summer."

"The droughts in southern Japan are well in the past," Hayoto said. "But looking at this sere landscape and imagining what it must have looked like there, I understand what drove many Japanese away from their farms, to America."

"Including your great-grandparents," Helena said.

Hayoto nodded. He admired her smooth handling of the unfamiliar car at speeds he'd seldom experienced and never driven. "I'm surprised the traffic is still heavy this far from the city."

Helena nodded, not taking her eyes off the stream of cars and trucks surrounding her. "It's Friday. People are getting an early start on their weekend."

They reached Carmel Valley just before lunch. The car's tires crunched on the gravel driveway that circled in front of a long, low house with a wide, vine covered porch across its front. Suki Franconi came out to greet them, a small brown and white dog bouncing around her feet.

"That's Zelda. She's ancient and half-blind from cataracts, but she is devoted to Grandma Suki," Helena said before climbing out of the car. "Grandma! You look wonder -ful. Zelda, too." The dog, a Jack Russell Terrier, bounced and yapped around Helena, then back to Suki.

Hayoto squatted in the gravel and held out his hand for inspection. Zelda dropped to the ground and rolled onto her back.

Suki laughed and mockingly shook her head. "Such a trollop."

After hugs and handshakes, they went through the house to the patio in back, where Paul sat in his wheelchair, awaiting them beneath a wisteria-covered patio.

Helena immediately went to her grandfather's side and dropped to her knees. "Hi, Grandpa." She hugged him.

Helena was so caring. Her emotions, like the affection between her and her grandparents, her cousins, and her aunts ran deep. What, then, lay behind the rift with her parents?

Helena stood. "Here is Hayoto, too."

Setting aside his thoughts, Hayoto went to Paul's other side. "Mr. Franconi. It is a pleasure to see you again."

Helena's grandfather held out his left hand, which Hayoto took in his own.

"I understand congratulations are in order, young man. You'd better take good care of our little girl."

Hayoto smiled. "Trust me, sir. I will."

"We'll take good care of each other, Grandpa."

A round wrought-iron table was set for four and lunch was served by a woman named Rosa. Rosa pretended to remonstrate about Helena being too thin, then began to cry. "First you go and move to Idaho, and now you're married and going to live in Japan. We will hardly ever see you."

Hayoto enjoyed seeing Helena surrounded by so much love. He admired the setting, as well—the shaded patio, the pool, where Helena had told him she learned to swim. In the garden, butterflies flitted between yellow and red roses. Birds called from several of what Suki identified as Monterey Pine trees bordering the yard. A steady breeze from the nearby ocean blew across everything.

That evening, Suki showed Hayoto photo albums filled with pictures of Helena growing up, while Helena entertained Paul with stories of her teaching days at Stanford. Her grandfather was, she assured him, still well-remembered there. During the next two days, when they weren't gathered on the patio or sharing a meal with Suki and Paul, Hayoto and Helena swam and lounged. They walked around Carmel, visiting her favorite shops, and later drove up to Big Sur.

Their time passed too quickly. "It is not a wonder you are so fond of this place," Hayoto said as they at last drove away.

Tears were still drying on Helena's cheeks. "I'm afraid I'm going to lose them before long. Grandpa looks so frail. I guess I should be thankful I've had him in my life for so long, given how much he's been through. He is Grandma's passion. When he dies, I fear she will soon follow him."

"Would that be so bad—they clearly have been everything to one another." Hayoto didn't think so. His Grandmother Nobuko had lived many years following the death of her husband, and she'd loved Masato dearly, but she had been very young when her husband died and she'd had a daughter to raise—Hayoto's mother.

"Probably not," Helena said, giving a final sniff. "But I will miss them dreadfully."

They drove east on an increasingly winding road, which made Hayoto think of the road up the mountain to Nishimi. "I saw a sign to Salinas when we drove from our hotel in Palo Alto. Why are we not returning on that highway?"

"It's quicker this way."

"I see."

The highway dropped down into the outskirts of a large town. At its center were many old-fashioned Victorian-style buildings.

"This is Salinas," Helena said. "John Steinbeck grew up here. I've spent many hours in that library." She nodded toward a modern-looking building surrounded by shrubs. A large statue of a man Hayoto assumed was the famed writer stood in front of it.

"The library is dedicated to him, but about eight years ago, it almost closed because of a budget short-fall. Can you imagine, the city of John Steinbeck's birth closing the library dedicated to him? A bunch of celebrities rallied around and eventually they raised enough money to keep it going. People need access to books."

"Speaking of books, have you heard from your publisher?"

"Nothing more than that the book will be out next spring. The galleys should be in Nishimi when we get back. I'll need to be in Idaho for the launch."

"We need to be in Idaho for the launch."

Helena flashed him a smile. "Thank you."

They drove southeast out of Salinas and followed a road through what appeared to be miles of vegetable gardens.

"Salinas Valley is known as the Salad Bowl of the World," Helena said.

Hayoto could see why. "It looks like they grow everything here."

He enjoyed their brief visit with Helena's Aunt Millicent. Unfortunately, her husband, Henry, a Vietnam war veteran, wasn't much of a conversationalist. As a boy, Hayoto had seen the same vacant stare from the grandfather of one of his schoolmates. His friend's grandfather fought with the sensei and Masato on New Guinea. Unlike his grandfather, who'd suffered physically and eventually died of liver failure, his schoolmate's grandfather had suffered mentally. War's victims continued, yet mankind continued to engage in them, Hayoto thought.

They were only able to stay a couple of hours, but before they left, Helena's aunt took Hayoto aside and cautioned him what to expect from Helena's parents.

"Don't be surprised if they do no more than say hello and goodbye," Millicent said. She was a tiny woman with apple-cheeks and smile lines. "A more self-centered, self-important couple is hard to imagine."

Hayoto had to lean down to hear her. "Thank you for taking such good care of Helena as a girl. Despite her parents, she grew up to be a wonderful woman. I'm sure you had a great deal to do with that."

Millicent beamed and bobbed her head. "Suki and Paul, too."

"Yes. Suki and Paul, too." But Suki and Paul had obviously gone wrong with their son, Helena's father.

Millicent watched Hayoto with her still-sharp eyes. "Don't blame Suki and Paul for Andrew," she said, as if reading his mind. "He held Paul and Suki at a distance from the day he was born, no matter what they did or how much they tried to love him. Strange baby, strange boy, strange man."

Helena grew quieter as they neared Palo Alto.

"Shall we go to the hotel first," Hayoto asked.

"No. I'd rather get it over. I texted them earlier to let them know we'd be there in time for happy hour. They never miss that." She looked at him and gave a nervous-sounding laugh.

"Helena. Do not worry. Whatever they dish out, I can take. You can, too."

9

HELENA

California

Helena was used to her parents' indifference, but her stomach twisted more the nearer they came to Palo Alto. Hayoto, her husband of only a few weeks, was about to witness how little his wife's parents valued their only child. She glanced over at him. He was gazing serenely out the window, seemingly unconcerned about what lay ahead.

He wouldn't understand. How could he? His mother was so kind and motherly, interested in her son's work, interested in everything he did. Helena's mother had the maternal instincts of a sea turtle. What a relief it had been for Helena to spend her summers with her grandparents. Or in Salinas with Aunt Millicent and Uncle Henry. Or on the farm with Lily and Nori. In Idaho, carefree day followed carefree day. How she'd envied them. In Palo Alto, she had as much freedom as her cousins, perhaps more. Lots more, in fact. But Nori and Lily had something Helena lacked— people who cared enough to worry about them.

Her grip on the steering wheel tightened as they turned into the drive. She stopped to punch in the security numbers. The gates in front of them slid open.

Hayoto looked puzzled. "What is this?"

331

"Home sweet home." The gates silently closed behind them. Helena drove down the rhododendron-bordered drive that eventually led to the house. She cringed inwardly, picturing it through Hayoto's eyes. By Japanese standards, the house was big enough for ten families. Instead, it housed two people, plus a housekeeper, two maids and two secretaries—all of whom were meant to take care of her parents' every whim. Not to mention a gardener or two for the acres of lawn and shrubs surrounding the house.

Such a waste. It might be different if her parents enjoyed the house. But it was only for show, to impress or intimidate the various people who came to call—lawyers, accountants, CEOs—people her parents were negotiating deals with.

"Never hurts to let them know we can buy and sell them, should we decided to do so," Helena's father frequently said.

Long ago, she'd stopped recoiling at his words, but what would Hayoto think of such shallowness? Too late to back out now. They'd arrived.

The housekeeper greeted them. "Your parents are dressing for dinner. They have an engagement this evening, but they will join you for drinks on the terrace. If you'll come this way."

Helena looked at Hayoto and rolled her eyes, pretending amusement, but knew her flushed cheeks betrayed her shame at being treated like an unimportant visitor in her childhood home.

The terrace was as impeccably furnished as the rest of the house. A drinks cart was already waiting. Helena poured two glasses of perfectly chilled white wine.

Hayoto took his glass and wandered to the edge of the terrace where he looked out at the park-like setting.

"You won't see a blade of grass out of place," Helena said. "If there were, the gardener would be fired."

"So, this is where you grew up," he said.

Helena took a sip of wine and tried to sound natural. "Yes."

"I'm glad you didn't stay…I never would have found you here."

Helena closed her eyes, savoring his words. Maybe she'd worried needlessly. Maybe the evening wouldn't be a complete disaster.

In a rustle of long, silk skirt, Helena's mother arrived, followed closely by Helena's father. Her mother air-kissed her on both cheeks. Her father nodded and went to the drinks cart. When he'd poured two gin and tonics, one for him and one for Helena's mother, Helena introduced Hayoto.

Her mother, who was dressed, made up, and coifed to the nines, all but batted her eyes at her new son-in-law. "You're so tall and handsome. No wonder you swept my daughter off her feet," she gushed. "Helena, you didn't tell me you'd married a hunk."

Helena suspected the gin and tonic was not her mother's first of the evening.

Her father refilled his glass and lowered himself into one of several deeply cushioned patio chairs. His eyes followed Helena's mother for a few minutes, then locked on Hayoto. His mouth drew down.

"So, you're a potter." He said the word potter as if he might have been saying street-sweeper. Helena's lips tightened.

Hayoto lifted his chin, his eyes unwavering. "Yes."

"I thought she might have the good sense to marry a man of business. She had the opportunity to meet plenty of them—someone who would keep her in the style she was accustomed to." He threw out a hand to indicate the house, the brick terrace, and the grounds. "Instead, she insisted on being influenced by her grandparents. Virginia, too, I imagine. Isn't that where you two met? Not that long ago, either."

Helena bit back the retort she wanted to fling at her father, but replying in kind would have been a useless gesture. Her father's face had grown flushed, whether from emotion or from the alcohol, Helena didn't know. He tipped back his head and drank the rest of what was in his glass.

"I hope you're not planning to drive, Father."

Her mother answered. "We have a driver."

"Good."

Her father ignored the interruption and returned his narrowed gaze to Hayoto. "I looked you up on the internet. It appears you have a decent reputation. I assume you plan to move here to the U.S. now you're married to an American. Don't expect me to fund you."

"We plan to live in Nishimi, Father."

"Hmm," he grunted. "I expect that will change."

Helena stood. "It's time for us to leave so you can get on with the rest of your evening."

Helena dropped down onto a chair in their hotel room. "Didn't I warn you it would be awful?"

Hayoto smiled at her. "You did. But you are not to worry—I won't hold your father against you, so long as you won't hold mine against me."

Just as she was about to tell him he was the most wonderful and understanding man in the universe and she would love him forever, Helena's phone lit up. Lily.

"Hello."

"Virginia is asking for you."

"We plan to be there in two days."

"She's dying, Helena. Two days may be too late."

"We'll be on the next flight."

Nori met them at the airport just after eleven the following morning. "She's still hanging on. My grandparents are already here. If they make all their connections, yours should be here in a couple of hours."

Amy, Nori's mother, greeted them at the door. "Everyone's in the living room."

Nori went to sit on the couch beside her father, taking his hand in her own. "Helena's here, Daddy."

Neil looked up, his nearly opaque grey eyes glistening with unshed tears, and smiled his thanks.

Helena greeted Nori's aunts. They murmured congratulations on her marriage to Hayoto, but tears filled their eyes, too. "Not the way you would have wanted to end your honeymoon, I'm afraid," one said.

"I'm just glad we could make it in time. I hope my grandparents will get here soon. Keiko and Mako?"

"They are upstairs in their room," Amy said. "Mama is having a hard time. She and Virginia have been friends for so long. A lifetime."

Virginia's nurse told Helena she could go in.

Grace knelt on the floor next to Virginia's bed, her face buried in the bed's blanket. Virginia's hand rested on Grace's tumbled hair.

A warmth flooded Helena when she saw them together, glad they'd finally made peace.

When she approached the bed, Grace straightened and tried for a smile.

Virginia's eyes fluttered open. "You've come." Her voice was nearly a whisper.

"Yes, I'm here. Grandma and Grandpa will be here soon, too."

"Good. I'm tired."

"I know."

"John is waiting for me. Marc and Leo, too. And my beautiful Bella."

"Just a little longer, Aunt Virginia."

Virginia's eyes fluttered closed again.

Helena knelt beside Grace. "Where is Lily?"

Grace shook her head. "I'm not sure. She was here earlier. This is the first time she's left Virginia's side."

Poor Lily. She must be devastated. Virginia had been everything to her—mother, grandmother, great-grandmother.

Virginia's breathing grew slower and deeper.

Helena wiped tears from her eyes. Please get here soon, Grandma.

Thirty minutes later, the door opened and Suki stepped inside with Keiko. The nurse brought two chairs to the other side of the bed.

Keiko stroked Virginia's brow. "Virginia?"

"We're here," Suki said.

After a moment, Virginia opened her eyes once more. "Just like old times," she whispered. "I'm a lucky woman."

Helena and Grace tip-toed to the door, just as Lily, looking wild-eyed, entered. Helena hugged her.

Lily's lips trembled. "I've already told her goodbye. I just wanted to come back once more. I'm glad Suki and Keiko made it."

"Shall we leave them?"

Lily nodded and took her mother's hand. "Let's go, Grace."

"What about Grandpa?" Helena asked. "Did you see him?"

"He's waiting for Keiko and Suki to say their goodbyes first," Lily said.

Helena joined Hayoto on the patio. They walked down to the river and sat near the bank. Helena thought about all Virginia had seen and been through in her long life—her terrible father, her mother's death when she was a teenager, the wars, the loss of her firstborn, kind and beautiful Bella. Her marriage to John Sato. The hard work of building the farm into what it had become—a huge and profitable corporation. The ups and downs, the good times and the bad. Soon, she would be with her John. And with Bella.

"Virginia didn't travel much—to Arizona and Mexico when she was young—but life came to her." And life would go on after she was gone.

Helena gazed at the gurgling river, winding its way through rock and sand. Its waters would eventually reach the Pacific and evaporate, then come back to fall to earth as rain or snow and begin the journey to the ocean once again.

She drew a deep breath and reached for Hayoto's hand. In a few days, they would return to Nishimi, where they would begin their life together. She gazed across the river to the rockface rising above it, the pocked granite surface glowing in the sun. "Virginia lived a long, satisfying, and independent life. She should be our inspiration to dare whatever we wish to become or do with our lives. I think she and your Grandmother Nobuko were very much alike. Both lived with tragedy, and yet both refused to let tragedy define them."

Hayoto lifted Helena's hand to his lips and kissed her palm. "Do you remember much about Virginia's husband, John Sato?" he asked. "There was a woman the old folks talked about when I was a boy. Some said she was a witch. Others said she was a spy, or that her husband was a spy. Whatever, it seems surreal that she was John Sato's mother. She'd died before I was born, but like Takeda Yoshida, she was a village legend."

"What I know about John Sato is that he adored Virginia and his kids. He and Virginia's brother were partners in the farm. Marc never married—my grandmother said he was engaged once, but that something happened to his fiancé. Both men were incredibly hard workers. Virginia managed the business end of things. You saw what the three of them accomplished."

"You should write their story."

"Maybe I will."

A few minutes later, her eyes closed and the corners of her lips tilted upward in a smile. Yes, she could do that. She would do that.

Nishimi, Japan
Six Years Later

Chieko knelt on a cushion. Incense burned in an urn on the low table in front of her. Next to the urn was a bowl with more incense. A rope of beads looped around her hands, Chieko bowed and took a pinch of incense from the plate, brought it to her forehead, then dropped the incense into the smoldering urn. The priest intoned a sutra.

Hirotaka, her beloved husband, now in the flower-draped coffin in front of her, had slipped away in his sleep, not stirring, not causing any sort of fuss. As had been his way all the years of their marriage. The son of a noble, he'd gone to war and come back a humble artist, with no other wish than to become one with the village of Nishimi.

Behind her were seated their son and daughter-in-law, their grandchildren, most of the villagers, all come to honor the man they called sensei, honored teacher.

So many were there, Chieko thought, including an emissary from the Emperor, but so many were gone: her good friend, Nobuko; Yoko Yoshida, whose bark was much fiercer than her bite; Yoko's awful husband, Takeda; their son, Kazuhiro; Toshio Hara; Kensai Hara; Mr. and Mrs. Mori. She thought of mousy Mrs. Tanaka, who, even when Chieko first met her, looked to be a hundred. She and Mrs. Mori had kept everyone in the village apprised of even the tiniest bits of gossip. Chieko had been foolish to think they didn't talk about her, the rich girl who'd married the poor, but noble, artist.

She brought her hands to her forehead and bowed three times then stood and returned to her seat. The priest's voice droned on.

Sachiko sat near the back of the room next to Hayoto and Helena. She remembered when she, Kensai and Hayoto had brought old Toshio's body to this same place, and how surprised she'd been to see the sensei stride down the aisle in his formal kimono, his family monogram on its back, his family sword swinging at his side. She looked at Hayoto and wondered if her son was thinking of that day as well. After paying his respects to the dead, the sensei had withdrawn something from his waistband and placed it in the coffin with Toshio. Long afterward, he explained it was a letter, begging Toshio's forgiveness for allowing Takeda to blow down the bridge in New Guinea that left so many behind, including Toshio. He said he'd made a yearly pilgrimage to the farm, but Toshio always refused to hear him. "Perhaps he will be more willing to hear my plea in the afterlife," the sensei had said.

Sachiko's mind went to Takeda, who'd disappeared soon after her marriage to Kensai. After his body was finally discovered, she'd wondered how he had felt when he knew he was about to die. Had he repented for all the terrible things he'd done, including raping her? She'd been convinced that Kazuhiro had killed his father in a fit of jealousy and rage—Takeda had disappeared soon after Sachiko had told him what his father had done. But it had been her husband's fingerprints on the knife they found with Takeda's body. Had Kensai been mad, even then? At least Takeda had given her something good. Hayoto.

They were all dead now, her parents, her husband, her mad father-in-law, Kazuhiro, whom she'd once thought to marry. And now the sensei. Before long, it would be her turn. She glanced at Helena, whose hand was placed protectively on her rounded stomach. Sachiko's face softened with thoughts of a grandchild. She wondered what hardships, what challenges, what joys awaited it.

Helena sat with her eyes closed. Wouldn't Virginia have loved this place, loved these people. Just as she did. She wished she'd had time to know the sensei better. Hayoto had worshiped him. They had visited a museum in Sakayama where much of the sensei's work was shown. According to a plaque on the wall, the museum and the beautiful landscaped grounds surrounding it had once been the sensei's childhood home. On display had been lovely platters and bowls from Nishimi Pottery with the sensei's sumi-e style painting depicting flowers, animals, insects and whole scenes, including one with a samurai atop a horse, the samurai wearing a hawk-like mask. Behind the samurai were the same mountains and crags surrounding Nishimi. As well as the pottery pieces, were his oil on canvas impressionist-style paintings. She'd been drawn to a delightful painting of a boy and a girl flying a kite, the wind blowing the girl's long black hair about. Helena could almost hear their laughter. Hayoto said the girl was his mother, the boy, Kazuhiro Yoshida.

The sensei would be sorely missed. The pottery factory may have been the heart of Nishimi, but the sensei had been its soul. She glanced at her husband, a man filled with passion and humanity, and knew in that instant the village had a new soul. Its future, along with hers and the child now filling her womb, would be in strong and loving hands.

About the Author
TONI MORGAN

Toni came home to Oregon from a summer as an exchange student in Denmark knowing two things: she loved history, and she loved traveling and meeting new people. Her parents collected early-American antiques. By their measure, anything over 75 years of age qualified. The house of Toni's host family in Denmark was 400-years-old, and the church where her host-father preached was 800-years-old. She saw where battles had been fought and where Danes had lived ten centuries before she was born. It was a revelation. Her writing career began with that trip, keeping the editor of her hometown paper apprised of all she saw. A former NYT editor, he convinced her that she should continue writing. Although a west-coaster by birth, marriage, and preference, Toni has lived in many places, including nearly four years in Japan. That rich experience led her to write *Echoes from a Falling Bridge*, *Harvest the Wind* and *Lotus Blossom Unfurling*.

(http://authortonimorgan.com)